# ALFIE

## & George

## RACHEL WELLS

This novel is entirely a work of fiction.
The names, characters and incidents portrayed in it are
the work of the author's imagination. Any resemblance to
actual persons, living or dead, events or localities is
entirely coincidental.

AVON

A division of HarperCollinsPublishers
1 London Bridge Street,
London WSE1 9GF

www.harpercollins.co.uk

A Hardback Original 2016
4

Copyright © Rachel Wells 2016

Rachel Wells asserts the moral right to
be identified as the author of this work

A catalogue record for this book is
available from the British Library

ISBN 978-0-00-818164-2

Set in Bembo by Ben Gardiner

Chapter headings and endpapers © Shutterstock.com

Printed and bound in Great Britain by
Clays Ltd, St Ives plc

**MIX**
Paper from
responsible sources
**FSC** www.fsc.org **FSC™ C007454**

FSC™ is a non-profit international organisation established to promote
the responsible management of the world's forests. Products carrying the
FSC label are independently certified to assure consumers that they come
from forests that are managed to meet the social, economic and
ecological needs of present and future generations,
and other controlled sources.

Find out more about HarperCollins and the environment at
**www.harpercollins.co.uk/green**

*To Jo with love*

# Chapter One

# Chapter
# One

'What on earth is THAT?' I looked at Snowball, my cat girlfriend, then at the creature. We were standing by the wooden fence that surrounded the garden of our holiday home, staring at the strange creature roaming around on the other side. It was quite plump, had a very sharp beak, spiky fur, which looked feathery, and small, mean eyes. It made a funny, high-pitched noise as it eyeballed us, pecking in our direction. I backed away nervously.

'Oh, Alfie, it's just a hen! You must have seen one before?' Snowball laughed.

I took offence, though in actual fact I hadn't seen a real-life chicken before. But I was supposed to be the man in the relationship so I tried to square up.

'Hiss,' I said. There, that'd show him who was boss. But then the hen rushed towards me, wobbling its tiny head and flapping its wings. I jumped back.

Snowball laughed again and tickled me with her tail. 'It's harmless, Alfie, honestly.'

I certainly wasn't convinced. 'Well, you don't get many hens in London,' I huffed, stalking away.

We were somewhere called 'the country', and very nice it was too. We were staying in a house in the middle of nowhere, with nothing around for miles except fields. My family – Jonathan, Claire and Summer – and Snowball's family, the Snells – Karen, Tim, Daisy and Christopher – had rented a house for a week, and they had brought both me and Snowball with them. Cats don't normally go on holiday so we felt very lucky. When I told my friends, the neighbourhood cats, they were shocked, but we were having a lovely time so far and I thought that perhaps us cats should holiday more often. A change is as good as a rest, my first owner, Margaret, used to say, and she was right – it was just what the vet ordered.

The house itself was large, with five bedrooms, and there was a lovely open fire in the living room, which Snowball and I curled up in front of in the evenings. It was very romantic – although we had to be careful as sparks jumped out every now and then, once nearly singeing Snowball's beautiful white tail.

We had been told that, if we went out, we mustn't leave the garden. Our humans were worried about us getting lost – as if that would happen – but so far we had obediently stuck to exploring said garden and doing as we were told. It was a good size; pretty, with lots of interesting bushes and flowerbeds. There was enough to keep us occupied, as it was much bigger than the small back garden I had to put up with in London. However, beyond the garden, where the chickens lived, was the lure of some very lush fields. It was a big temptation for an inquisitive cat like me.

Snowball was less impressed. She'd been a rich cat before she moved to Edgar Road (my street in London), and her family had had an enormous garden in their old house in the country. She didn't boast about it anymore, but when we first met (a time when she had done her best to be rude to me) she did a bit. But anyway, I had won her over and captured her heart and we'd been together for two years now. The best two years of my cat life.

People always seemed surprised by our relationship at first, but then cats can fall in love just as easily as humans, if not more so. I should know, as I've had an awful lot of experience of humans.

Being a doorstep cat, I have a wide variety of humans I call family. I visit more than one home and have many 'owners'. As well and Claire and Jonathan, I regularly spend time with Polly and Matt and their two children, Henry and Martha, and my Polish family, Franceska, big Tomasz and their children, Aleksy and little Tomasz. I am one busy cat.

I've managed to bring my families together so they are all the closest of friends. In my time with them, on Edgar Road and beyond, I've seen so much change. Humans seem to change a lot, or at least their lives do, and us cats are often the bystanders that have to sort out the inevitable debris. I take care of my humans, it's what I do, and I've seen the ups and downs, the good and bad, and even the downright ugly, but I have always taken my role of looking after my families very seriously.

'We ought to go in, I'm getting hungry,' I said to Snowball, licking my lips. I could have almost eaten the hen, had it not been so formidable. But then I'm not much of a hunter, and neither is Snowball; she's far too beautiful to kill anything. I still remember how mesmerised I felt when I first laid eyes on her. Even now, after two years, I am one smitten kitten – or smitten cat, more accurately.

'Race you back,' she said, giving herself a head start. I bounded after her and we arrived at the open back door at the same time, both slightly breathless from the run.

'Ah, there you two are,' said Claire, smiling at me as we

5

padded into the kitchen. Summer, who was two and a half years old, was balanced on her hip. Claire put a bowl down on the highchair and wrestled Summer expertly into the seat as she wriggled in protest. Summer, my human sister, was what Claire called a 'madam' and what Jonathan called 'spirited'. Although she could sometimes be a pain, and tried to pull my tail a bit too often for my liking, I loved her very much. And she compensated with some lovely cuddles.

Summer smiled, picked up her spoon and threw it on the floor. She never tired of this game, although in my opinion she was old enough to know better.

'Toast,' she said, in her lispy voice.

'Eat your porridge, then you can have toast,' Claire replied sternly.

'NO!' Summer screamed, throwing her bowl of porridge on the floor. As usual, I had been standing too close to her highchair, and I carefully licked some of the stray porridge from my fur. When would I ever learn?

Summer was my charge, I felt. I had to look after her, even when she was being a madam. It amused Jonathan, our dad, who said he liked a woman with a strong will. I did too, which is why I liked Snowball and my best cat friend, Tiger. However, Claire found it a bit annoying, I think, although since having Summer she was so happy that I didn't worry about her too much anymore. Not like I did before anyway.

When I first came to live with Claire she had just got divorced, and she was quite broken. It took a lot of time and effort to put her back together. But then eventually she met Jonathan, one of my other humans, and now they are happily married with their child, Summer, completing our family.

'Alfie, Snowball, breakfast,' sang Daisy, Snowball's teenage owner, putting bowls of tuna down for us.

'Miaow,' I thanked her. Daisy was beautiful – tall and lovely. She and Snowball actually looked alike in that they both had almost white fur – or hair, in Daisy's case. Since Daisy had turned eighteen she'd been working as a model. She was becoming fairly successful already, and that was why she'd come on holiday. She might be too busy to come away with her family in the future, if all went to plan, so she needed to take the chance while she could. Snowball missed her when she was working but was very proud of her, which was touching.

Christopher, Daisy's sixteen-year-old brother, sat at the table eyeing Summer suspiciously, making sure he was far enough away from her to avoid being hit by any food. He was much more sensible than me.

As I enjoyed my breakfast, I basked in happiness. Although my other families weren't sharing my holiday, it was almost perfect. I had all the other people I loved around me and of course my beloved Snowball. As the humans ate their breakfasts, happily chatting and making plans for the day, I couldn't help but feel my heart swell. Life didn't get much better than this.

After breakfast, the sun slowly emerged, heating the morning into a warm spring day. Summer was playing with some teddy bears on a picnic blanket in the garden, whilst Claire and Karen sat beside her, drinking tea and chatting. Daisy had gone for a run and the men and Christopher had gone to the local town to do some grocery shopping – although Claire said they'd really gone to find a pub. Meanwhile, Snowball and I were relaxing, sprawled out on a warm patch of grass.

'This is the life.' I stretched my paws out and rolled onto

my back, letting the sun warm my fur.

'It really is,' Snowball replied. 'Shall we go and see if we can find some butterflies to chase?'

I didn't need asking twice.

This place was certainly different than London. Not only were there more animals around, but there was a sort of peacefulness that I hadn't really experienced before. And the wonderful thing was that it was rubbing off on all of us. All the humans seemed relaxed, which was nice because that didn't happen often in London; they were usually too preoccupied with work and other stresses. We had all been through some trying times in the last few years; my humans had faced many challenges. Adjusting to life in a new country, trying to have babies, post-natal depression, bullying at school, secrets, heart-ache – you name it, we'd been through it. I've been with them through each experience and have helped to resolve many problems, if I do say so myself. I think the problems brought my families closer together, and it was nice to see that we had finally entered a harmonious phase. Long may it last.

Snowball and I found a flowerbed, which looked as good a place as any to find butterflies.

We sat silently, side by side. We were so happy together that we often didn't need words. I actually felt as if I knew what Snowball was thinking, and vice versa. In the event, there were no butterflies, but we both dived into the flowerbed when a noisy bee appeared. We tried to lay low as the bee took what it needed from its chosen flower. I knew bees were good – I'd heard enough people saying that – but if you got too close, a sting could be pretty nasty. After the bee buzzed off we rolled around, enjoying the sun and the soft scents of the flowers. It was a pretty romantic time.

'Alfie, being on holiday with you is the best thing I've ever done,' Snowball purred, putting her paw on mine. I felt quite emotional as I looked at my love.

'It's the best thing I've ever done, too,' I replied – and I meant it with all my heart.

# Chapter Two

Summer was playing ball with Christopher. Although he treated her with suspicion when she had food, he could be quite good with her at other times.

'Throw the ball, Sum,' Chris said. Summer clutched it to her chest and shook her head. She then put it on the ground and sat on it. Christopher laughed. I went over to her and nudged the ball with my paw. Summer giggled and wobbled, rolling off it. She laughed as I lay next to her on the grass, tickling her with my tail. Out of the corner of my eye, I could see Jonathan approaching us.

'Honestly, neither of you will play for Chelsea at this rate,' he said, laughing. He scooped Summer up and swung her around.

'Jon, she's just had breakfast, she'll be sick,' Claire said, joining them. I stood up and stretched, brushing some grass off my fur with my tongue.

'Sorry.' Jonathan rolled his eyes. I gave him a conspiratorial look; Claire did fuss sometimes.

'Ready?' she asked.

Jonathan nodded. 'Right. Alfie, Snowball, we're off for a day trip, so you guys need to stay here and keep out of trouble.' He looked at me when he said the last bit.

'Miaow,' I said, indignantly.

'Do you think it'll be OK to leave the back door open?' Tim asked as he went to put some bags into one of the cars.

'Don't see why not, it's pretty deserted here,' Jonathan said.

'Gosh, I love that we can do that. We'd never be able to on

13

Edgar Road would we?' said Karen. She and Tim exchanged a look; I wondered if they were thinking about their old homes, as Snowball sometimes did. I would catch her with a faraway look in her eyes, and as much as I knew she was happy, she did miss it. I understood – I still missed my first home at times and, although I loved my home and all my families now, I would never forget it. It wasn't bad to miss things, I realised. Although it meant you had lost something or someone, it also meant you loved them in the first place. It was hard, but that was how life worked.

We sat by the stone steps that led up to the back door as we watched our families go out for the day. I was quite excited, as it meant a day for us to have our own adventures without worrying about the humans for once.

'Do you think we should go and explore a bit?' Snowball asked.

'Well, the humans said we shouldn't in case we get lost,' I replied. I was sometimes a foolhardy cat, but the last thing I wanted to do was get lost in the country. I might never be able to find my way back home!

'Oh, come on, let's live a bit. And anyway, I've got a good sense of direction.' Snowball nuzzled me, which meant she knew I was going to give in. However, I couldn't forget the time that she had got horribly lost, and I had had to launch a rescue mission as a result. I didn't dare mention it though – I wasn't looking for an argument or for Snowball to sulk, which she was rather good at when she was cross.

'OK then, let's go.' After all, I told myself, what could go wrong?

We headed out of the garden for the first time and into the neighbouring field. The long grass pleasantly tickled my legs as we ran through it side by side. There were insects buzzing around us, and as we travelled further from the house, we found some more chickens. These ones were actually quite friendly, clucking and scratching at the ground as we crept near them. I got quite close to one actually, trying to demonstrate my bravery, although inside I was like cat-food-in-jelly.

We went through another field and jumped onto a fence.

'Are your legs OK?' Snowball asked gently as she saw me grimace. I had an old injury that sometimes affected my back legs, but they weren't too bad, despite the odd twinge.

'Yes,' I said. 'I'm fine, thanks.' I jumped down from the fence smoothly to show her that I was all right. Then, feeling my confidence growing, I ran into the field. I was having a lovely time, the wind in my fur, the sun gently smiling down at us. I could get used to living in the country, I thought. Little did I know I was about to get a rude awakening.

'Moo,' a voice said angrily.

'Yelp!' I screamed, stopping suddenly. I found myself level with a leg, and as I looked up I started shaking. I was facing a monster, and he didn't look happy to see me. He stared down at me with big, dark eyes, snorting loudly. 'Yelp,' I screamed again.

'Snort,' the monster said, sounding angry. I realised that he was unhappy about us being in his field. He started to stomp and, as I saw the grass being flattened, I started to imagine being squashed beneath those big hooves. He shook his head, violently, as he eyeballed me again. Surely he was about to pounce. I managed to spring back, bouncing off Snowball and back in front of the cow again.

He lifted his head, snorted loudly again and swished his long tail from side to side.

'It's OK, Alfie.' Snowball was beside me. At the sight of her the monster seemed a bit less aggressive. She gently led me a safe distance away. 'It's just a cow,' she continued. 'They're big, and seem aggressive, I know, but they're really quite gentle.'

I had never seen a cow this close up before and it seemed anything but gentle to me.

'But it's… it's… enormous,' I stammered, unable to take my eyes off the black-and-white patchy creature. I could feel my back legs trembling with fear, although the cow had turned away, flicking its tail and eating grass as if we didn't exist. I was flooded with relief.

'They're harmless,' she explained. It seemed I had a lot to learn about these farm animals.

I gladly followed her away from the monster cow. It certainly didn't look what I would call 'harmless'.

The rest of our trip passed without incident, although I felt as if I was more skittish than I had been when we set off. But it was also one of the best days ever. We romped through fields, found some lovely trees to admire and were not attacked by any other farm animals, although we saw some sheep and I thought that one of them seemed to take a fancy to Snowball. But they were the same colour and maybe she thought Snowball was a lamb. After all, as Snowball explained, sheep weren't known for their brains. Not like cats.

Later that evening I was having a catnap, curled up in front of the fire. I needed a rest after our expedition. Although I was generally an active cat I was totally worn out. Maybe it was the country air, whatever that was. Claire kept referring to it, so it must have some effect. Jonathan said it was ridiculous to have an open fire when it was so warm but Karen and Claire wanted it lit, as we didn't have fires like this at home. I wasn't complaining; I loved being toasty warm. Snowball was with Daisy, in her room, I think, and I must have nodded off as I started to slowly awaken to the sound of soft voices.

'Are you sure?' I heard Karen say. I opened one eye to see her and Claire sitting on the sofa.

'Pretty much. I'm afraid it's definitely the case.' Afraid? What was this? As far as I knew all was well with my families.

'Oh, honey, I am sorry, I don't know what to say.' Karen's voice was rich with sympathy.

'Well we have Summer and she's perfect, even if she is a little diva, but you know I would have loved another child, and Jon would too, but it hasn't happened. Our doctor has run tests, but it looks as if we've been blessed with the only child we're going to have.' Although Claire sounded a little bit sad, she wasn't crying. I hoped that this wasn't the start of something. I worried about all my humans, but Claire especially. After the dark times she had faced in the past I knew she was prone to sliding into depression.

'But you had no problems with Summer,' said Karen.

'No, it's just one of those things – nature. It's funny, but with Summer I was so desperate to have a baby that I really got into a state before I conceived her, but now we've been trying for over a year and a half and I'm still quite calm. I guess I feel lucky having such a gorgeous little girl, and of course Jonathan, that I have to count my blessings rather than dwell on what I can't have.'

'Have you thought about IVF?'

'I did do some research but I'm not the most balanced person and with the hormones and injections and stuff, I worry that

I'll become unhinged. Not to mention that it might not work, and would cost a fortune. No, I need to be a good mother to Summer, and with working part time now, I need to be on top of things. To be honest, I'd love to adopt a child, but Jon's reluctant.'

'Adoption?'

'Yes, my dad's a social worker and I kind of always grew up thinking that giving a child a home would be a great thing to do. I hadn't thought about it in years but when we found out we couldn't conceive naturally, my mind immediately turned to adoption. But unfortunately Jon just doesn't see it the same way.'

I stayed perfectly still as I listened. Of course I knew they wanted another baby, and there had been quite a few hushed conversations behind closed doors, but because everything had been so good for us all, perhaps I had turned a blind eye to the struggles they were having. Or maybe I had been more caught up with Snowball than I realised…

'Ah, the whole man thing, wanting their genes to run through the veins of a child.'

'Probably, but he'll come round, I know he will. We have so much to offer a child, I just need to persuade him that it's a really good idea,' said Claire.

'You know how it is with men, you need him to think it's his idea.' They both laughed.

'Glass of wine?' Claire suggested.

'Why not? We are on holiday after all.'

As Karen and Claire drank their wine I marvelled at how far Claire had come. When I first met her she had been a mess – divorced, heartbroken, drinking too much and miserable. But now she was so happy and not even this setback, something that would previously have threatened to derail her, could defeat her. She wasn't a victim anymore, and I was so overjoyed that I jumped up onto her lap and touched my nose to her hand. I wanted her to know how proud I was of her.

'Oh, Alfie, I love you.' She kissed the top of my head. I snuggled into her, thinking that this holiday lark wasn't bad at all. Despite the monster cow.

# Chapter
# Three

This holiday was making me love Snowball even more. Before we left Edgar Road, both cars full of cases and me in my cat carrier in one car, Snowball in the other, I wouldn't have thought it possible to love her more. Yet I did. Spending this time away together, away from the day-to-day stresses of Edgar Road, had brought us even closer.

If cats could get married like humans, I would have married Snowball in a heartbeat. I knew it wasn't possible, but when I told her as we lay by the fire she said it was the most romantic thing she had ever heard. Which gave me an idea. As a very organised cat, I do like to make plans, and I thought that in order for us to always remember this holiday, the first one we'd had together – and also the best holiday any cat could ask for – I would plan something for us.

The humans were going to the beach for the day. They had packed up lots of food, fussed a lot, and made it seem as if they were going for days rather than a few hours. Finally though they left the house, and Snowball and I were alone. I wanted to have a lovely day with her, and that meant being brave, bold and taking a risk. This cat was ready to do just that. I wanted to put a smile on Snowball's face and for us have a day we would both remember. Of course, I wasn't sure where the day would take us. When we went out the other day, we hadn't ventured too far. We still didn't know the area but I figured if we headed towards the big farm there would be lots of fun to be had. I outlined my plan to Snowball. We would leave the garden – hopefully avoiding the giant cows – and explore the luscious green fields that led to the big hill. Once at the top of the hill we would admire the views that our families had been talking about. I thought if we just headed off in one direction we would be fine, there would be no way we'd get lost. In fact, I was quite excited and feeling adventurous.

'I love it, Alfie. Although I thought you were still worried about the cows and getting lost?'

'Not me,' I replied, with more bravado than I felt. I just hoped those cows would keep away.

When our families had finally piled themselves into their cars and driven off, Snowball and I finished our ablutions and got ready for our own adventure. My legs were almost trembling with excitement; I just knew we were going to have the best day ever.

We headed towards the farm, greeting the hens as if we were old friends. They wobbled their heads and clucked but weren't very interested in us. I don't know why I was ever scared of them: they were quite sweet really. We watched them for a bit before heading off. Before too long we came across a field with incredibly long, green grass. It was even taller than us. We made our way into it, and at one point I couldn't see Snowball at all.

'Yowl!' She jumped out at me and I almost fell over.

'Yeah, nice one, this is meant to be romantic – not scary,' I pointed out, smoothing my fur.

'Sorry, Alfie, I couldn't resist. This grass is the longest I've ever seen. It's so much fun! Come on, let's go.' She started running and I joined her. We ran through the grass, letting it tickle our fur, until we emerged on the other side of the field. I felt invigorated as we looked around, deciding where to head next.

'Let's avoid that way. Remember those sheep? I really think that one wanted to kidnap me,' Snowball said, looking a bit worried.

'As if I would ever let them do that,' I replied, with a raise of my whiskers.

'Alfie, would you ever want to live in the country?' Snowball asked as we trekked through another field.

'I don't know. I mean… it's very nice. But it's quiet. And all these animals… I'm not sure it's for me, to be honest. I'm a Londoner through and through.'

'When we lived in our old house, it was a bit like the country, but not as much as this – it was far more built up. I think it was a nice compromise.'

'I know you miss your old home, Snowball,' I said, trying to be understanding and not feel hurt. You see, I didn't like to think of Snowball before me. It sounds silly but I felt jealous that she had a life that didn't have me in it.

'I do a bit, but I would never want to go back, not without you, Alfie.' I felt my heart melt as I looked into her beautiful eyes.

A big black cloud loomed, interrupting our moment.

'Oh no,' I said, as I felt a drop of rain land on my nose. It seemed to have come from nowhere. Just a minute ago we had been enjoying the sun on our fur.

'We might have to make a run for it,' Snowball shouted, as rain started to patter all around us; neither of us liked getting wet. As Snowball bounded off I followed her, not thinking about where she was going. After a bit of a run we came across a building and hurried inside. There was straw on the floor; it was a bit scratchy, but at least we were dry.

'Thank goodness, Alfie,' Snowball said. 'It's a proper rain shower out there.'

'But what is this place?' I asked.

'Some kind of barn.'

'Oink.' We both looked up to see a group of fat, pink pigs moving towards us. They shuffled and snorted and didn't look very friendly. Five of them descended, all pink skin and rounded bellies. Although they didn't move quickly, as they banded together I could see we were in trouble.

'Oh dear,' I said, as Snowball and I backed away, until we were huddled in the corner of the barn.

'Pigs seem very mean,' Snowball said, not reassuringly at all. 'I've never been this close to any but I've heard all sorts about them. Apparently they eat anything and everything.'

'Which could include us…' We were literally backed into a corner. They were coming closer, heads shaking a little, feet stomping beneath their immense weight. They looked at us with hungry eyes. Snowball cowered behind me. We were going to be pigswill at this rate. I had to get us out of this mess. After all, I was the tom here. I took some deep breaths, trying to calm myself down even though the animals were almost upon us.

'OK, they aren't as big as cows. How about we run through their legs?' I suggested. Although I was terrified, I couldn't see another way out.

'We could try, but look at those feet, the weight they carry. I wouldn't want to get trampled under them.' Snowball shivered. We were both cold and scared. This romantic day wasn't turning out quite how I had expected.

'I know,' I said, 'but look, we have no option – they look like they want to eat us!' I tried to be the man of the relationship – the pigs were only inches away from us. I had to act, so I sort of pushed Snowball a bit and then darted between the legs of the nearest pig, looking behind to check she was following. 'Come on, Snowy, it'll be fine,' I encouraged, as one of the pigs gave an angry snort.

Snowball didn't hang around; she ran for it and joined me. The pigs looked a bit confused but luckily their bulk slowed them down as they tried to come after us. We were far quicker and after a couple more pig-dodges we emerged triumphant, relieved, and thankful to be safe. The rain had eased off and was now more of a drizzle.

'Shall we risk going back home in this?' I asked.

'Best do, I don't fancy my chances with those pigs.'

'You've been so calm around the farm animals so far,' I pointed out. Snowball looked even more terrified than I felt.

'I know, but pigs… As I said, I don't have much experience of them, but I've heard things.' Her eyes shone with fear.

'They did look as if they'd be happy to eat us both.' I looked around so we could start our journey home and my heart sank yet again. 'Snowball?'

'Yes, Alfie?' She was trying to clean some straw from her fur.

'Which way is home?' I asked. She stopped what she was doing and looked at me. I stared glumly back at her. I had no idea where we were.

'Oh no, we were in such a rush to get out of the rain, I didn't even notice which direction we were going,' she cried.

Could this day get any worse? I looked around again but

all I could see were fields. Fields in all directions – and they all looked the same. We were well and truly lost.

As we discussed what to do next, I led us to a nearby hedge so at least we could shelter from the rain while we argued.

'I think we just head off and hope for the best,' I said.

'Great, Alfie, you always have a smart plan and now you're saying that we just head off with no idea where we're going,' Snowball snapped. I knew she was cross but I felt that was unfair. It wasn't just my fault we were lost after all. I was nestling further into the hedge when something – or rather someone – stopped me, and I found myself nose to nose with a rather large, shabby tabby.

'Hiss,' he said.

'Hello.' I kept it friendly. He was much bigger than me after all. That said, I liked to pride myself on staying trim and taking care of my appearance, and the same certainly couldn't be said for this cat.

'Who are you?' he asked.

'I'm Alfie and this is Snowball. We're on holiday with our families.'

'Don't be ridiculous, cats don't go on holiday.' He grimaced, showing quite sharp teeth, and for a moment I wasn't sure if he was going to attack. I tried to keep calm, my ears moving sideways with nerves and my tail swaying. I wasn't an aggressive cat but I did have my girlfriend to protect.

'I know it's quite strange, but honestly we are,' Snowball replied, stepping forwards. The tabby took one look at her blue eyes and white fur and immediately preened himself, sitting up straighter and waving his tail in a friendly gesture. A bit too friendly, if you ask me.

'How are you doing?' he asked, grinning. 'Let me introduce myself. I'm Roddy and I'm a local resident. I'm sorry if you think me rude but, well, I'm not used to visiting cats.' He blinked at Snowball, which is our equivalent of blowing kisses. Just who did this Roddy think he was?

'We live in London,' I replied haughtily. Anyone who thinks that cats don't flirt should have seen him as he stretched out his paws and wrapped his tail neatly round his body. I decided he was too big and scruffy to be considered good-looking, which was a relief. I, with my blue-grey fur and svelte figure, was often complimented on my handsomeness. In any case, I was pretty secure in my looks and I knew Snowball was loyal, so I tried to relax a bit.

'London, you say? Well I don't know anything about that.' He was looking directly at Snowball.

'The thing is,' Snowball said, a little bit too flirtatiously, 'we're a little lost. We tried to shelter from the rain and ended up trapped in a barn with some rather unfriendly pigs and now we don't know how to get back to the holiday house.' She tilted her head, and I saw that already Roddy was smitten.

'Where are you staying?' he asked, puffing his chest out. 'I'm a bit of an expert on these parts.'

'A big house,' I replied, not exactly enjoying this exchange, though I acknowledged he was probably our best hope.

'That narrows it down,' he said sarcastically.

'Well Roddy,' purred Snowball, stretching out her paws, 'it's near the farm, we have hens on the edge of the garden and there's a field of cows directly in front of us.'

'Ah, I know where you mean. Right, city cats, follow me and I'll have you home in no time.'

\*\*\*

Despite us getting a bit wet and being a little bit stressed from our adventure, Roddy got us home safely, and although I was still a bit annoyed at his flirting with my girlfriend, I thanked him graciously. I was relieved. As we left him at the door, he was still marvelling at how odd it was for cats to go on holiday.

The fire wasn't lit as the house was empty, but it was warm as we lay down in front of it to dry off. I decided that, as our romantic trip had been my idea, I would be magnanimous.

'I'm sorry that our day went a bit wrong,' I said, nuzzling into Snowball's neck.

'And I'm sorry I snapped. I was just scared. But you took care of me, like always,' she said, returning the nuzzle.

'Well, it was Roddy who saved us,' I pointed out.

'Maybe, but you're my hero, not him,' she said, and I couldn't have felt happier.

The door opened and our families, dripping wet, walked into the living room.

'Let's light the fire and get ourselves out of these wet clothes before we catch pneumonia,' Karen said.

'Look at those two, just relaxing by the warm hearth while we nearly drowned on the beach,' Jonathan said, getting the kindling into the grate. With our eyes half closed, Snowball and I grinned at each other. How little they knew.

# Chapter
# Four

'Hope it hasn't been too boring for you two,' Jonathan said, as everyone breakfasted together on our last full day of the holiday.

'Nah,' Christopher replied. 'It's been good.' He looked a bit sheepish, but then he was a teenage boy and apparently they are all somewhat monosyllabic.

'I've enjoyed doing nothing,' Daisy answered. 'If it all goes to plan I'll be busy with work when we get back.'

'According to Polly, you're going to be the next Kate Moss,' Claire said.

'If I could be just a fraction as successful as she is, I'll be over-joyed,' Daisy laughed. She didn't realise how stunning she really was, I thought – a bit like Snowball. Although Snowball had been aloof when I first met her, it wasn't because she thought she was a beauty, and even now she was still unaware of the effect she had on other cats and people. Like Roddy, most male cats started drooling like dogs when they first saw her. Myself included, I have to admit.

'So what shall we do today?' Karen asked as she buttered another piece of toast.

'How about we hang out here, maybe go for a walk, and then have lunch at home?' Tim suggested.

'Sounds nice,' Claire said, trying and failing to spoon cereal into Summer's closed mouth.

'TOAST,' Summer shouted. Claire looked exasperated but Jonathan laughed indulgently.

'I wish she could learn to say fruit or porridge at least,' Claire said.

'My girl knows her own mind,' Jonathan replied. 'Chip off the old block.' Claire swiped at him with her arm.

'God, then I'm in trouble,' she joked.

'I'm going to do some computer stuff,' Christopher said, looking bashful. He was turning out to be quite a chip off his old block himself, if that means what I think it does. He was following in his father's footsteps by being a computer genius, or something along those lines.

'Hey, Claire, I know you've got that book you keep trying to read, so I'll take Summer out round the farm this morning. She loves the animals and you can stick your head in your novel,' Jonathan said, giving her a kiss on the cheek.

'My God, now I remember why I married you.'

'I'll come with you, Jon,' Karen said, and Tim nodded.

I looked at Snowball. It would be just the two of us again; maybe we could go for a romantic meander in the garden. After our adventure on the farm the other day we had stayed close to the holiday house, and I wasn't sure that it would be a good idea to explore.

For a while, Snowball and I stayed in the garden, close to where Claire sat in a lawn chair, reading. Chris was inside, Daisy had gone for a run, and the others had gone for a walk. As the morning drew on we decided to visit the hens. We nodded at them in greeting – I was no longer afraid – and they wobbled their heads in response. I knew they weren't scary now. Being in the country was an education about other animals, ones we didn't really get in London.

'All right, city cats,' said Roddy, suddenly appearing from

behind the hen enclosure.

'Hey, Roddy,' said Snowball.

'We need to thank you again for the other day,' I said, remembering my manners.

'You're welcome. Anyway what are you guys up to?' Roddy asked.

'It's our last day here, we leave tomorrow,' I explained, feeling relaxed and friendly. I definitely found the country enjoyable, though I missed many things about London, like my friends, especially Tiger, and my other families. I also missed the hustle and bustle, the constant noise. At night here, it was eerily quiet, but back home I could hear cars, voices and the odd siren. Silence took a bit of getting used to.

'In that case, how about I take you to my favourite place?' suggested Roddy.

'What is it?' Snowball asked.

'You'll see, it's lovely. Come on, come with me.' He ran off and we sprang after him. As we crossed a different – and thankfully cow-free – field, I realised how nice the country smelled. I breathed in deeply, enjoying the fresh scents. I was happy that we were having a last adventure and with Roddy with us there was no danger involved. Well, I hoped not anyway.

We set off and took a route that we were more familiar with, passing the outskirts of the field where we'd met the giant cow. There were a few cows there, but they were at the other end of the field and were so busy eating grass they didn't pay us much attention. I can't say I was sorry.

'Come on, let's keep going,' Roddy said, as we followed close behind him.

I blinked at Snowball and she blinked back as we came upon a stream.

'I am not a fan of water,' I stated.

'Nah, me neither, Alfie. But look, there's a bridge just up here. Come on.' Roddy led us across a small wooden bridge and then came to a halt. As I looked around, I almost felt my breath being taken away. We were standing in a clearing on the edge of a wood, trees densely surrounding us. Sunlight glinted between the branches and reflected off the leaves, it was beautiful.

'It's a forest,' Snowball exclaimed.

'Yeah, it's my forest,' Roddy said, although I was pretty sure it wasn't.

'Wow, it's beautiful,' I stated. 'Almost as beautiful as you.' I nuzzled Snowball. She smiled coyly and raised her whiskers.

'It reminds me a bit of my old home,' Snowball said. 'We had a big wood just outside our garden and I would chase squirrels, although they could be mean. They were particularly protective of their nuts.'

'I can see why you'd miss it,' I conceded. As much as I loved Edgar Road and London, I did see the beauty of this place.

We stood at the bottom of a large tree. Roddy said that if we climbed up it we would see the most spectacular view. Snowball looked at me questioningly and gestured towards the tree. I shook my head – I was staying on the ground. I'd been stuck up a tree in the past, twice in fact, and it wasn't fun. So I stayed put and watched as Roddy and Snowball climbed higher and higher, feeling a little bit jealous and half wishing I could join them. But ultimately I was glad to be on firm ground where I found some leaves to play with.

After a while I saw Snowball scaling back down and I was

relieved that she was managing it easily.

'Right, let's get back before you're missed,' Roddy said, bounding off.

He took us a different route home, and I felt so energised by the journey, with the wind in my fur, the warming sun above and the tickly green grass beneath my paws, that I started fooling around a bit. I turned and walked backwards.

'What are you doing?' Snowball asked, raising her whiskers.

'Hey, I can go backwards, look at me,' I said, showing off. I started trying to run backwards, which wasn't as easy as I thought – in all honesty, I'd never tried it before. I felt my legs tangle and I tried to turn around but ended up falling on my bottom. Luckily, something soft broke my fall.

'Yelp!' I said. But what was that smell? I stood up and, trying to get away from the smell, ended up running round in circles – wherever I went, it seemed to follow. I heard laughter from Roddy and saw that Snowball was hiding behind her paw.

'What?' I asked.

'You fell into a cow pat!' she said. I looked down and saw that the soft thing that had broken my fall was in fact the source of the terrible smell. Those monster cows had left a monster mess, and I was now covered in it! As I walked dejectedly home, my earlier energy deflated, I knew that there would be only one thing for it: a bath. I really dislike baths, or actually water in any form – even rain upsets me, and don't get me started on puddles. But I knew I had no choice.

We said a fond farewell to Roddy back at the house.

'You're a lucky guy,' he said to me, gesturing towards Snowball. She purred and looked coy.

'I know I am – she's wonderful. Thank you for everything,'

I said, as I bade him a warm goodbye.

I was still covered in mess and I didn't dare enter the house. 'Maybe if you go inside, you can miaow loudly and get some-one's attention?' I said to Snowball. As much as I hated baths, I really wanted to get this mess off me as soon as possible.

Snowball went off and returned after what seemed like ages with Claire. I was beginning to really hate the smell. It was another reason for me to add cows to my list of things to be avoided.

'What on earth?' Claire said. 'Snowball was making such a racket, I thought something was wrong.' She took a closer look at me. 'Oh God, Alfie, did you roll in something bad?' I miaowed to show my disagreement – as if I would do anything like this on purpose!

Claire wrapped me in a towel to carry me inside, holding me at arm's length as she took me straight to the bathroom. I could see that Snowball found the whole thing amusing; we would be having words about that later. As Claire ran a shallow bath, muttering about the way I smelled, I stayed very still. She gently put me in the water and I tried not to squirm, but as the warm wet stuff started to engulf my body, I found it so uncom-fortable that I wriggled a bit. I wasn't sure which was worse, the bath or the smell. Actually, it was definitely the smell.

'Keep still, Alfie,' she said crossly as I squirmed. I couldn't stay still. Eventually, after what felt like forever, Claire carefully lifted me out and dried me off. 'Go and lie by the fire, you'll soon be all dry and warm,' she said. She didn't need to ask twice, and I quickly ran out of the room.

I curled up by the fire and Snowball joined me.

'You smell much better, thank goodness,' she said, nuzzling into my neck.

'You know, I'm going to miss a few things about this holiday but the fire is definitely one of the things I'll miss most,' I said, yawning. What an eventful day we'd had. I closed my eyes, and soon I was dreaming of pilchards.

A while later, I was aware of voices as I woke up, and sensed the presence of everyone in the living room.

'I can't believe we have to leave in the morning,' said Jonathan. I kept my eyes closed, enjoying the warmth in my fur as I listened. I could picture him, stretched out on the sofa. He sounded quite mellow. Jonathan was often uptight, and it was clear the holiday had done him good.

'It's been a good holiday though, mate,' Tim said.

'I'm just worried about how Alfie's going to be you know, if…' I heard Claire say. I pricked up my ears. I could tell that Snowball was still asleep next to me. She made this really sweet noise as she slept. Some called it snoring but to me it was music.

'And Snowball,' Karen added. 'It's weird, I never thought cats were like that, we've always been led to believe they're solitary creatures, certainly not animals that mate for life.'

'Like lobsters,' Tim said.

'What?' Jonathan asked. I was trying to follow this conversation but it wasn't proving easy.

'You know, lobsters, they mate for life,' Tim explained.

'But look at them,' Claire said, sounding sad. 'Snuggled up together. They definitely love each other.'

'God, I feel guilty already,' said Tim. 'But this time, it's not my family I might be letting down, but my cat.'

'It might not even happen,' said Karen.

I gave Snowball a gentle nudge, but she was fast asleep. This conversation made no sense to me, and my fur suddenly felt freezing cold.

'It'll be such a shame if you did,' Claire said.

'Anyway it might not happen,' Karen repeated, indicating that that was the end of the conversation.

What on earth were they talking about? It was as if they were talking about something that would be bad for me and Snowball. I tried to put it out of my mind but I couldn't.

As the humans all went to sort out dinner that evening, and Jonathan put Summer to bed, I finally got Snowball on her own.

'I heard something weird when you were sleeping. Your family were talking about something strange, but I didn't understand what. It sounded like something that might happen to us. Do you know anything about it?'

Snowball surveyed me with her cool blue eyes. 'What do you mean?' She sounded shocked; she obviously didn't know anything.

'Tim said something about letting his cat down if it happened. Karen said it might not happen, but I don't know what "it" is. I didn't like the sound of it though.'

'Alfie, you're talking in riddles! I have no idea what you're going on about. We both know what you're like, always looking for drama.' Snowball yawned and stretched. She didn't seem worried but I couldn't shake the feeling that all wasn't well.

'OK, if you say so, but let's see if we hear anything.'

'Of course, Alfie. I love you, and I love that you worry so much, but we've had a wonderful trip together. Let's just focus on that.'

I couldn't argue.

# Chapter
# Five

I was suffering from what I had learnt were called post-holiday blues. Being home was exciting at first. I saw Tiger and my other friends and was reunited with my other humans on Edgar Road, which of course was lovely. Still though, I was fed up. I missed spending all my time with Snowball; I still saw her but not as much. I also missed the country walks, the fresh air, the romance, the fire we slept in front of… Even the hens. And of course it had rained every day in London since we'd been home, so after my initial visits to all my friends I had been largely stuck indoors. I felt as limp as the weather. I was totally bored and listless.

And there was something bothering me. I was still a little perplexed by the confusing things I'd heard on the last day of the holiday. No one had said anything about it, so I still had no idea what they had been discussing. Snowball and I had been listening out for any more clues, but apart from the usual hushed conversations that humans were so keen on, I hadn't noticed anything amiss and neither had she. Perhaps she was right, we should just ignore it and not worry. It was probably nothing… So why did I still feel so unsettled? I tried to tell myself it was the post-holiday blues that were making me feel so rattled, nothing more.

As I sat on the living room windowsill, I saw a man putting something on a nearby lamppost. Soon after, I saw Tiger approaching my front gate. I ran to the kitchen, dived through the cat flap and made my way round to the front of the house. My blues were momentarily cheered at the sight of my friend.

'Hey, Alfie,' Tiger said, a bit breathlessly.

'What's going on?' I asked. She lifted her head towards the lamppost and I saw that there was a picture of a tabby cat on it, along with some words – which, of course, being a cat, I couldn't read. 'What is that?' I asked.

'Not sure, there were two others that went up on lampposts while you were away. None of us cats know what they mean.'

'I'm not sure either.' I felt puzzled. 'Let's go and see the others,' I suggested. 'See if they know anything.' Something was bothering me, but I wasn't sure what. As we made our way to the end of the street, we saw the other two cat pictures, but we didn't recognise the cats.

'Are these the only other two?' I asked Tiger.

'Yup. Weird, huh?'

We found Elvis and Nellie at our usual meeting place. They were sitting away from the damp grass, on a strip of concrete that was relatively dry.

'Guess what?' Tiger said.

'What?' Nellie loved drama and looked excited.

'We just saw a cat picture going up on a lamppost,' said Tiger.

'Another one? What can they mean?' Elvis asked.

'I'm not sure,' I said. 'But something is niggling me.'

'I think we should definitely keep an eye on it. This all seems very strange,' Tiger said. As we lapsed into silence, Salmon, our nemesis cat, approached.

'He might know,' hissed Nellie, although we were all loath to ask him.

'What are you up to?' Salmon asked, narrowing his eyes and flicking his tail in a hostile way. Salmon was the meanest of cats and never missed an opportunity to be horrible to us.

'Just hanging out with friends, something you know nothing about,'Tiger replied. She was the only one of us not scared of Salmon.

'Very funny, Tiger.'

'Salmon,' Elvis cut in quickly. 'We just saw another cat picture going up. Do you know what they mean?'

Salmon flicked his tail again. 'Of course I know, but I can't possibly tell you.'

'Which means he doesn't have a clue,' I cut in.

'I do! I know far more than you think,' he hissed. 'Why don't you find that girlfriend of yours and ask her what's going on.'

'What do you mean?' I felt angry now – how dare he bring Snowball into this.

'I just heard her owners talking to mine, and let's just say it doesn't look good for you.' He licked his lips, looking pleased with himself.

'Salmon, tell me right now, or I'll, I'll…'

'You'll what? Set your girlfriend on me?' he laughed, and before I could say anything else, he bounded off.

'What could Salmon mean by that?' Nellie asked. But as my cat friends looked at me, worry in their eyes, I knew there could only be bad news to come. I had to get to Snowball.

I found Snowball waiting by my front gate. As soon as I saw her, I knew that something was very wrong.

'We're in trouble, Alfie,' she said.

'What have we done?' I asked. I was prone to a bit of trouble but I didn't think I had done anything lately.

'No,' said Snowball, wiggling further into the bush. It was

45

still a bit damp from the rain but she looked so serious that I didn't complain. 'Not that sort of trouble. You know that conversation you heard? Well, it seems it wasn't nothing after all.'

'Snowball, slow down, you're not making any sense at all.'

'OK, well, Tim and Karen were talking to Daisy and Christopher last night. It seems that we're moving away, because Tim's been offered a really good job.'

'Moving away?' I asked, my heart sinking into my paws. The Snells had been through a terrible time when they first moved to Edgar Road. It had taken quite a while and a lot of planning from me to make them part of our community, but we had done it in the end. Surely they wouldn't move away now?

'The worst thing is that the job is in Cheshire.' Snowball looked glum.

'Cheshire? Where is that? Is it far away?' I asked, fearing the answer.

'Yes, it's hours away. Christopher will have to go to a different school, although he doesn't mind, and Daisy said she would be travelling for work so much that it didn't matter to her. And she has friends in London she can stay with. Of course, no one asked me what I thought.'

'Of course they didn't. Humans can be so selfish. Hold on, does this mean you're leaving me, Edgar Road, us?' My eyes were so wide I thought they might ping off my face. Salmon had been right.

'I don't know when exactly, but it sounds like it.' Snowball looked sad and I started to panic. She couldn't go, not when we were so in love. Not when we'd had such a wonderful holiday together. Though I knew full well that although human life worked very differently to cat life, there was no way they could be so cruel to us. It had to be a mistake. It just had to be.

Snowball and I moped around for the rest of the day.

'I don't want to go home,' she said. She was angry and confused, as was I. I did try to be positive, but there's only so much of that you can do in such a dire situation, especially when you have the post-holiday blues to boot. I led Snowball into my house and we curled up in my basket in the living room, both of us upset and worried and trying to take some comfort where we could. We must have fallen asleep because when we woke up, Claire, Jonathan, Summer, Tim and Karen were all staring at us.

'It's as if they know they're going to be separated,' Claire said.

'Alfie is a very perceptive cat,' Jonathan added.

'But how can they know? They're cats,' Tim said.

'Miaow,' I objected.

'See,' Jonathan said. 'Alfie knows.'

Snowball glared at her owners as, now fully awake, we sat side by side.

'Maybe...' Karen sounded uncertain. 'Maybe you should try to explain it to them, properly. You know, man to cat?'

'Really?' Tim asked. 'You want me to talk to the cats and tell them?'

'I think it's a good idea,' Claire concurred.

'Yes, go on, Tim.' I wasn't sure if Jonathan was goading Tim because he found it amusing, but he was smirking a bit. I gave him one of my looks and thankfully he had the grace to look ashamed. After all, this was clearly no joking matter.

Tim cleared his throat. Snowball and I looked at him expectantly.

'We love living here, on this street, and we've made some great friends.' Tim looked really uncomfortable. 'But just as moving here was a big decision for our family, and far from ideal at the time, actually, we have had to make another difficult decision. You see, Snowball and Alfie, I've been offered a dream job, a really amazing opportunity. It means we can buy our own home again, so I can give my family the security they need and deserve.' He was a bit pink. I looked at Snowball, who looked at me. I felt a sense of disbelief. Although I had heard they were moving already, having this confirmation from Tim wasn't making it any easier. I had been holding onto the hope that the rumours weren't true.

'As much as we hate to leave here,' Tim continued, 'having spoken to the family, we feel we have to take this opportunity. We'll be leaving in a few weeks. It's all happened very quickly actually.' He looked at us expectantly but we just stared back at him. 'And I never wanted to part you two,' he added.

'Oh, Alfie, it'll be all right,' Claire said, scooping me up in her arms. But I knew it wouldn't. As I looked at Snowball sitting in my cat basket, her manner changed from sad to angry, I knew it would never be all right again. I felt a sense of rage building inside me. How could they do this to us?

I thought about running away. Maybe Snowball and I could run back to the country, to where we'd been so happy, but I knew we wouldn't. I couldn't do the homeless thing again, no matter how much I loved her, and I knew that even though I was angry with our families right now, we both loved them very much. It was an impossible, impossible situation.

All I could hear as the humans began trying to reassure us was the sound of my heart breaking.

# Chapter Six

It was the day before they were due to leave. The day before my true love was to be ripped away from me. I had been beside myself since Tim's chat a few weeks ago. Snowball and I had snatched as much time together as we could but something had changed: it was awkward between us, because we knew that it was coming to an end. When we spent time together, it hurt badly. We both felt so sad that our time together was almost over. Yet again, I was losing someone that I loved; how much could my cat heart take?

Claire looked glum as she picked me up and gave me a kiss on the top of my head. Jonathan looked sombre. I had heard them talking, and although they were sad for Snowball and me, I knew they'd also miss the good friends they had made in Edgar Road. I didn't have the energy to feel sorry for them; I didn't even have the energy to miaow. I just wanted to curl up in my bed and cry silently.

Saying goodbye is one of life's biggest cruelties and I had spent a lot of time in my short life saying it. It never got any easier, and this looked set to be the worst one yet.

Claire carried me next door to say a final goodbye to the Snells and Snowball. Tim answered the door, and everyone hugged awkwardly as we walked into the house. It was almost all packed up and the sight of the boxes made me want to wail. Claire gently put me down.

'Snowball's in the garden, she's very unhappy,' Karen said as she led the way.

I went into the garden and sat next to Snowball. The humans stood on the other side of the patio door but I could feel their eyes on us. For a few minutes neither of us spoke.

'So this is it then,' Snowball said. She raised her whiskers but I could see the despondency in the gesture.

'I just don't know what to say,' I replied. 'I wish I could say that we could do something to stop this, but for a cat who is used to solving problems, I have nothing here.' I felt the pain of her impending departure in every fibre of my fur.

'Remember how awful I was to you when I first met you,' she said.

'Yes, you weren't very nice. Even after I rescued you, when you accidentally got yourself lost all those years ago. But I never gave up.'

'And you taught me so much. I don't want to go, Alfie. I don't want to leave you but at least I can say I learnt a lot from you.'

'I can't even begin to tell you how much I'm going to miss you,' I told her. She rested her head on mine. I almost felt as if I would stop breathing.

'Alfie, don't come and see me tomorrow. I don't know if I could bear it,' she said. I could feel her pain as a mirror to my own.

'I'm not sure I could either. But remember I will always love you and you are in my heart forever,' I said.

'And mine.' Her voice broke and we stayed like that for as long as we could bear it, before we had to tear ourselves away.

Cats might not produce tears, but believe me, we were both weeping. And when I slowly made my way back inside, I saw that Jonathan, Claire, Karen and Tim all had tears in their eyes.

Our 'purrfect' love had touched everyone. I just wished it didn't hurt so much.

I sat in my front garden staring at a big removal van. I normally loved the sight of removal vans, as they heralded the arrival of a new family, an area of fascination for a doorstep cat like me, but today as I smoothed down my grey fur, I hated that van. It was taking the Snells' furniture away, followed by the family and my beloved Snowball. The nightmare we had first heard about on holiday was actually coming true.

I didn't know how to cope with the despair I was feeling as I stared at the removal van. I wanted to tear myself away and run inside, but I couldn't stop watching. I was both horrified and mesmerised.

I heard a noise as my best cat friend, Tiger, squeezed under my gate. Although Tiger could be feisty and she hadn't exactly been Snowball's biggest fan when they first met, she had thawed towards her and the two cat women in my life had formed a rapport, almost becoming friends.

'Oh dear,' she said, looking at me. Tiger wasn't known for sugar-coating anything.

'Look, they're filling the van, and by the end of today they'll all be gone,' I said, wanting to yowl with pain.

'I know and I am sorry, Alfie, it's really tough. Oh boy, I don't know what to say. Look, I know you and Snowball have already said goodbye but don't you want to see her one last time?'

'Tiger, every day since we heard the news it's as if we've been waiting to say goodbye and it's been horrible. I would rather be chased by a dog and get stuck up a tree than go

through this again. Besides, we said goodbye properly yesterday. I promised her I'd stay indoors today – but I couldn't.'

'Look, come on, I'll take you to the park and we can chase
birds, or tease dogs, it's your choice.' She patted me with her
paw. 'I promise I won't let you get stuck up a tree.' I knew she
was trying to cheer me up but I couldn't feel anything but
gloom at the idea of never seeing Snowball again.

'OK, but I can't promise I'll be good company. In fact, I
know I'll be terrible company.'

'Yeah, well, I'm used to that,' Tiger said, but she gave me an
affectionate look at the same time.

I tried to take my mind off Snowball, and goodness knows
Tiger did all she could, but it was still too raw. Tiger tried
everything to cheer me up: finding butterflies for me to chase,
telling me how Nellie tripped on something – she's a bit
clumsy – and landed on Rocky, which apparently was funny
if you were there. She even tried to involve me in the mystery of the pictures on the lamppost, but I couldn't muster up
enthusiasm for anything.

I felt as if I would never be happy again, but I was clinging
onto the hope that one day I would start to feel better. I knew
I would eventually; I had been through enough in my life to
know that although heartbreak never fully went away, it did
fade – you just had to give it time. I was quite wise, having
accumulated much life experience during my eight cat years. I
would never stop loving Snowball or missing her, but the way
I was feeling right now would get easier. The pain of losing
someone you loved never totally disappeared, but you did get
used to living with it. That was how I saw it.

'I'm sorry, Tiger. I'm so miserable. I'm just not great company,' I said as I lay down by my favourite flowerbed. A leaf flopped on my head and I brushed it away listlessly.

'It's fine, I understand. Remember when Tom went away?' Tom was a grumpy cat who used to live on our street. He was sort of Tiger's boyfriend, although she never seemed to like him that much. His owner had died and we had all rallied around trying to figure out where he could live, but a relative took Tom to live with them and he was happy to go. Tiger had been a bit sad but then she didn't exactly love Tom the way I loved Snowball, although for a few days she had been like a cat with a sore head.

'Yeah, you were really scratchy,' I said.

'OK, yeah, so you're miserable and I was scratchy but the principle is the same. We're friends, and friends stick together no matter what – even when they're not the best company. So if you want to wallow or sulk or cry or even be angry, I'm here for you. Whatever you need, Alfie, I'll always be here for you.'

'Tiger, you're such a good friend and I really appreciate you. I hope you know that.'

'Well, good, and luckily for you I'm not going anywhere.'

'Please don't, I couldn't bear to lose you as well.' And then I crumpled. To preserve what little dignity I had left, I shuffled fully under the nearest bush and then I yowled. I could feel the pain in every sound that escaped my mouth. Finally, when I was exhausted and could make no more noise, I emerged, tired and feeling as if I had lost something of myself. Tiger, who had been waiting patiently, put her paw on mine.

'Come on, Alfie, I'll take you home,' she said.

\*\*\*

The van had left by the time we got back to my house and so had the Snells' car. They had gone. Tiger walked me to the back door and bade me farewell at the cat flap. I went through it, although even that felt like a major effort. I padded sadly to the kitchen. Claire, Jonathan and Summer and Polly, Matt and their children – Henry and Martha – were all there. They looked at me and I saw the sympathy in their eyes. Well, not the children – they just played on the floor, oblivious to my pain. I noticed that my favourite food, pilchards, sat in my bowl, but I had no appetite.

'Alfie,' Claire said. I just looked at each of them, sadly, and walked out, ignoring the food and going upstairs to my bed on the landing. I curled up in it and begged for sleep to come.

# Chapter
# Seven

I sat on the sofa, listlessly watching the sun stream through the window. It had been a week since Snowball left, and the longing I felt, just to see her, speak to her, hear her voice, was all consuming. I had barely been out; I didn't even want to see my friends. I just wanted to be alone with my poor, aching heart. Even Summer's lovely smile had been unable to cheer me up, although I did put on a brave face for her, letting her cuddle me and even pull my tail, although that took all the energy I had.

This evening, my Polish family – Franceska, big Tomasz, Aleksy and little Tomasz – were all coming over in yet another effort to cheer me up. It was Claire's idea. I wanted to try to be more like my old self, if only for my humans' sakes, as they were being so kind and trying so hard, but I was oh so tired. It was like I had an illness of the heart.

'Alfie?' Jonathan sat down next to me, interrupting my thoughts. I nudged my head lethargically against his arm. It was the most I could offer.

'Right, Alfie,' he said. He was wearing his work clothes, the smart ones he normally kept away from me in case a bit of my fur snuck onto them, and he had a beer in his hand. This must be serious if he was risking his best clothes, I thought, and I couldn't resist rubbing my head against his suit sleeve. I might be a bit down in the dumps but still… Especially as he didn't even tell me off! He took a sip of his beer and then, looking solemn, he put it down on the coffee table.

'I know that this sucks,' he said, looking slightly embarrassed. 'We were very sad that Snowball had to go – we knew how close you two had become. But it's human stuff. Jobs, houses, schools, it all added up to the Snells having to move away, and unfortunately you're a casualty of that.' He paused to lean forwards and take another sip of beer. I looked at him; I had no idea where this was going. 'The thing is that women, well, we love them and we lose them sometimes – but then you might find someone like I found Claire.' He beamed as if he had solved all my problems.

'Miaow.' *He* found Claire, really? I think he'll find I handed her to him on a plate! I rolled my eyes, as I thought back to my careful matchmaking when I first arrived on Edgar Road.

'Claire is wonderful, and I love her deeply. She may have her moments, but when I think about some of the women I have been with… Goodness, I still shudder to remember them.'

No, I still had no idea where this was going.

'So, anyway, the thing is, you need to dust yourself off and get back out there. You know, back in the game. Stalking alleyways for new cats the way we go to bars.'

Was he for real? Was he telling me to go down an alleyway?

'You see,' Jonathan continued. 'The best way to get over heartbreak is to put yourself out there, even if it's just for a bit of fun. Oh yes, the rebound is actually quite healthy, and you must have ways of meeting cat ladies. That Tiger down the road is pretty cute for a stripy cat. Anyway, it's like they say, you need to get back on the horse.'

He looked pleased with himself as he downed the rest of his beer and stood up. I looked at him. Was he mad? Horses?

Tiger? I might be heartbroken but Jonathan had lost the plot. If I could talk to humans I would have had a lot of questions to ask him. Instead, I put my head down, even more exhausted than before.

Claire came into the room.

'Oh, there you are.' She came up to Jonathan and kissed him. 'How did it go?' she asked.

'Yeah, I think I got through to him,' he said as I lay down on the sofa and curled myself up into a ball.

'Really? He still looks sad,' Claire pointed out.

'Give him a bit of time. We had a chat, like you asked me to. You know – man to cat. It's all good.'

As they both left the room, Claire looked back at me – she clearly wasn't convinced. But then again, neither was I.

After a short catnap, I got up and greeted my other families. Although the adults could deal with my heartache, I knew the children couldn't, especially my first-ever child friend, Aleksy, who was nearly eleven now and had always been a sensitive boy. He would hate to see me sad. Little Tomasz, who wasn't so little, nearly as big as Aleksy despite being three years younger, was more of a physical child, and he didn't really pick up on emotions. Polly and Matt's children, Henry, who was almost five, and three-year-old Martha, were too young to under-stand my pain. As I played with them, mainly with a ball and ribbons, I made a huge effort. It wasn't easy, but to see my friends smiling and hear them laugh was a tonic. I made a spe-cial fuss of all the children, especially Aleksy, and it did cheer me up just a tiny little bit. It was lovely to be surrounded by the love of my families. Having all of them there was such a treat, and I just about managed to be like the old me for a short while.

My families got together frequently. Polly and Matt lived on the same street and I often spent time at their house, where they had been kind enough to install a cat flap for me. Frankie and Tomasz lived a few streets away, above the restaurant they owned. The restaurant food was delicious.

Talking of food, I was distracted by the smell of it. Tomasz had brought a feast from his restaurant for everyone and he'd brought me sardines which, even though my appetite wasn't quite what it normally was, were quite welcome. I tried my best to appreciate the food and count my blessings, although it wasn't easy. Nothing at the moment was easy – it was as if my paws were stuck in mud.

'So how is Alfie?' Franceska asked Claire. I could hear them, as they had a habit of talking in front of me as if I didn't understand. They did the same with the younger children.

'Sad. He seems sad. He's been off his food and he's barely been out. I know he'll recover but it's heartbreaking,' Claire said. She liked to read books, and lately she had been reading classic romances, which seemed to have made her even softer than normal. 'I just feel so terrible for him, to love and then to lose. We've all been there, haven't we?'

'He'll be fine,' Jonathan cut in. 'He's a man, he'll soon bounce back.'

'Typical male point of view,' Polly added.

'I'm sure Jon's right. He'll soon be his old self,' said Matt.

'Hey, why doesn't he come and stay with us for a couple of days,' big Tomasz suggested. 'A change of scene might help.'

'That's not a bad idea,' Claire said. 'Maybe next weekend?'

I gave up eating and curled up by Franceska's feet, nestling into her legs. A weekend away wouldn't solve my problems, but it would be nice to be with them all and it would mean I wouldn't have to look at the empty house next door. Plus, I'd have the boys to keep me occupied and I'd get to spend time with my cat friend Dustbin. I felt something akin to hope for the first time since I had heard that Snowball was leaving.

'Yeah, can he come?' Aleksy said, sounding excited. It seemed it was all settled. I would take my broken heart away for the weekend.

That night, I was thinking about my weekend away when I heard Jonathan and Claire arguing. It was a funny kind of argument though, because ever since Summer was born, they rowed in whispered voices. I was worried. After all, whilst I had enough problems of my own, I didn't want anyone else to be unhappy – I wasn't sure I could bear it. I crept closer to their room to listen.

'Look, we can get a second opinion,' I heard Jonathan say.

'You mean a third opinion. Jon, I am trying to tell you, it's pointless, and it's time we faced facts. I'm OK, really. We were lucky with Summer, but there aren't going to be any more babies. I'm sorry I can't give you another child but at least we have her.'

'I know, we've got Summer and Alfie… It's fine, as long as you're all right. I mean… OK, yes, I would ideally love another child but it's more important that our family – you, me, Sum and Alfie – are all right. I love you.' I felt a bit relieved, it seemed they weren't really arguing after all.

'No, I'm fine. Please don't worry, this isn't going to send

me back to my black days, it really isn't. I'm disappointed, but I think deep down I knew, the tests just confirmed it.' Claire did have dark moments, which made us all worry terribly, but it was only when things went wrong. She seemed to be coping with life so much better these days – there was no doubt that Jonathan and Summer had brought great joy into her life. It was if they had taught her how to be happy.

'So we're OK? Then why are we arguing?'

'I don't know.' I saw Claire sit down on the bed. 'Jonathan, I don't want Summer to be an only child.'

'But you just said you were OK?'

'I am, but that doesn't mean we can't adopt. There are so many children out there who need a good, loving home. We've got all that and more. We have space, we can afford it…'

'I don't know.' I could hear the doubt in Jonathan's voice. 'But why not?'

'Because.' I could almost hear Jonathan folding his arms across his chest. He could be such a child sometimes.

'Because why, darling?' I saw through a crack in the door that Claire had put her arm on his.

'It's complicated. I just think it's a big step, taking in some-one else's child. And then the adoption process is gruelling, we might not even be accepted.'

'Oh, Jon, I'm sure we will, I've spoken to Dad… We might not get a baby, but I know that they are crying out for homes for older children. We're not criminals or insane…' She attempted a laugh.

'I'm not so sure. I mean about adopting, not being a crim-inal. Or insane.'

'OK, but will you at least agree to let me look into it?' I

heard Claire's pleading voice and then Jonathan's sigh.

'If you really have your heart set on it then we can look into it, but I'm not promising anything.'

'Hey, like you said, we might not even be accepted, but at least let me find out. I don't want to wonder about it, that's all.'

'Hey, I'd be more agreeable to you adopting a new girl-friend for Alfie,' Jonathan joked. He often did this when he was uncomfortable, tried to make a joke. A pretty poor joke, in my opinion.

'Jon, that's not funny. But now you mention it…'

'I was joking,' he said.

'I know you were. OK, let's go to bed.' As I saw them settle down for the night, I went back to my basket, thankful that everything was fine and there was nothing to worry about. Apart from myself of course.

# Chapter
# Eight

'So you've never been in love?' I asked. I was in the small yard behind the restaurant with Dustbin. Dustbin was my friend and the cat who sort of worked for Tomasz's restaurant. He was what he referred to as feral; he had never lived in a house before and liked it that way. He lived in the yard outside the restaurant and Franceska and big Tomasz's flat and he kept the vermin under control. We'd known each other since I had started visiting here and he was also one of the wisest cats I'd ever met.

It was nearing the end of the weekend and I have to say that it had done me the world of good. I'd eaten well, having found my appetite, and I found it easier not to pine, being a bit further away from Snowball's old house.

'Can't say I have,' Dustbin replied, eating some leftovers that Tomasz had put out for him, baring his teeth at a foolhardy mouse who had come a bit too close. Dustbin was the master of multi-tasking. 'I'm not that kind of cat. I like my own company most of the time. I like hanging out with you and passing the time of day, and I don't mind hunting with some of the other cats around here, but romance and all that – nah, it's not for me.'

'But love is wonderful,' I continued, feeling quite poetic, despite the fact we were surrounded by bins and rodents in a pretty ugly yard. It certainly wasn't like my last time away, in the country. A picture of Snowball and me popped into my head, running through the long grass without a care in the world, and I yowled.

'That's as maybe, but you're not feeling wonderful now,'

Dustbin pointed out. I couldn't argue with that. 'Look, mate, I know you loved that cat. I remember when we rescued her when she ran away, I saw how much she meant to you then. I'm sorry it's been so tough for you.'

'Thanks, Dustbin. And you're right, but spending the week-end here has been such a tonic, I do feel a bit better.'

'Yeah, well, I think it's good for you to have a break from home, and sometimes a bit of distance can give you perspective. I know that when I have a problem, going off to roam away from here often gives me clarity.'

'You're a wise old cat, even if you've never been in love,' I said, and I meant it. 'But I'd better go now, I think my visit here is nearly over.'

'Ta, Alfie. Right, make sure you come back again soon, now you've got a bit more time on your paws. And maybe I'll teach you to hunt,' he grinned.

'No. I mean, yes, I'll come back, but no to hunting. It never ends well for me.' I shuddered. The last time I had been bitten by a cheeky mouse. It was too humiliating.

'OK, but we can hang out nonetheless. I have to get on now, there's this awful rat who thinks he can come here whenever he wants, and it's time for me to show him who's boss. Unless you want to come with me?'

'Um, as tempting an offer as that is, I think I'll give it a miss,' I said, backing away.

Yes, the weekend had done me some good. The boys had been fun to hang out with: we'd played football – or paw-ball – at the park and I had been given plenty of treats. I felt as if the adults were being extra kind to me, especially food-wise, like they were trying to feed me up. I missed my other humans, especially little Summer, but I was happier than I had been since Snowball left. Although missing Snowball was still occupying most of my time, the weekend had proved a distraction. I couldn't stop hurting, and I wasn't sure if I wanted to. I loved her so much that the pain was a reminder of that, and in some ways it comforted me – although I understood that that made little sense.

I made my way back up to the flat where Aleksy and little Tomasz were playing a game on their games console. Franceska was sitting down, which was rare for her, and having a cup of tea. Big Tomasz was sitting at their small dining table, planning menus for the following week. It was a lovely, harmonious family scene.

'Ha ha, I win,' Aleksy shouted, punching his arm in the air.

'You cheated,' little Tomasz replied.

'I didn't, how could I cheat?' Aleksy looked at his brother who threw the game controller down in a huff. OK, maybe not so lovely.

'Enough, boys,' Franceska said. 'If you can't play nicely together you lose the games. And anyway, we have to go soon to take Alfie home.'

'Oh no, does he have to go?' Aleksy came over and picked me up. Little Tomasz stroked me, all arguments forgotten as I nestled into the boys and purred.

'Yes, unfortunately, then we'll come home and you have to do homework. It's school tomorrow.' The boys started complaining and big Tomasz shushed them as Franceska went to get my things together. They decided that, as it was warm, we would walk home, though I got carried some of the way as I still hadn't fully regained my strength. I was glad to be in big Tomasz's arms when we walked past the Snells' house. There was a 'To Let' sign outside it now, which made me feel terrible all over again; I was almost as empty as that house.

We stood on the doorstep and Jonathan opened the door.

'So glad you're here,' he said. 'Can you all stay for a bit?'

'Just for half an hour,' Franceska replied. 'The boys have homework.'

'I'll put the kettle on then,' Jonathan said. As I walked in, I immediately knew something was different. I could sense something, or I could smell something – I wasn't sure what it was. As big Tomasz put me down in the hall, I knew that something was wrong.

'Oh my,' I heard Franceska exclaim from the kitchen. I stayed where I was, trying to figure out what was going on. The boys stayed with me.

'My goodness, what on earth?' I heard big Tomasz say as he too entered the kitchen.

'It was Claire's idea and I'm not sure it's one of her better ones,' Jonathan replied, sounding tetchy.

'It's gorgeous,' Franceska said.

'I tried to talk her out of it but she wouldn't budge,' Jonathan moaned. 'I mean really!' He didn't sound happy. Just what was going on?

'Well, you gave me the idea. You know, when you said you wished we could adopt a new girlfriend for Alfie,' Claire said.

'Yes, but I was joking and I certainly didn't mean this.'

Oh boy! I couldn't move. Had they got me a new girlfriend? That was crazy. But it made sense with the smell I could detect. Although it didn't exactly smell like a female cat but, yes, there was a definite scent. There was another cat in this house! Oh, what had Claire done now?

'Well, of course we couldn't get him a new girlfriend, you don't just get over love like that,' Claire snapped.

Phew! I was relieved, but if it wasn't a female cat, what was it?

'No, but I'm not sure this is going to help him – or us, for that matter,' Jonathan snapped back.

'Oh, ignore him. It was fate. I saw an advert on the local Facebook "for sale" page. So we went to see him,' Claire said.

Went to see who?

'It was just such brilliant timing. He was supposed to go to a family who had paid a deposit and everything but then changed their minds, so he was ready to go.'

'How old is he?' big Tomasz asked.

'Fourteen weeks.'

I felt my fur stand on end.

'It does sound like fate, and he's very, very beautiful, little *kochanie*,' Franceska said. I heard a tiny little mewing sound.

'Where's Alfie?' Jonathan asked.

I was full of trepidation as I finally walked into the kitchen, terrified as to what I would find. And there, my worst nightmare was confirmed. OK, maybe not my worst nightmare – I mean, it wasn't a dog! But still I shuddered. Claire was cuddling a bundle of fur. A small, orange-and-black striped bundle with grey eyes. Oh, what had she done?

'Alfie, kitten,' Summer said, pointing at it.

'Alfie's kitten?' Aleksy asked, coming up beside me. 'Wow, look at him, he's so cool, I love him!' We all looked at the kitten. The kitten stared at me. He was tiny, and he was in my kitchen, in my house.

'Yes, darling, that's right. Everyone, meet George. Alfie, he's your kitten.'

73

# Chapter
# Nine

My paws were rooted to the spot as Claire bent down to bring me nose to nose with the kitten. *My kitten.* I felt a wave of panic, as he, George, eyed me suspiciously. He really was incredibly small, and somehow also mesmerising. The children were all so excited by him, but I didn't know what to do.

'Can I see?' little Tomasz said, saving me, as the three children crowded round and took turns having a cuddle. George made these quiet and very cute mewing sounds, and I wanted to both take care of him and run away in equal measure.

I used the distraction of the children fussing over him to head to the back door. I needed some fresh air, time to breath and think. Yes, that was what I should do, just take a few moments to clear my head and then I would come back and deal with the situation. What on earth was Claire thinking? How was I supposed to cope with George when I couldn't cope with myself?

At times like this, I couldn't help thinking that Jonathan was infinitely the more sensible of the two. How on earth could Claire think that getting me a kitten would help me in any way, shape or form?

I needed to get out. I wanted to go and see Tiger and tell her about this terrible turn of events, so I ran to jump through my cat flap.

'Yowl.' I hit the cat flap with force, but it didn't move and bounced me backwards, taking me by surprise as I landed on my tail. Ouch, that hurt.

'Oh goodness, sorry, Alfie.' Claire rushed forwards. 'We had to close the cat flap because of George. It's not forever, only until he's allowed out.' She looked a bit guilty at this, at least.

'So how is Alfie going to go out?' Aleksy asked, echoing my thoughts. He was holding George and cuddling him. Normally I might have been put out by the fact that they all seemed far more interested in this striped kitten than me, but I didn't have the energy to be jealous. Especially as I now had a sore tail and no idea how to escape.

'Well, we'll just have to kind of figure it out I guess,' Claire said, looking as if she hadn't thought this through. 'We'll let him out if he stands by the door and then when he wants to come in, he can miaow loudly so we hear him. He is a clever cat after all.' She sounded as if this was the most normal thing, which for me it certainly was not, and Jonathan rolled his eyes. I wished I could do the same; it seemed I was to be a prisoner in my own home. On top of everything else, I had lost my freedom.

'And anyway, he's been out all day. Alfie, you need to stay in and bond with George,' she said. Great. I'd had a lovely weekend away and now I was trapped with a kitten. He might be adorable, but still... This was not what I wanted, not at all.

However, showing my displeasure would have taken energy and, despite the fact that Claire had just managed to make my terrible life even worse, I still loved her. I guessed she was trying to do the right thing. I could hear Franceska saying what a great idea it was and even big Tomasz seemed to agree. It seemed only Jonathan and myself had any reservations about this George. And anyway, what kind of name was that for a kitten?

As we saw my friends out, I nuzzled the boys, wishing in a way that I could go back with them. How simple my life had been that morning: just me and Dustbin, playing with the boys, sardines on tap, heartbreak. But now… Now I had a kitten and no idea what I was supposed to do with him.

I went to the living room and Summer came bounding in after me. She cuddled me, a little roughly, as she always does, but I knew she meant well. I worried fleetingly for George. Summer wasn't the gentlest child and he was so small and fragile.

'Sum, you have to be really careful with George,' Claire said. I felt immediately relieved. She carried George in and put him on the floor. He stood up, not quite as tiny as he had first seemed now that he was on four legs. I tried to remember being that young but my memory failed me. I remembered when I went to my first home, feeling scared, and then having to face the formidable Agnes, my owner's other cat. Though she didn't like me for a few weeks, she eventually became like a sister to me. But that was all I could recall. As George came right up to me, sniffing me, I looked kindly at him. It wasn't his fault. He was just a helpless kitten. Oh goodness, he was my helpless kitten now. I nudged gently at him with my nose. I didn't have it in me to be anything but kind to the poor little thing. As he looked at me with those eyes, waving his little tail gently, I knew that, somehow, I had to take care of him. He *was* my kitten.

'Look, Jonathan, look, Alfie already loves him. I knew it!' Claire sounded triumphant. George looked at me questioningly. Although Agnes had eventually come round, it had been diffi-cult and scary for me at first, and I couldn't do that to George.

I wouldn't do it to anyone, but especially not this little chap. But then I'm a tom and we are typically far less difficult than women. Well, I think so anyway! George came closer to me and then Summer approached with a piece of ribbon in her hands. He was wide-eyed as he bounded over to play with it.

As Summer giggled and George chased the ribbon, Claire looked on happily. Even I couldn't stop a smile finding its way onto my face.

'I knew it would work out. Adding to our family isn't a bad thing, Jonathan. In any way we can,' she said pointedly, giving his cheek a kiss.

He hugged her back but he didn't reply.


That evening we ate our first supper together. Though George had his own bowl of food he kept looking longingly at mine.

'Hello,' I said warmly, when the humans were out of earshot.

'Hello,' he replied in his little voice.

'This is your first tea here. I hope you enjoy it.'

'Thank you.' I could hear his voice shake a little and I thought he must be terrified; he certainly looked it.

George had special kitten food, which meant they couldn't leave my food down on the floor in case he ate it. Claire had told me that if I wanted it I had to eat it all at once. This kept getting worse! I, like many cats, liked to graze, not always licking the bowl clean straight away. But now I had to eat it all or lose it. George ate from his bowl tentatively; the poor thing really did seem confused, and after tea, he followed me to the living room.

'Aren't you going to clean me?' he asked, as I began my ablutions.

'What? No,' I replied. 'You clean yourself.' I immediately felt guilty for sounding so irritated. It was enough effort to keep myself spick and span, but that wasn't George's fault. He looked at me, wide-eyed, and I melted a bit. Damn, he was just so cute.

'My mum always cleaned me,' he said, sounding so forlorn I wanted to wail. 'I miss her.' I almost crumpled. This poor kitten was in a strange home for the first time, and although it happened to all of us, it would take some getting used to for him. Yes, he was lucky to have ended up in such a loving home, but that didn't mean it was going to be easy for him. I needed to be the strong one for him. I had been thinking about myself too much and someone else needed me more: George.

'Look,' I said, more gently this time. 'Watch me and then you can learn how to do it.' I slowly cleaned myself while he looked on.

Later that night, Claire announced she was going to bed, picking up George, who had been sleeping on her lap. He yawned and blinked. I followed them upstairs. His tiny bed had been placed next to mine. I climbed into mine and Claire placed George in his. I closed my eyes and drifted off to sleep.

Some time later, I was woken by distressed mewing. As I opened my eyes and pricked my ears I saw it was George, crying in his bed.

'George? What's wrong?' I asked, sleepily.

'I miss my mummy,' he cried, and I felt very sorry for him. I don't remember my cat mum, and I knew that George would forget over time, but now he was distraught and I felt my already broken heart break some more.

'I understand,' I said. 'I know plenty about missing those you love, but you've got us now – me, Claire, Jonathan and Summer and the other families. You'll be OK.' The poor mite deserved comfort, so I tried to sound reassuring. I stretched across and climbed into his bed, curling up and wrapping my tail around him, in the way I hoped a parent would.

'Are you my new mummy?' he asked, looking at me hopefully.

'No, George. I'm male, a boy. A mummy is female.'

'So you're my dad?' he persisted.

'Well, no. I mean, not really. But if you like, you can think of me like that. But now it's time for sleep.'

'OK, Dad.' George closed his eyes and I curled tighter around his little warm body, feeling an overwhelming need to keep him safe.

I had suddenly and unwittingly become a father.

# Chapter
# Ten

'Tiger, it's not funny,' I said the following morning, swishing my tail in annoyance as she carried on regardless. I'd managed to get out, although the minute I did, I worried about George. I worried about all my humans, especially the little ones, but this was different; somehow I felt even *more* responsible for him.

I told him I had to go, which he didn't seem to understand, but I promised him he'd be fine. He'd quivered as he made me promise I'd be back soon. It was upsetting but I reassured him as much as I could. Poor kid. But Claire and Summer were home, so at least I hadn't left him on his own. I couldn't have done that.

'But it is quite funny,' Tiger said, swishing her tail back at me, when I recounted how I'd had to show George how to use the litter tray. Claire had tried putting him in it yesterday evening but each time he'd been terrified and scrabbled straight back out. Then little Summer tried to play with the tray, which sent Claire crazy, and so she had to explain to Summer to keep out at all costs while trying to encourage George to use it. Humans! They really had very little idea sometimes.

So when no one was around I explained to George what it was used for, why he had to use it for now, and how it wouldn't hurt him. Embarrassingly, I then had to pretend to do my toileting in it by way of a practical demonstration. Although he had been caught short in the kitchen this morning, he had almost got the hang of it already, thanks to me.

'Just the idea of you in the litter tray,' Tiger finished, still laughing.

'Tiger, listen, yesterday all I had to do was indulge my broken heart and now I'm responsible for a kitten. I can only go out when someone lets me out and ditto back in, which is no good for a doorstep cat is it?'

She tilted her head in sympathy. 'When can George go out?'

'Claire said a few weeks. He has to have some stuff done at the vet first. I didn't listen past the word vet.' I shuddered.

'Sounds as if you're fond of him already.'

'Well, you can't help it. Oh, Tiger, you should see him – he's a bit like a mini you actually. So cute, and I know he's going to be very handsome when he grows up. And clever! I mean he picked up the litter tray so quickly, and he's got these lovely eyes and such sweet whiskers, I can't wait for you to meet him…'

'Oh, Alfie, you sound like a proud parent. You'll be getting the photos out next.'

'Don't be silly, cats can't take photos,' I snapped, but I saw what she meant. I had been put under George's spell. I sounded like Claire when she talked about Summer, or Matt when he talked about his two. It seemed I had definitely taken to parenthood, and although I still wasn't happy in myself, I had to admit that George kept me so busy I barely had time to pine for my beloved Snowball.

'By the way, Alfie, another picture went up yesterday. That makes four cat pictures on lampposts.'

Again, I felt something niggling at me. I felt like I knew

what this was but I couldn't quite remember. 'Are the cats from Edgar Road?' I asked.

'No, none of them, or if they are we've never seen them,' Tiger said. It seemed unlikely that they were from Edgar Road: though not all the cats on our road were friends, and some kept themselves to themselves, we would still recognise most of them.

'I wonder what it is.'

'Well, the others think it's some kind of cat beauty contest. You know, the owners putting the pictures up of their cats as a way of boasting.'

I narrowed my eyes at Tiger suspiciously. 'Tiger, you do know that that makes absolutely no sense don't you?'

'Well, I'm not sure.'

'If it was then don't you think my picture would be up there?'

'Oh, Alfie, you are one vain cat.'

'OK, fine. But they would have put up a picture of the new kitten, George, at the very least. He's the best-looking cat around. Next to me.'

'I get your point. Perhaps your owners will put your pictures up soon, and then we'll know. And if it's not some weird competition among humans, then what is it?'

'Look, I have enough on my plate with my new charge but I'll figure it out, I promise.'

I reluctantly left Tiger to go and play in the park and then I popped into Polly and Matt's house to say hello. I couldn't neglect my families totally for my kitten. In any case, I was sure that Summer, who seemed to think George – or Deorge, as she called him – was her new toy, would be taking care of him, or terrorising him, but hopefully the former.

I felt amazingly free as I leapt through the cat flap and padded into Polly and Matt's kitchen, where to my surprise they were both sitting at the table. I knew Henry would be at school and Martha at pre-school, but Matt would normally be at work at this time and I'd have Polly to myself. She had been doing something called 'interior design' for the last two years and had just finished her course. Apparently she was very good at it, which you could tell because their house was incredibly beautiful, and it was all down to her. She had also helped Claire make our house much better, although she had had to try and combine the Jonathan's minimalist taste with Claire's love of scatter cushions, which apparently wasn't easy. More recently, she had helped big Tomasz redesign his restaurant. Although she didn't work too much, she had picked up some freelance work now and then, as the children weren't at home so much.

I went up to Polly first but she looked at me and blinked as if she hadn't really seen me.

'Hi, Alfie,' she said eventually, bending down to stroke me, although it was clearly half-hearted. Matt didn't even acknowledge me. I immediately knew something was wrong, I could feel it in my fur. I felt my heart drop even further – it would be in my paws at this rate.

'Look, love, it's not the end of the world. I know that you loved your job but you're so talented and you'll find another one,' Polly said, giving Matt's hand a squeeze. I rubbed Matt's legs in reassurance but he didn't seem to notice. He'd lost his job? How? This seemed to have come from nowhere.

'Maybe. I mean, I will, yes, but you know what the

economy's like right now, it's going to take time. And we have two kids, a mortgage… How the hell are we going to manage?'

'Well,' Polly started. 'I know it's not ideal but I did get that offer from DF Design. I know I turned it down, but—'

'I thought you didn't want the job?' Matt looked surprised.

'I wanted to work for them but the job was full time and I was hoping for part time so I could work around the kids. When I told them I couldn't do it, not with the kids, they said to call them if I changed my mind. I didn't want to work full time, but it's on a contract basis so maybe, just until you sort yourself out, I could try it? It's not as much money as you were earning but at least we'd have something coming in.' She didn't exactly look thrilled, but then this was a shock.

'I can't believe this has happened, no warning, the whole company gone under. None of us even saw it coming'. Matt clenched his fists. He was normally so laid back but he was definitely angry, and hurting, and I immediately felt upset for them both.

'I know, love. I'm sorry. But if I can go and work for DF then at least that'll be something.'

'So I have to be a househusband?' He sounded crosser than I'd ever heard him. I snuck under the table. I wanted to hear the end of this conversation but I also didn't, if you know what I mean.

'God, Matt, it's not the 1950s! Men do look after their children and the house now. And you know full well that if we had a choice then no, you wouldn't need to – I like being with the kids. At least we have an option – a lifesaver even,' Polly snapped.

'But I've always worked. I just don't know if I know how

not to work. What am I meant to do, make you a packed lunch and wave you off every day?' Matt was shouting and Matt never shouted.

'No, you make terrible sandwiches.' She tried to laugh. 'Look, Matt, we don't have many options. I'll take this job – it's a rolling contract so it seems like the perfect solution until you find another role.'

'Right, so I look after the kids and the home? Play house?' Matt asked again. It seemed to be his sticking point.

'They're your kids and it's your home so yes. It's not the end of the world, Matt.' Now Polly sounded angry. 'Do you realise how patronising you sound? I've been doing this job for five years now and you seem to think it's beneath you.'

'Sorry, Pol, I don't think that, it's just that I've always worked.' He kept repeating himself but I could tell he was still in shock.

'I know.' Her voice softened. 'But now I have to. Listen, love, you'll have plenty of time to look for a job and go to interviews when the kids are at school, and at least this way the bills will be paid. It won't be so bad, you'll see.'

'I know, I'm sorry. It's just that I'm still in shock.' Ah, I was right. He put his head in his hands. Polly leaned over and put an arm around him.

'I know, love, but thank goodness for DF Design. Someone is looking after us at least.' Polly smiled sadly and I slunk off. I was looking after them too, although I couldn't take credit for the job offer.

Back at my house, I hit my head as I lunged at the cat flap. I was so preoccupied with Matt and Polly that I forgot about it being closed. I'd have a very sore head if I kept doing this. I jumped onto the kitchen windowsill and tried to tap the glass, miaowing very loudly. It wasn't too long before Claire saw me. I jumped down and ran to the back door.

'Oh, thank God,' she said as she opened the door. I tilted my head. 'We've got a problem, Alfie. It's George.'

Summer came running towards me. 'Deorge, Deorge, Deorge,' she kept shouting. I felt my heart beat faster, my fur standing on end. What had happened?

'We can't find him,' said Claire. 'He can't have gone out – he was here after you'd gone and I haven't opened the door since, but I can't find him anywhere.'

I made my way into the house, my tail bushy with fear. Claire had opened all the cupboards and emptied them, covering the whole kitchen floor with their contents. I carefully manoeuvred my way through the mess and tried to stay calm. He had to be here somewhere, but I felt scared for the little baby. It was my fault. I shouldn't have left him. He'd only just moved here. I should have gone out, done what I had to do and then come straight home. What kind of parent was I? I began to feel slightly hysterical as I hunted for him. I could smell his scent but it was everywhere he'd been. I checked the ground floor before climbing the stairs and trying not to panic.

I miaowed loudly but heard nothing in reply. My heart pounded. I checked under Summer's little bed, which was a cosy hiding place that would be perfect for a kitten, then I looked in all the other rooms, but I couldn't find him anywhere.

I lay on Claire and Jonathan's bed to take a break and think of a plan. I'd been hunting for quite a while with absolutely no luck. I was fretting as to where the lad could be. I stretched out and sniffed at the bedding, wracking my brain as to what I could do next. Bingo! I figured it out in my very clever cat way. Claire had obviously just changed the linen on her bed. It was invitingly fresh – just the sort of thing that a little kitten would like. I realised what must have happened and hurried to the linen cupboard. I could hear a gentle snoring – well, more of a snuffle – coming from inside, but the door was closed.

'MIAOW,' I shouted with all my might, which brought Claire running towards me. Honestly, humans. It was lucky George had me, I thought, as I nudged at the door.

'Thank goodness!' Claire exclaimed as she opened the door. 'Ahh, look at him, he's so cute.'

'Oh, bless,' I thought, as we both stared at George curled up on a pile of freshly laundered towels, fast asleep.

'I used to watch Summer sleeping for hours,' Claire said, and as we both stood and stared, I knew exactly what she meant.

'So what happened?' I asked George as we sat side by side on Claire and Jonathan's bed later that evening.

'It smelled so good in there that I decided to lie down. Then it was so comfortable that I fell asleep and Claire must have closed the door,' he said. It sounded simple. I'd been shut in cupboards before – it was easily done. I knew it wasn't his fault, but I had learnt a lesson from my mistake and George needed to as well.

'OK, I understand. But they were worried about you and so was I. You shouldn't go into any open cupboards, you risk getting shut in and, well, you were lucky that I could smell you. Claire was too busy emptying all the kitchen cupboards to think of looking for you up here. You could have been in there for hours, days even, if I hadn't found you.'

'Days?' His beautiful eyes were as wide as saucers.

'Living with humans isn't always easy, George. But don't worry, I'm here to teach you.'

'Thanks, Alfie – Dad.' When he said that my heart melted.

Summer bounded into the room and dived onto the bed. She scooped George up and ran downstairs, babbling about a new game she wanted to play.

I smiled as I watched them go. Summer was like a human sister to me, and now that George was my kitten I had two little ones to take care of. I was overwhelmed with a need for them both to be happy, but right now I was glad that Summer was there to play with George. Apart from all the human business, running around and having to take care of little ones, plus the cats on the lamppost mystery, I also needed a bit of time to myself to think of Snowball, who I still missed with all my heart. Or the bit of it that George hadn't stolen anyway.

# Chapter
# Eleven

George had officially been with us for just over a week, and what an exhausting week it had been. I was suffering from sleep deprivation – George still woke most nights – and constant worry. Looking after him had taken its toll on me. This parenting lark wasn't as easy as I had always assumed. I know humans moan about how hard it is, but I had just assumed that was because they weren't cats. It seems I was wrong.

The whole house was besotted with George, myself included. Us grown-ups would marvel at the way he would lie on his back and play with his paws, like Summer used to do when she was a baby. It made us all smile. Or the way he would nestle into Jonathan's neck while he watched TV, his gentle purring making his fur tremble slightly. Or when he lay on the sofa, asleep on his back, and Claire stroked him – he would put his paws over his head, stretching out to be stroked even more. It was the sweetest thing ever.

After the linen cupboard incident I barely let him out of my sight. I needed to teach him how to fend for himself, which he definitely needed. Despite my lesson on the importance of staying out of cupboards, I had to drag him out of a kitchen cupboard the following day. He said he wanted to explore, which I understood, but I seemed to be constantly warning him of the dangers. And suddenly dangers were everywhere. I wasn't sure if I could kitten-proof the house, let alone the world – an even more terrifying thought.

He had also been pinching my food; I caught him with his

nose in my tuna, and, well, let's just say I'm not used to sharing. But I couldn't bring myself to get angry with him, not when he looked at me with those cute eyes, that smile and his little whiskers. I was putty in his paws. I found telling him off difficult already, but I knew I had to, because that was a part of parenting.

I was proud of him at the same time; he was doing so well using the litter tray, there had only been one terrible incident when he had done his business in Jonathan's slipper. Jonathan acted as if someone had committed murder – they were Italian leather slippers, apparently – and Claire had to pacify him for ages. When we were alone, I explained to George that Jonathan had always been a bit hot-headed and his bark was worse than his bite – excuse the dog reference, which was another thing I had to teach George all about. Although he still couldn't go out, I needed to prepare him for when he did. We spent our evenings before bedtime having lessons about life. I was taking my parental responsibilities very seriously. George had a lot to learn and teaching him was really taking my mind off Snowball. By the end of the day I was often so tired that, once I had settled George into bed for the night, I fell straight into a deep, dreamless sleep myself.

After me sleeping in his bed the first night, we both now slept in mine, which was a bit bigger and more comfortable for the two of us. Claire thought it was adorable and took photos to put on something called Facebook. As George nestled into me, the warmth of him was undoubtedly comforting. It reminded me of when I used to sleep next to Agnes, back in another of my nine lives. I was still unsure that Claire had been sane, getting George and thrusting me into the role of parent, but on the plus side I had no time to indulge in my heartbreak anymore.

I'd hardly been out, but I had managed to snatch some time with Tiger, who was keeping me abreast of any cat news in the neighbourhood. We were still no clearer on the cat pictures, but apparently she had seen another one on the way to the park the other day. It was getting more and more mysterious.

I missed seeing my other friends and planned on spending some time with them the following day. As Summer and Claire would be at home, I was hoping it would be OK to leave George for a little while. I also hadn't been to Polly and Matt's, although I had seen Polly and the kids at our house – Martha was just as obsessed with George as Summer was. Henry wasn't as interested, so he and I watched TV together while they played, treating George like one of their cuddly toys. George loved it – he didn't mind even being manhandled. I hadn't seen Matt, who was busy job hunting, though I worried about him, of course. Polly seemed OK, albeit not quite her usual self, but I was trying to keep that worry on the back burner for now.

Early evening, I was in the garden. Claire had left the cat flap open for me as she was taking George into the bathroom with her while she bathed Summer. I remember when Summer first arrived, Claire had moaned to Jonathan that she didn't have any time to herself – even going to the loo and showering had become a luxury. I had thought she was exaggerating. Well, guess what, she wasn't – as I was quickly finding out. So I decided to make the most of this rare time alone. The cool breeze of the summer evening felt wonderful on my fur and I enjoyed it thoroughly before reluctantly returning inside. I wanted to make sure George ate a good tea and cleaned himself before bedtime… I realised there was so much to do as I ran upstairs, just in time to hear a disturbing noise.

'YOWL!' I heard his little voice cry out.

'Deorge, Deorge,' Summer cried. I panicked and ran to the bathroom door, bashing against it until Claire finally opened it.

George was sitting on the bath mat, dripping wet, and Summer was standing up in the bath. Claire was trying not to laugh. I allowed myself to breathe again.

'Oh, Alfie, George fell into the toilet. I didn't realise he could jump up that high but he must have climbed up onto the loo seat while I was washing Summer and then fallen in,' she explained.

Of course he could jump up, I thought, he was a clever kitten.

'Right, now, Sum, I'll get you out of the bath and then pop George in, we don't want him smelling of toilet cleaner.' As Claire wrapped Summer in a towel and gently bathed George, he looked far from happy. I gave him a knowing look; tonight our lesson would be about water.

By the time George had recovered and dried off, it was tea-time. Jonathan had come home from work and was soon laughing at George's antics, which was lovely to hear – he hadn't been laughing much lately, although I hadn't had a chance to get to the bottom of that yet. Claire told him that they had to make sure the loo lids were always down now, which was a relief; there were so many hazards to think about when you had a kitten. Anyway, Jonathan was smiling as he changed his clothes; he was going to Matt's house for a boys' night while

Polly was coming here. Franceska was joining us too, so I was excited. Normally I would move between the two houses for boys' night and girls' night, but as George needed me I would be with the ladies tonight. Hopefully I'd pick up some new information about everything that was going on around here.

'Don't want go bed!' Summer shouted as Jonathan tried to coax her upstairs.

'If you come to bed now I'll read whatever story you want, but if not then no story,' he said. I watched her face as she weighed up the situation. Summer didn't like to concede anything, so it was hard to tell which way it would go.

''K,' she said in the end. 'But only if Deorge comes.' I felt a little stab of jealousy at all the attention George was getting, but I adored him too much to really mind. I had had a lot of attention in my day after all. Perhaps it was time to step aside for the lad.

'Magic touch,' said Jonathan as he picked George up. 'But, Claire, couldn't you have named the kitten something Sum could actually say,' he said, laughing as Summer kept saying 'Deorge' over and over.

'Right, George,' I said later, when the living room was empty, with Summer asleep upstairs and Jonathan gone. 'Are you ready to go to bed yet?'

'No. I want to see the others.'

'OK, you can stay up a bit later tonight, but you must tell me when you're tired. And we need to talk about water. And the hazards of the toilet.'

'I didn't like it much,' George admitted.

'No, us cats should avoid water if we can, apart from

drinking it of course.' I went on to tell him about my past experiences. I had once nearly drowned, after all, and I didn't want George to be in any danger. They say cats have nine lives, and I reckon I've used up about three or four of mine, but I didn't want to take any more chances and I didn't want my little boy to either.

The doorbell interrupted our discussion and I ran to the door with George on my heels. As Claire opened it, and Polly and Franceska came in, with wine and hugs, I felt happy. We followed them into the kitchen where Claire poured wine and I drank some water before settling on Franceska's lap. Polly scooped up George and he purred as she cuddled him.

'So, I have big news,' Polly announced.

'Not another baby?' Franceska asked. I shot a worried look at Claire but she didn't appear upset.

'No, don't be daft. It's more complicated – Matt lost his job.'

'Oh no, Pol, I am so sorry,' Claire said.

'Now I feel the stupid,' Franceska said. Her English was brilliant but when she got upset or stressed her accent became stronger and she sometimes put words in the wrong places.

'No, honestly, I'm used to the idea now.'

'But I've seen you loads lately and you didn't say anything.' Claire sounded worried.

'I think I wanted us both to get our heads around it a bit before we told anyone. He's talking to Jon about it tonight. But anyway, he went to work and they simply told everyone it was closing down – the company's gone bust. They're sorting out packages now but Matt says he'll be lucky to get a couple of months' pay. But the thing is, just before we found out, DF

Design offered me a job.'

'Wow, Polly, that's great.' Claire smiled at her.

'Yes, well, I turned it down at first because I didn't want to work full time because of the kids, but things have obviously changed. It's a rolling six-month contract, and it doesn't pay as much as Matt earned, but we can manage, at least until Matt gets another job.'

'It all sounds complicated,' Franceska said. 'But you OK?'

'Yes, the main thing is that we'll be fine – financially anyway. But the thing is, Matt and I are arguing because he's miserable about not working. He says he doesn't want to be a househusband but I don't even know if that's the real issue.'

'Oh God, Pol, it could be the role reversal… I shudder to think how Jonathan would cope with that. If I told him I was going to work and he was staying at home, he'd wonder what the hell he was supposed to do. He thinks Summer and the house get sorted by magic. Anyway, at least the kids are a bit bigger now.'

'Yes, Henry's at school and Martha will be soon,' Franceska added.

'I know, I know, but I'll miss them, and the idea of working full time, well, let's be honest – I was a model before so I've never actually had a nine to five. Now I will, five days a week, and Matt will be at home, making packed lunches and cleaning the house. Well, hopefully cleaning the house!' They all laughed.

'Is he taking it that badly?' Claire asked.

'I keep telling him that it's only until he finds another job, which will hopefully be sooner than he thinks. Then goodness knows what I'll do if he gets a job, but we'll cross that bridge when we come to it.' She sighed. 'Right, enough about me, what's going on with you two?'

'Well, we're well underway with the adoption process,' Claire told them.

'Claire, that is the biggest news! Why you haven't told us?' Franceska asked, giving her a hug and nearly sending me flying off her lap.

'I was waiting for tonight. It's a long process, and Jonathan still isn't exactly keen... I'll keep you posted but having George has made me want a sibling for Summer even more. She thinks that Alfie and George are her brothers and she talks about them at nursery as if they're human!'

'That's so cute, although perhaps a bit worrying when they find out she's talking about cats,' Polly pointed out.

Franceska then told the other two that they were now ready to open a second restaurant. Tomasz had a partner, a friend from Poland who had moved here a while ago, and they were expanding the business together. The restaurant was really popular so it made sense, although I worried that big Tomasz worked too hard already. I didn't want him to be too busy for his family.

'I'm worried that we'll see less of him, but he assures me that he's going to put managers in so he can concentrate on the food side and not have to be there quite so often. Well, we are hoping,' Franceska said. I knew that Tomasz found it hard to let go and delegate to others – his wife had worried about that since he had opened his first restaurant.

I looked at George, who was fast asleep on Polly's lap, then at my three human women. They were all so strong and had come a long way since I had first met them. Claire with her broken heart, Polly with her post-natal depression after giving birth to Henry, and Franceska struggling to settle into a foreign country. But I knew that it wasn't plain sailing and once again it felt as if issues were mounting up for each of them. Changes were happening and change always threatened to cause problems, I knew that. I just hoped we would all be able to keep it together, and that my families would weather the storm I had a horrible feeling might be brewing.

# Chapter
# Twelve

The first storm came not from my main families but from someone else I was very close to. Though all my families were a bit rocky, there was nothing that was an immediate concern to me. After the girls' night, Claire and Jonathan had had a bit of a row, but that wasn't anything new. When Jonathan went over to his house, Matt had been upset about his job loss, understandably, but Claire commented on how lucky they were that Polly had been offered something. Jonathan said she didn't understand how unsettling it would be for Matt to have to slip into a housewife role and then Claire accused him of being sexist, which Jonathan quite happily admitted he was… It was just one of their usual annoying bickers. But it unsettled little George, who still had a long way to go before he understood.

'I don't understand why they shout,' he said, his voice quivering.

'Humans do that sometimes. It's very complicated and it doesn't mean they don't love each other.'

'But why?'

'Well, sometimes people – and cats, for that matter – don't agree.'

'But why?' he asked. And on and on he went, until I had to cover my ears with my paws, because I couldn't hear 'why' one more time. Again, I knew how the human parents felt; Martha was going through a 'why' phase right now and Polly said it made her want to tear her hair out. Parenting this kitten was almost harder than taking care of my grown-up humans. But of course this cat had to do it all.

The next day, Claire and Jonathan had made up and were doing that yucky thing they do when they keep kissing and being soppy. Poor George looked at me, eyes full of confusion, and I wondered how on earth I was supposed to teach him about life when it made so little sense sometimes.

'Yuck,' Summer proclaimed, watching her dad kiss her mum as they made breakfast. 'Yuck, yuck, yuck.' Claire and Jonathan laughed but I had to agree with her – it was pretty embarrassing to see them put on such a public display!

George was stationed underneath Summer's high chair, where he was enjoying licking off the yoghurt she kept dropping onto him. It was his new favourite thing to do. I was eating my breakfast, having ensured George had eaten enough of his by telling him he wouldn't grow up as strong as me unless he did. I had heard many a human parent saying this so I knew it was true. But we were having lovely family time together and it made my heart swell with love, a feeling that had been lacking since the loss of Snowball. Don't get me wrong, I still missed her when I had time, but I was also happily counting my blessings too.

The doorbell dinged, interrupted our lazy Saturday morning. Jonathan and Claire looked at each other, and Claire went to open the door. I gave George the 'stay there' look I had mastered and followed her.

'Oh God.' Claire and I stood back as she opened the door. Tasha, her best friend and one of mine too, stood on the doorstep, holding her son, Elijah, who was only a bit older than Summer. She was crying with such force, it suggested she might fall over.

'Tash, come in,' Claire said. She grabbed Elijah, almost dropping him; he was only a few months older than Summer but he was about two children heavier. She shouted for Jonathan, who came running, thrust Elijah at him and told him to take him into the kitchen with Summer. Jonathan looked shocked but didn't argue as Claire led Tash into the living room with me at their heels, where Tash immediately collapsed onto the sofa.

'Tash, darling, what on earth is it?' Claire wrapped her arms around her friend as she sobbed. Not quite knowing what to do, I curled up next to her. At least she would know I was there for her.

Tasha and I had met when I started living with Claire on Edgar Road, a long time ago. I had loved her straight away. She was a good friend to Claire and had seen us both through some tough times. Claire and Tasha used to work together and had quickly become best friends. Now, with the children so close in age, they spent loads of time together and she remained one of my favourite humans. I didn't go to her house, as it was too far away, but she was nevertheless part of my family.

'It's Dave, he's gone!'

Dave was her partner. They had never married, and although he seemed an all right kind of bloke, he was allergic to cats, so we always had a bit of an issue between us. He used to take pills when he was around me but he still never touched me, so our relationship was far from close.

'Gone? Gone where?'

'He's, he's…' She hiccupped. 'He's left us. Moved out.'

'What? Tash! What on earth?' Claire took hold of her friend's hands, looking as shocked as I felt. I might not have been Dave's biggest fan but I thought they were solid in their relationship. Immediately, I felt a kinship with Tash – we both were suffering heartbreak, after all.

'He said last night he couldn't do this, this relationship with me. He said he loved Elijah but this wasn't how he thought family life would be and he wasn't cut out for it. I tried to ask him for reasons, he just kept saying that he didn't love me anymore. I tried to talk him out of it, but he, he didn't change his mind. I cried, I begged, I didn't sleep all night and this morning he packed a few bags and went. What am I going to do?'

'Oh, Tash, I can't believe it.' As Tash sobbed in Claire's arms I came to the sad realisation that I had been right all along not to trust a man who was allergic to cats.

Claire was good in a crisis, a bit like myself. She mobilised the troops. She told Jonathan to look after the children while she took Tash into a different room. She ordered Jonathan to call Dave and try to get to the bottom of it, then she said that Tash and Elijah had to move in with us for now. She drove Tash home to get some of their belongings so they could stay for a few days at least. Basically she did exactly what I would have done, if I were a human. I had taught her well.

I felt sad for my lovely friend. Why did humans continue to hurt each other? It was something I didn't understand. I knew how Tash felt, a little bit, having lost Snowball. But at least Snowball hadn't abandoned me – she didn't have a choice but to leave.

I knew I needed to be there for Tasha; I had to help her heal and let her know I understood how she felt. As I pondered how I would do that I heard George miaowing urgently from the kitchen. I had only taken my eyes off him for a second but

I ran in to find him standing in my food bowl. In the crisis, Claire and Jonathan had obviously forgotten to put our food away as they usually did.

'What are you doing?' I asked, exasperated. He had flakes of tuna on his head.

'I wanted to try your food, then I thought how much bigger your bowl was than mine, so I thought I'd see if it was bigger than me. I got in but I can't get out again.'

'George, if the humans find you they'll be cross,' I admonished as I helped him get out. 'Quick, clean yourself up before they get back.' I supervised his clean-up and tried not to be annoyed that he had used up the rest of my breakfast with his experiment. After all, I had more important things than food on my mind right now.

'Yum, I liked that,' George said, licking his lips when he was clean again.

'But that was my breakfast. You have special food because you're little. Like Summer,' I explained.

'I'm going to get big now so I can eat like you,' George declared before scampering off. I checked that there was definitely no food left – there wasn't, George had either eaten what I had left or worn it – before chasing after him.

I found him running round in circles.

'What are you doing?' I asked, mildly amused.

'I'm trying to catch my tail but it keeps running away from me.'

Oh, how I laughed as he determinedly ran round in circles. I didn't have the heart to tell him he'd never catch it. In the midst of all the doom my kitten was cheering me up. He had this magical power and I wondered now if it was time for me to pass the baton. Should I train George up to help people the way I always did? It seemed like a good idea, and perhaps George could help me help Tash. I was already teaching George what I knew, so when it came to my families, and being a doorstep cat, George would be my apprentice. I grinned – what a nice thought that was.

I looked around the living room. Tash was lying on the sofa, cuddling Elijah, who was asleep. George was curled up at her feet, which was sweet. I had asked him to spend time with Tasha and, actually, when he did the chasing-his-tail thing she had laughed for the first time, so it had worked. My gorgeous kitten was a tonic for us all, it seemed.

Summer was napping in her bedroom, so I joined Claire and Jonathan in the kitchen, where they were talking quietly.

'So he's not going to change his mind?' Claire asked.

'No, the idiot's met someone else. I suspected it already, so I tripped him up and he admitted it. Typical story, she's younger, no kids and he probably thinks she'll never make the demands of him that Tash does. Anyway, he was too cowardly to tell Tash. I'm afraid he's moved on. He's even talking about selling their place and splitting the money. It's only been five minutes!' Jonathan looked incredulous – angry and red faced. What made me most proud of Jonathan was how honourable he was as a person. He would never do that to Claire; I would put all the pilchards in the world on it.

'Oh God, what are we going to tell Tash?' Claire asked.

Jonathan shook his head. 'He really doesn't care that she's in pieces. He just seems to ignore that he's hurt her, and when I tried to talk about Elijah he said that plenty of kids grow up with parents who aren't together. He doesn't seem to think he's done anything wrong. I wanted to punch him – it was lucky he was on the other end of the phone.'

Jonathan and Dave had never really been friends. They spent time together because of Tash and Claire but I heard Jonathan say he thought he was missing a few brain cells, and apparently he had committed an even worse crime than being allergic to cats: he supported Arsenal. Jonathan could never forgive that but I didn't really understand why.

'So what do we do?' Claire was distraught. Jonathan held her.

'Well, she can stay here as long as she needs to. I'll tell Dave to get the rest of this stuff out of the house. And I know she might not be ready, but I'm going to get her a solicitor for when she is. He's not going to do the right thing, so I'm going to take him on.' Jonathan sounded pretty certain.

'Oh, Jon, thanks, we have to help her. I can't imagine how it must feel…'

'Hey, you know I'd never leave you and Sum, don't you?' He looked at her as he spoke and, as I said before, I knew with certainty in my heart that, no matter what, he wouldn't leave them. He was nothing like Dave.

'I do, and I love you. But for now we need to get Tasha back in one piece. She did the same for me when I first moved here, and I didn't have a child to think about like she does.'

'Hey, baby, we'll do whatever it takes to sort her out. Don't worry.'

I nuzzled against both their legs. I was going to help too, of course.

'Oh, Alfie, I forgot how much you love Tash too. Well, between us all we'll get her back on her feet,' Claire declared, sounding determined.

Satisfied, I miaowed and then went to the back door.

'OK, Alfie, you can go out, but come to the windowsill when you want to come in,' Claire said.

'Miaow,' I agreed.

I found Tiger under a bush in her front garden.

'Hi, Tiger, what's going on?' I asked. It had been a couple of days since I'd last seen her, and I realised that I'd missed her. I was so used to seeing Tiger almost every day, I wondered if I took her for granted a bit.

'Well, hello, stranger. I'd almost forgotten what you looked like.'

'This not going out lark isn't easy. Nor is having a kitten to take care of. I can't wait for you to meet him though, he's so cute.'

'Oh, Alfie, you keep saying that, you proud father. Stroll?'

'Yes, I'd love to. I haven't had nearly enough exercise lately.' We rubbed noses and set off. We hadn't gone far when a big cat shadow loomed over us.

'Great,' I said. 'First time out in ages and we have to bump into *him*.'

'Well, fancy seeing you two here,' Salmon said, baring his teeth at us.

'We do live here,' Tiger replied, flicking her tail angrily.

'Well, I'm patrolling to check everything is OK. Can't be too careful you know.'

'Right, Salmon, and what trouble have you happened upon?' I said, humouring him. Salmon's owners ran the local Neighbourhood Watch; they were real busybodies and Salmon was cut from the same cloth.

'Well, like my owners have noted, number twenty have put

so much rubbish in their garden that they're attracting vermin. They're holding a meeting about it, you know.'

'Great, and what about the cat pictures, do you know anything about that yet?'

'I do,' Salmon replied. 'But unfortunately it's classified information.'

'What? What on earth does that mean?' Tiger asked.

'I am not at liberty to discuss it with you.'

'Which, once again, means you don't know anything,' I retorted.

'I see your girlfriend left you,' he said, unkindly.

'She didn't leave him, she moved away,' Tiger hissed. She glared at Salmon in her most aggressive way. Tiger was my best friend and also my self-appointed bodyguard.

'Yes, well, same difference,' said Salmon, hissing back at us before walking off.

'That cat does not get any nicer,' I said, fuming.

'But he's not important. Look at him, he has no friends, and you have loads. Speaking of which, let's go and find them.'

We made our way to a strip of grass surrounded by bushes at the end of Edgar Road, where our little cat community would sometimes converge. I was lucky: Elvis, Nellie and Rocky, three of my favourite cats, were hanging out there when we arrived. They all stood up to greet us.

'Alfie, it's been ages,' Nellie said, yawning and raising her whiskers. 'Is there any news?' Nellie loved drama.

'I'm sure Tiger told you, I've been preoccupied with a kitten.'

'I know, fancy you having a real kitten and not a human to worry about,' said Rocky. He was an older cat, well-meaning but sometimes a tad interfering.

'Oh, I still have plenty of humans to worry about, but the kitten can't go out yet so I'm restricted as to what I can do at the moment,' I explained.

'How are you, Alfie?' Elvis asked kindly. 'You know, after Snowball leaving?'

'I miss her, of course I do. You don't just get over someone that quickly.' I felt emotional as I thought of her beautiful white fur and blue eyes. 'But George, my kitten, he's keeping me busy.' I smiled sadly, tilting my head to one side.

'Well, we're all looking forward to meeting him when he's allowed out,' Nellie said. 'But try to come here more often, now the weather's nice. There are some new neighbourhood cats you should meet.'

'Really?' I hadn't even noticed any new families. I had obviously been neglecting my doorstep cat duties with everything going on.

'Oh, not new families, just new cats. Two, actually, and nice they are, as well. One is so pretty we think she'll probably get a picture up there soon,' Elvis said.

'Elvis, do you really believe there's some kind of cat beauty competition going on?' I asked.

'Can't see why not,' he replied. 'And as I said, I'm guessing at least one of the new cats will be entered soon.' He sounded sure but it made no sense to me.

'Have you met them?' I asked Tiger.

'Yes,' she answered shortly, slowly blinking her eyes to indicate the subject was closed. 'Right, I want to sunbathe while it's still hot.' She found the best spot and lay down. I had time to stay for a little while, so I settled down, stretching out next to her, and enjoyed the feeling of the sun warming my fur. I thought about the new cats and how Tiger had been so keen to change the subject. She could be a funny one, I thought, but it would be nice to meet new cats, it was something else to look forward to. After all, I always say, you could never have too many friends.

As I left the others and walked back on my own, I saw some of the posters. I had seen four in total now. I looked at the pictures of the cats and had to admit that, yes, they were all nice looking cats. But still I was annoyed with myself – I knew somewhere deep down that I had the answer. As I reached the front door, I experienced a sudden flashback. My memory suddenly fell into place. When my families had thought I was missing, they'd put a picture of me on the lampposts (I wasn't missing at all, I was ill at the vet, but that's another story). Yes, I had figured it out. These cats were missing for some reason and their owners were trying to find out if anyone had seen them. Of course, it all made sense now. I remembered Aleksy showing me the picture he drew of me and telling me how he had put that up. That was what the lamppost cats were – missing cats! I would have to tell the other cats my discovery, but first I had to go and check on George.

# Chapter
# Thirteen

'Where's George?' Claire asked me. I looked at her and blinked. I had just been out into the garden for a few minutes to attend to my needs. How could they have lost him in that short time? I went off to find him. It didn't take me long – he was under Summer's bed.

'George,' I said, 'come out.'

'No.'

'George, I am not going to tell you again. Either you come out or I come to you,' I warned.

'No,' George repeated. I wondered if he'd been taking lessons from Summer when my back was turned. I crawled under the small toddler bed and saw he was tied up in what look like a ball of wool.

'George, what have you done?' I asked, eyes widening.

'Nothing,' he replied, trying to back away and bumping into a wall.

'Well, what's this wool all over you?' He tried to wriggle away from me but his legs were all tangled up with wool. I had to push him with my paw to get him out from under the bed. When I examined him, I saw that he had what remained of Jonathan's scarf trailing behind him and the rest of it wrapped around him. He looked like a cat's cradle. Ah, was that why it was called that?

'What have you done?' I asked in my sternest voice.

'I was just playing with this thing.' He gave me his most innocent look.

'The scarf.'

'Yes, if that's what it's called. I was playing with the scarf and suddenly it started to unravel and somehow it unravelled all around me and I couldn't get it off. I was in Summer's room anyway so I hid.' He spoke as if it was the most normal thing in the world.

'That's Jonathan's scarf,' I said, wondering how much trouble we'd be in. Claire had taken up knitting when she was pregnant and had decided to practise by making Jonathan a scarf. It was the first and last thing she'd knitted but she was proud of it and insisted that Jonathan wear it all winter. Goodness knows how George had got hold of it.

I tried to get it off him but he was more tangled than he looked, and I seemed to be making things worse. Reluctantly, I went to get Claire. She was in the kitchen preparing supper for later. Summer was at nursery, as was Elijah, and Tash was at work. I rubbed against her leg.

'Hi, Alfie. Did you find George?'

'Miaow.' Yes. I nudged her leg with my head.

'What? What's wrong?'

'Miaow.' I repeated and led the way upstairs.

'Oh, George!' Claire said as she saw the tangled mess that was George and the scarf. She tutted and started trying to free him, but he was properly tangled. 'Oh goodness, I'll have to get scissors.' She returned with Summer's nail scissors and started carefully cutting. I saw George close his eyes and knew how he felt. I hoped he wasn't going to get a fur-cut at the same time. When he was eventually free, George sprang away quicker than I'd ever seen him move. I guessed he didn't want another telling off.

'Well, I don't know what Jonathan will say, that was his favourite scarf,' Claire said as we left the room.

That evening, after dinner, Claire took Tash out for a drink. She thought a change of scene might do her some good. I thought it meant that at least she wouldn't be crying. Poor Tash, she held it together when Elijah was awake but as soon as he was asleep she would crumble. I spent as much time with her as I could spare, but nothing I did seemed to make her feel better, not even one of my special snuggles. I knew she must feel like I did when Snowball left, so I understood her pain, and I knew that nothing would really help apart from time. Although she had her kitten, Elijah, and he would help, as George helped me.

I sat with Jonathan on the sofa. George was asleep, curled up on an armchair. It was nice to spend some quiet time together, just the two of us; we hadn't done that for a while.

'Oh, Alfie,' he said as he put his feet on the coffee table, switched the TV on and sipped a beer. 'Boy time. I have to say I was over the moon that George ruined my scarf. I hated that thing, I only wore it because Claire insisted, but it was really itchy and far too long. And thankfully she's given up knitting so I know she won't replace it. I might get a lovely cashmere one instead. I should buy that kitten some pilchards to thank him.'

'Miaow!' But what about me?

'And you, of course. Right, well let's enjoy some peace and quiet from the madness that is this place at the moment.' I nodded and yawned. It was lovely to relax; it was something that had become very rare in our house.

***

I was woken a little later by the sound of the door opening. I could hear someone giggling and a loud 'shush'.

'Oh God, they're drunk,' Jonathan said, bracing himself. Tash and Claire stumbled into the living room. Claire hugged Jonathan, almost falling on him and then me.

Tash fell down on the chair, almost sitting on George who shot up in surprise and then settled back down next to her. As Tash stroked him, George purred with joy.

'We have a plan,' Claire announced. Now I was sure she had too much to drink, as she was speaking very loudly.

'Yes, we do,' Tash slurred.

'And are you going to share this plan?' Jonathan looked amused.

'Yes, Tash is going to see the solicitor you found, I'm making an appointment tomorrow.' Jonathan had found a good recommendation from someone he worked with. 'She's then going to sell the house and move onto Edgar Road. Genius!'

'Yes, it's time for me to pull myself together,' said Tash. Then she burst out laughing. I never understood humans and alcohol. I mean, I like a bit of catnip as much as the next cat but we never let it get this out of control.

'OK, but is there a house available on this road?' Jonathan asked.

'No idea,' said Claire. 'But it's a big road.'

I was excited by the idea; it would be nice to have Tash nearby and I'd have another home on Edgar Road, a bit like the old days.

'Well, that sounds good. Look, Tasha, are you sure?' Jonathan asked, gently. 'It's still early days.'

'Yes, I am. Dave isn't coming back.' She suddenly burst into tears, showing the sudden swing in emotions I had learnt was quite common with humans. Then George licked her face and she laughed as if to prove my point. 'Oh, George. I love this kitten. And you, Alfie,' she said, almost as an afterthought. But that was all right. I was used to George working his magic on everyone, and I was now sort of in second place. I had thought it would bother me, but actually, I was really happy, because I was under George's spell too.

'Right, well that's all good then, and of course I'll help out with whatever you need,' Jonathan said. 'But for now, you both need to drink a big glass of water and get to bed.'

I led George up to bed and left Jonathan to organise the women. I was pleased that Tash was looking towards the future, despite her tears. And I felt the same for me. I was taking little steps. I would never forget Snowball, but life did go on. When I was hurt, I wanted time to stand still, but it didn't: life didn't do that.

However, I wished I could see Dave and rub my fur all over him. That would serve him right for hurting one of the loveliest women I knew.

# Chapter Fourteen

Today was a big day for us. Claire was taking George to the vet to get his vaccinations, which meant he would finally be allowed outside. Although I have a severe vet phobia, I wanted to go with him but annoyingly I wasn't invited. I had been very careful not to share with George my aversion to the vet. Vets meant well but they prodded in places they frankly had no business to. I told him he'd be fine though, and got him excited about seeing the outside world. I was keen to take my boy out: I couldn't wait to show him off to my friends and take him round the neighbourhood.

The good news was that as long as they were at the vet's, the cat flap would be open. It was also very important that I tell my cat friends what I had figured out about the lamppost cats. It was a worrying turn of events, and I knew the posters were still on everyone's mind. I was also hoping I might get to meet the new Edgar Road cats. Since becoming a parent I had barely had any time for myself, and I was now realising how precious that was. Just being able to do what I wanted to do, something I had previously taken for granted, was now a luxury. I was so busy looking after George that I wasn't looking after myself, and it was a while since I'd been my usual cat-about-town self.

I called for Tiger, who came out when I bashed her cat flap, our way of ringing the doorbell. She was just finishing cleaning her whiskers.

'Did I interrupt your lunch?' I asked.

'No, I was only having a snack,' she replied. Tiger liked her food, though since we'd been friends, I had made her take more exercise, and she was far less lazy now than she used to be.

'I need to talk to you about the lamppost cats, but I think we should go and see the others so I can talk to you all,' I said.

'Really? You know something?' Tiger was interested.

'Yes, I've figured it out – there's lots to fill you in on.'

I started strolling with Tiger by my side. From a distance, I saw Elvis and Rocky, and with them was one of the new cats. I was excited – Tiger was right, it was the curiosity I always felt for new people and new cats that I loved. I smoothed my fur down and approached. I couldn't help but notice instantly that the new cat was beautiful. My heart may have belonged to Snowball but my eyes were still working! I saw Tiger glance at me sideways and I thought maybe she was jealous; she could be a bit possessive of me, although I didn't think she thought of me in *that* way anymore. Did she? I tried to give her a reassuring look. I mean, I couldn't even think about another woman right now, and probably not for a very long time. Maybe not ever.

'Alfie, Tiger, glad you came. This is the one of the new cats I was telling you about, Pinkie,' said Rocky.

'Nice to meet you, Pinkie,' I purred. She was a similar colour to me, but with a very cute round face and a bright pink collar.

'You too, Alfie,' she grinned. She was quite stunning. 'And Tiger, nice to see you again.' What lovely manners, I thought. Tiger made a sound but didn't say anything.

'You're new to the area?' I asked.

'Yes, my family moved to somewhere called "overseas",

and they couldn't take me with them so they found me a new home.'

'That's rough,' I said. 'Although I know all about that, having suffered something similar.'

'Yes, Elvis told me a bit about your background. But the lady I live with now is very nice, and she has great taste in food.'

'Anyway,' Tiger interrupted. 'We have more important things to discuss than food. Go on, Alfie, tell them what you know about the cat pictures.'

'Ohh, you know something?' asked Nellie, moving closer. I raised my whiskers as all the cats surrounded me.

'Yes, I do. The lamppost photos aren't a beauty contest. It means that they are missing.'

'Missing?' Rocky asked. He looked shocked.

'Yes, the owners have put up pictures asking if anyone has seen their cats. Which means they aren't at home.' I felt quite knowledgeable as the others hung on my every word. 'It happened to me once, when Jonathan and the others thought I was missing. But it was all a misunderstanding, as you know, because I was with the vet. So we need to try to figure out if these cats are really missing or if they've left their homes of their own accord.'

'You mean like they just got fed up and ran away?' Nellie asked.

'Found new owners, maybe?' Pinkie suggested.

'But there does seem to be quite a lot of them,' Rocky pointed out.

'You're all right. This may be a case of missing cats, but we need to figure out why. After all, they could just have found nicer homes. It does happen.' I was loyal to my families but

133

they were good to me – not all humans were.

'So we need to be vigilant?' asked Elvis.

'Yes,' Tiger replied. 'We don't think there is anything to worry about but we do need to keep our eyes on the situation and we should discuss it at various intervals. It's only right.'

'Tiger's right,' I concurred.

'Guess where I met Pinkie, Alfie?' Elvis said, changing the subject and sounding proud. His attention span really was very short. I wondered if they were an item, but I didn't think so as Pinkie seemed far too young and pretty for him.

'Where?' I asked. I saw that Tiger was chasing her shadow and pretending not to listen.

'In my fridge.'

'Your fridge?' I asked, incredulous.

'I happen to like fridges,' Pinkie said. 'When I first moved here, my owner kept me inside, but when I was allowed out I went to Elvis's house by mistake.'

'Well, it is only next door,' Elvis said kindly.

'Anyway, his fridge was open, and I just can't resist an open fridge.'

'Yes, but then my owner closed the door, trapping her. Luckily she forgot to put the milk back so when she opened it again, Pinkie jumped out. Gave my owner a bit of a fright you know,' Elvis laughed.

'Wow, that's some story. Don't you find fridges cold?' I asked.

'Of course, but then I don't plan to spend that much time in them. It's what you get out of them that counts.' She said this as if it were the most normal thing in the world.

'Anyway, I escorted her home and now she's become a

friend,' Elvis finished. Tiger made a sound that sounded a bit like 'hmmph.'

'Well, it's nice to meet you, although maybe you ought to keep out of fridges, they can be dangerous,' I warned. 'And if you get stuck in one they might have to make you a lamppost cat.'

'Anyway, as I was saying to Pinkie, Alfie is single,' Rocky interrupted.

'What?' I said.

'You know, Pinkie's new to the area, you're a single tom, you two could step out together. Just a thought.'

So now my cat friends were trying to matchmake? Had that been their plan all along?

'Sorry, Pinkie, but you know I'm still nursing a broken heart from my last relationship. I can't think about courting another cat.' I felt embarrassed all the way to the tips of my whiskers. This was awkward.

'Hold on a minute,' Pinkie cut in. 'Thanks, guys, for thinking of me, but Alfie, well, to be honest, you're not my type.'

'He's not?' Tiger had now stood up and looked interested.

'No, I like my toms a bit more manly, if you know what I mean.'

I was affronted. More manly? What on earth did she mean? Tiger was trying and failing not to laugh, and Rocky and Elvis couldn't hide their smirks either.

'Well, although I like to think of myself as quite macho, actually, at least we're on the same page. And I'm sure we can be friends,' I said, mustering all the dignity I had left. 'But I have to be getting back. I have a kitten to check on. Don't forget to be vigilant about those lamppost cats.'

I left my friends where they were and walked home. Not

manly enough, what on earth? I strutted and swaggered to show just how macho I could actually be.

When I got home, the house was quiet and I enjoyed some time on my own whilst they were still out at the vet. I padded from room to room, enjoying the silence and the space. Just like the good old days, when Claire and Jonathan went to work and I had the whole house to myself. I would never wish for life to go back to what it was – I couldn't imagine life without either Summer or George – but a bit of peace was nice.

I pondered the missing cats. I certainly felt as if something strange was happening, and there might be a mystery to solve. It did seem an odd coincidence that four cats had now decided to leave their homes, but then it wasn't impossible. Maybe their owners were mean, or gave them terrible food, or made them sleep in a shed? Any of those reasons would be justification for running away.

I was dozing on Claire's bed when I heard the door open. I stretched, yawned and licked my paws before making my way downstairs.

'It's OK, George, you're home now,' Claire was saying gently. The door to the cat carrier was open but George was refusing to come out. I leaned in and rubbed his nose to let him know I was here.

'I don't like the vet. Why didn't you tell me?' he said.

'Because we all have to go. They are what we call a necessary evil. And now you've had your vaccinations you won't have to go so often – hardly ever, in fact, if you stay healthy and out of trouble.'

'Really? But I might have to go again?' He looked at me with his big eyes full of terror.

'I'm afraid all cats do from time to time, but listen, it gets easier.' It really didn't, in all honesty, but I wanted to be positive. 'And the good thing is that now you'll be allowed outside and you'll love that.' Although suddenly I started fretting. There were all sorts of dangers outside and I didn't want to think about what might happen to my kitten. 'But you don't go out without me or a human, not yet anyway. Promise?'

George looked at me with those big eyes that melted my heart every time. 'I promise, Dad.'

Was there anything sweeter than that word?

'I love hearing Summer call me Daddy,' Jonathan said that evening as he and Claire were having dinner. The kids were in bed, as was Tash, so it was just the three of us in the kitchen.

'I know. And you know what, you'll love it when our next child calls you that too.'

'Claire…' Jonathan's voice had a warning edge to it. I knew this issue was far from resolved but, what with everything that had been going on with Tash, it had been put on the back burner – or so I thought.

'Look, Jonathan, I'm going to be positive about this. We have the adoption workshop tomorrow and then after that we'll get allocated our own social worker. It's early days, I know. We've got a long way to go, but I refuse to feel disheartened.' Claire looked determined and I knew there was no arguing with her when she was like this.

'Right, well how's Tash doing?' Jonathan seemed to agree with me that an argument with Claire was a waste of time right now, and obviously decided a subject change was easier.

'I wanted to talk to you about that. The solicitor is great, thanks, and she suggested that Tash buy Dave out of the house. She said they have quite a lot of equity, because they bought it so long ago, and the prices have rocketed in their area, so her idea is that she buy him out and then if she doesn't want to live in it she can rent it out.'

'That makes sense,' Jonathan said. 'It'll be a good investment for her and Elijah.'

'I think at first she wanted to fight Dave a bit, you know, because he thought she'd just hand over half the money and she'd believe his half-baked promises to pay child support. And especially as he hasn't made much effort to see his son since he moved out. But now she just wants to move on. So the solicitor is going to be firm but fair with Dave.'

'Good for her. And if he does anything, I'll go and see him. Or maybe a solicitor's letter would be better. I never exactly took to Dave but I didn't think he was this much of an idiot. What about finding her a new home?'

'Well, there's a flat coming up at the end of the road, a bit like Polly's old one, which would be perfect for the two of them. The tenants are moving out in a month.'

'Are you sure you didn't kick them out?' Jonathan raised an eyebrow.

'No, although I admit I was asking around. I actually went to see the curtain twitchers.' That was their name for Salmon's owners, Vic and Heather Goodwin.

'Blimey, you must really want her here, to have done that! Though it would be lovely to have them down the road. What does Tash think?'

'I haven't mentioned it, I wanted to talk to you first.'

'Well, darling, I think it's great. She can stay here until

she's ready to move somewhere else, either Edgar Road or wherever.'

'See, you are such a compassionate man, Jonathan, you'll be fine with this adoption.' His smile quickly vanished, but Claire didn't push it.

'Oh, and Heather and Vic were talking about something else. You know there's been a few cat posters going up on the street?'

'This is London, unfortunately there are always cat pictures. I see loads on my way to the tube station. Maybe they've been hit by cars, or just run away,' said Jonathan.

'I know, but there is a bit of a spate of them at the moment. Anyway, Heather and Vic are going to mention it at the next neighbourhood watch meeting, as they think it might be a bit sinister.' I felt my fur shiver. I hoped it wasn't something bad, but I couldn't help but feel they might be right.

'Well, you know what those two are like, I'm sure there's nothing to worry about,' Jonathan replied.

'I hope you're right, darling.' Claire sounded worried, which made me feel even more worried. I had a feeling we were on the cusp of something; I had to make sure the local cats all kept their eyes and ears well and truly open.

Claire wanted an early night with her latest book club book, so after checking that George was fast asleep, I sat with Jonathan and we watched a film. Or he watched a film and I snuggled up and got a bit lost in my thoughts.

'Oh, Alfie, I know there's no stopping Claire when she makes her mind up, but I just don't think I can do this adoption.' He actually looked sad and I think I understood. Jonathan was a lovely, honourable man but he did struggle with his emotions a bit sometimes.

I snuggled into him to try to reassure him that he could, but I was pretty sure that it wasn't enough. I would have to think of another way. There were more changes a-paw, I could feel that, and suddenly I felt even more exhausted. Heartbreak, in whatever form, takes its toll and now it looked as if it might also be spreading its wings over all the people I loved.

# Chapter
# Fifteen

'What's this?' George looked at me in wonderment as he tentatively padded his paw onto the lawn.

'It's grass,' I replied. 'You can walk on it.'

'It's soft and springy and a bit damp!' he exclaimed. Seeing things through his eyes did open mine to what I usually took for granted. Maybe that was the point of children and kittens? It certainly made having them make more sense. I smiled at him indulgently. Could he be any more adorable?

'It's very good for walking on, and it's only damp because it's still early, although when it rains it will be wet too.'

'So it's safe and not like a bath?'

Educating George was still a bit of a chore. I watched him leap off across our small lawn. He was allowed outside now but only in the garden until he got used to the area. Claire and Jonathan were talking about getting a lead for him – honestly, we cats are not dogs – which was a terrible idea as I could do that just as well. I tried to tell Claire as much by miaow-ing very loudly and giving her my disapproving look but as Jonathan said, when she makes up her mind...

George flipped onto his back and rolled over in the grass. He was so happy with such simple pleasures; it was yet another thing I loved about him. I could remember when all I wanted to do was to sit on a warm lap or relax in a sunny spot, but those simple days had ended prematurely for me after my first owner died when I was still young. I now wanted that sim-plicity for George, and to protect him from the complexities

143

of life. That was when I knew that I was definitely a parent.

'Hey, Alfie,' I heard Tiger hiss quietly as she jumped over a fence and into our garden.

'Tiger!' I was delighted to see her.

'I know the humans might not like it but I had to come and see you.'

'They won't mind, they know we're friends. I don't think they'd even mind if they found you in the house – Snowball used to visit all the time.'

'Yeah, well, that was a bit different. Anyway, I wanted to meet George, plus I have something else to tell you.'

George, on hearing another voice, approached us, hiding between my legs and looking a little scared.

'Hey, George, there's no need to be worried. This is Tiger, my best cat friend,' I announced, feeling proud of my charge.

'George, I am so pleased to meet you,' said Tiger.

George stepped out from between my legs and gave Tiger his most charming head tilt. 'Hello.' He sounded so sweet.

'Gosh, you are gorgeous!' Tiger walked closer to him and rubbed him with her neck. I had never heard her sound so tender. Not with me anyway, that was for sure. Honestly, she'd only spent a few seconds in his company and she was already smitten.

'Are you my mummy?' George asked. 'I don't think you are, but you look a bit like her.'

Tiger looked at me and I knew we both felt our hearts soften even more; I could see it in Tiger's eyes.

'No, George, but I am going to help Alfie take care of you, if you'd like me to.' Tiger cuddled into my kitten, and George seemed to love that, stretching his paws out into the grass.

'Do you have a kitten?' George asked.

'No, I've never had a kitten of my own… but maybe you can be my kitten.' Tiger looked at me hopefully.

'Hey, it goes without saying, Tiger. We're like family and families take care of each other. That's what I try to teach my humans and that's what I'm now teaching George.'

'Now I have a mummy and a daddy!' George exclaimed. I looked at Tiger and was hit by an unexpected bolt of emotion.

'Right, well then, George, when you're allowed out more I will help you, with Alfie, get used to the area and the other cats. And if you feel like hunting then I can take you.' I had never heard Tiger sound so excited. 'Oh, think of the things we can do!'

George bounded off and started jumping around at the other end of the garden, where he had spotted a low-flying bird. I looked at Tiger.

'Do you think he'll want to hunt?'

'It's natural for us cats, Alfie. Just because you're rubbish at it doesn't mean the boy won't want to,' Tiger teased.

'It's not just that. When I had to hunt, when it was the only way I got food, I still really didn't like it. I'm just not that type of cat – so it's lucky you're around for George.'

'Yowl!' George tried to climb a bush and promptly fell off, landing on his tail and covering himself in blossom. Tiger and I smiled indulgently but let him get himself up again. My instinct was to rush to him whenever he fell but he had to learn to land properly.

'Alfie, he is so lovely, I know exactly what you mean now,' Tiger cooed.

'Isn't he just? Oh, what was the thing you said you had to

tell me?' I asked, suddenly remembering.

'Well, I didn't want to worry you but when I was on my early morning walk I heard Polly shouting at Matt as she left the house. She stormed down the road muttering to herself. She looked really cross.'

I looked at Tiger thoughtfully, grateful that she had told me. It was the second week of Polly going to work and Matt staying at home, and although I hadn't been able to visit them to find out how it was going, I had heard Claire and Jonathan saying that they were both finding it tough.

'Thanks, Tiger, I'll go and see them. Any other gossip?'

'Well, the cats miss seeing you as much as they usually do, but you'll be able to bring George by soon and it'll be like old times. There haven't been any more posters for a couple of days, which is good, so maybe that whole missing cat thing will blow over.'

'Thank goodness.' I had enough to worry about with my humans and George, I certainly didn't want to worry about other cats as well.

'The funniest thing is that Salmon has taken a liking to that Pinkie. You know, the one who thought you weren't very manly! Anyway, he keeps trying to find excuses to see her and I'm not sure she feels the same way. Actually, I'm sure she doesn't, she hides whenever he approaches, but seeing him try to flirt is the funniest thing ever. I think she's scared to come and join us much now.'

'Ha, serves her right for rejecting me,' I said.

'I thought you weren't interested?' Tiger's eyes narrowed.

'I'm not, but that doesn't mean she shouldn't have admired how handsome I am.'

'Oh, Alfie, you're such a vain cat. Please don't pass on that trait to George.'

We both looked at George. He was staring at his reflection in the glass door, preening and turning his head to look at himself from all angles.

'Oh dear, it might be a bit late for that,' Tiger laughed, before bidding us goodbye as Claire, Summer and Elijah all ran into the garden. Summer scooped George up and squeezed him tightly. Honestly, I did worry that she would stop him breathing sometimes.

'Eli?' Summer said.

'Yes?' he replied. He was used to being bossed about by her and didn't seem to mind too much.

'You pat Deorge now.' She thrust my kitten towards Elijah and he obligingly stroked him. I smiled, George purred, and I felt content for the moment.

A little while later I left George, who was still playing with Summer – or rather, Summer was dressing him up in her dolls' clothes. He didn't look exactly thrilled, but I had to go and see Matt, and I knew that being bossed around by Summer would at least keep him out of trouble for a while.

I pestered Claire to let me out. Despite the fact George had had his vaccinations, his outings were still being monitored and so the cat flap wasn't always open. I no longer worried about being let back in: if I sat on the kitchen or living room windowsill someone usually saw me. Although it wasn't quite as convenient as the cat flap, it wasn't too bad. I had cat friends who refused to use the cat flap, preferring to get their owners to let them in and out as if they were their butlers. Which I kind of understood now – it was pretty nice having my humans run around after me.

I padded slowly to Matt and Polly's house. It was early afternoon so I knew Polly would be at work and the kids probably at school, or at least Henry would be anyway. I let myself in and found Matt at the kitchen table, alone, with his laptop open in front of him. He didn't look great. He hadn't shaved, which wasn't like him – he was usually as well-groomed as me.

'Miaow,' I said, loudly. He jumped a bit, looked up and smiled sadly.

'Alfie, how are you?'

'Miaow.'

'I haven't seen you in ages. Hey, have some tuna.' I licked my whiskers; not only was I a bit peckish but it would be nice to eat without the threat of George stealing my food.

He took a bowl out then opened a tin and emptied it in, placing it on the floor. He then got me some water. I was in for a feast.

'It must be funny seeing me here in the middle of the day,' he said as he watched me eat. I had learnt in my years of experience with humans not to interrupt them when they needed to talk. If I carried on eating quietly I knew he would say all he needed to say. 'I'm not used to it either,' he continued. 'I miss work. I feel useless, Alfie. Don't get me wrong, I love spending more time with the kids but, well, I'm just not feeling myself.' I could tell he wasn't himself just by looking around. The sink still had dishes from breakfast and there were crumbs all over the kitchen floor; usually their house was immaculate. Polly would never have let that happen.

'Miaow,' I concurred.

'I know, it's normally immaculate and Polly is much tidier than me. Don't worry, I'll sort it before I pick the kids up from school. Like I need to give Polly any more excuses to nag me! I haven't done the washing and the place is a mess, but I am trying to find a job, you know. And it turns out housework is harder than I thought. The other day I tried to empty the hoover and I managed to tip it all over the kitchen floor. Honestly, I am not cut out for this.' He looked so upset.

He slumped down onto the kitchen chair. I quickly cleaned myself and hopped onto his lap. I looked at him, trying to tell him that he could do this. He was a strong man and this was only temporary. He would get the hang of the hoover, I was sure of it. He stroked me and I purred to give him some support. I wonder if he understood.

'And so far there are no jobs around. I've applied for a couple but I know they're not right and probably won't want me. God, everything was so great, how on earth did it come crashing down on me? I really don't understand, Alfie, and now it all feels as if it's falling apart.' He actually had tears in his eyes and I suddenly felt the seriousness of their situation.

I wanted to yowl again, the way I had when Snowball left. It was so sad and it was as if my worst fears were being confirmed yet again. All I wanted was happiness for my families but we were getting the opposite. Matt looked so miserable, not like the man I knew at all. It was funny how life could change so suddenly. He used to look smart, stand tall and laugh all the time, nothing fazed him, but now he seemed diminished. Now I knew why he and Polly had been arguing. But, I wanted to tell him, if he cleaned up the house and himself, he would feel better. I had learnt that from Claire. I had an idea. I jumped up onto the draining board and miaowed loudly, over and over. Finally Matt laughed.

'OK, Alfie, I'll load the dishwasher and clean up. You're right, at least then Polly won't shout at me again.' I kept him company while he cleaned the kitchen. Although he didn't exactly look as if he felt brilliant, as he said, at least Polly and the kids would have a clean house to come home to.

Matt also went to clean himself up before picking the children up from school. As I watched him shave and then put some jeans and a T-shirt on, he began to look like his old handsome self. He smiled at his reflection.

'Thanks, Alfie, you've somehow managed to cheer me up a bit.'

I rubbed his legs to let him know that he was most welcome, and then I left to go home to my kitten.


Claire was at the sink when I appeared on the windowsill, making her jump. She laughed as I hopped down and waited by the back door, which she soon opened.

I bounded in and found Summer in her booster seat at the kitchen table, eating carrots – or rather, sucking them and then throwing them on the floor. I wondered where George was; he was nowhere to be seen.

'Miaow?' I asked Claire.

'Oh yes, Alfie, look, we have to be so careful, but I didn't like to move him.' I looked at her questioningly and followed her to the utility room. The washing machine door was open with some clothes inside and on top of them, fast asleep, was George. I shuddered: what if they'd put the machine on? I miaowed my disapproval. It was dangerous! Didn't Claire know that?

'Don't worry, Alfie, I always check before I put the machine on and I'll check even more carefully from now on. I think he was trying to get away from Summer. But he does look so comfortable there. I even took a picture. I daren't put it on Facebook in case someone calls the RSPCA, but I'll show Jonathan.' I again miaowed my disapproval.

'He's fine, Alfie, don't worry.' That's as maybe, but I wasn't happy and it wasn't like Claire to be so laid back. This was no place for a kitten; what if he'd been washed and drowned? I know she said she was being careful but what if Jonathan decided that today was the day he'd do the washing for the first time? I stayed in front of the washing machine, guarding it and waiting for George to wake up. There was no way I was taking any chances.

Ow! I woke up with a start as something heavy landed on my head. I looked up and saw it was George.

'Hi, Dad,' he said.

'You're getting heavy,' I complained. He jumped down. So much for guarding him, I'd fallen asleep! Although no one would have put the washing machine on with me lying in front of it.

'I like my new bed,' he said.

'No, George, it's not your new bed and you mustn't go in there. If someone put the washing on you'd be in trouble.' I know I sounded like a broken record, but that was parenthood for you. I was finding I had to say the same things over and over again.

'Oh, but I can go to sleep looking at my reflection in the door.'

Oh boy, maybe Tiger was right – my kitten was as vain as me.

'That's as maybe, but it's not safe. Now promise you won't go in there unless you tell me first.'

'There seem to be a lot of rules,' George protested. 'I might not be able to remember them all.'

'Well, that's life. And anyway, they're all for your own good. Now go and have a drink of water, you need to keep hydrated.'

'Yet another rule,' George muttered, as he went to have a drink, only just dodging a flying carrot on the way.

'Yowl,' he protested quietly.

'Summer, stop throwing food,' Claire said sternly. I looked at Claire in understanding. This parenting lark wasn't easy. It wasn't easy at all.

# Chapter
# Sixteen

There was a flurry of activity. Tash was finally moving into Edgar Road. She'd been living with us for well over a month now but Claire had found her a flat. It was ground floor, two bedrooms, small but with a back garden. Although her old house was far from sorted, Claire and Jonathan were helping her out. That was what friends did.

'I just can't see myself living there again, but I have to think of Elijah,' Tasha had said one evening when talking about her old house.

'Exactly,' Jonathan had agreed. The three of them were sitting round the kitchen table, having supper and discussing Tasha's future. 'And it makes sense to buy the idiot out of your house, rent it out and keep it as an investment.'

'And if I rent the flat down the road, I'll have enough to cover the rent and money left over. Although right now, when I'm still paying the mortgage and the house is empty, I'm not exactly quids in.'

'We can help you, Tash,' Claire had said. 'The main thing is to get a new home for Elijah and yourself, at least for a while anyway. You can see how it goes from there.'

'You guys have been amazing.' I had jumped up onto Tash's lap then. 'And you, Alfie. Me and Alfie were best friends already but we've really bonded over heartbreak lately,' she said with a sad smile. I rubbed my nose against her hand; we really had. But like me, Tash was slowly getting back to her old self. Not all the time, but there were glimpses, which was all we could hope for in these early days. She didn't sleep as much as she did when she first moved in and she had stopped crying quite as often. And, most importantly, Elijah was so happy; he was as laid back as Summer was bossy.

Later that day, I was relaxing at home with George. Jonathan had gone to Tash's old house to organise the removal, Tasha had taken Elijah to the flat to get used to it, and Claire was tidying the house. We were all going to go to Tash's new flat later, but Claire said that Tash and Elijah needed some time to be alone. The good news was that George was allowed out properly now, as long as he was on the lead, which he didn't seem to mind but that was because he didn't know better. I was overprotective but I did think that Claire should let him go out with me now. I was sure he was ready, I just had to find a way of letting her know. And he would be with Tiger or myself at all times, I had already decided that would be the rule.

The doorbell rang and Claire opened the door. Polly stood on the doorstep with the children.

'Hey, Pol, come in,' she said, ushering everyone inside. Martha and Summer immediately ran upstairs, with George following them. He loved being spoilt, and sometimes terrorised, by the two girls. Henry wandered into the living room and started trying to put the TV on.

'Henry, you spend all your time watching TV, go and play,' Polly said, sighing.

'I'm not playing with them. They're girls!' Henry said. I couldn't blame him; not only were they bossy, but they liked to play dress up, and were always trying to make Henry be a princess. Polly shrugged and put the TV on for him.

'I just don't have the energy to argue,' she said to Claire as they went to the kitchen. I gave Henry a bit of a snuggle and then went to the kitchen.

Claire put the kettle on and Polly sat down.

'Are you all right, Pol? You look exhausted,' Claire said.

'Oh, where do you want me to start? Working full time for the first time in my life is so tiring. And then I come home and the house is a bombsite most of the time, but I'm trying not to nag Matt because he's so miserable. I just feel like it's all going to explode on me. The poor kids are caught in the crossfire. I mean I try not to shout at Matt, but honestly, Claire, I get home and he's done nothing, yet he acts like he's been run off his feet. And then he says the job hunt is taking all his time – but he's only applied for two jobs! What on earth am I supposed to do?' She looked terrified.

'Hey, it's probably just temporary, it's a massive adjustment for both of you.'

'I know, and I can't tell Matt this, but I'm really enjoying my job. I feel like a grown-up again and I'm loving it much more than I thought I would. But I miss the kids. When I get home I just want to play with them, and spend some nice time with my husband, but then I have to clean up and get everything organised for the following day as well as tiptoeing around Matt. I feel like I'm doing it all.'

'I know, honey, and you are, but I think Matt might be a bit depressed. Maybe I can get Jonathan to have a chat with him, not about anything in particular, but just to see how he is?'

'That would be good. Maybe if Jonathan could take him out to the pub one evening?'

'I'll arrange it. Although I'm not saying how useful he'll be, Jonathan doesn't exactly do domestic very well!'

'It's worth a try,' said Polly. I purred my agreement. 'Oh, Alfie, I miss seeing you every day!'

'Tonight, to cheer us up, we're going to Tasha's. Frankie's meeting us there, she's managed to get a babysitter, and we're going to drink champagne and celebrate despite any misery!'

'I'll put some lipstick on and a smile on my face. Sorry to go on about myself when Tash is having such a hard time.'

'Don't be silly, everyone has problems. But I do want to make sure that the first night in the flat isn't too awful for her.'

'You know, it hits home, doesn't it? I can't imagine losing Matt and yet I feel that if we don't do something I might.'

'You won't, but it does make you appreciate how lucky we are to have someone we love, even if they do drive us mad,' Claire said, smiling.

'I know, I just wish we could be a bit more like we used to,' Polly sighed. 'I just want him to be happier. I wouldn't mind the mess if he was cheerful. Well, I would, but maybe not quite so much.'

'You'll get there. It's early days, honey, so just try to be patient.'

I agreed with Claire: hopefully they would get used to it soon and then everyone would be happy again. Or happier, at least. I sighed to myself – so much of life was out of our control. A bit like George, I thought, as I saw him run down the stairs wearing a big yellow hat that had slipped over his eyes. He was shaking his head wildly, which made Claire and Polly laugh, before he banged into the wall. Still chuckling, they went over to him and gently removed the hat.

'Yowl,' he said sadly. He seemed a bit dazed.

'What have those girls been doing to you?' Polly asked, giving him a cuddle. He nestled into her and was soon purring again. If only all life's problems could be solved so simply.

Later on, we left Jonathan babysitting Summer and George as we called for Polly and made our way to Tash's new flat. I'd told George that he was to stay home and spend time with Jonathan. When Claire saw me walking down the road next to her she smiled indulgently.

'You probably deserve a night out,' she said. As we walked along the street, I used the opportunity to look out for more lamppost cats. As we approached Tasha's new flat I saw another notice. This time the picture was of a Siamese cat, who looked a bit mean but quite attractive. I stopped and peered at it.

'Oh no,' Claire said. 'Another missing cat.'

'Don't you think there's been a few more than usual lately?' Polly asked.

'I guess. I mean, that's what Heather and Vic were saying anyway but I just don't know… As Jonathan says, it's London and cats do go missing here or get run over.' She shuddered. 'Not Alfie and George though, thank goodness.'

'I don't know. I mean I know Heather and Vic are a pain but I do wonder if there's something in what they've been saying,' Polly said.

I felt a bit relieved. Vic and Heather were terrors but if anyone was going to get to the bottom of the mystery of the lamppost cats, then I was sure it would be them – after all, they were very good at poking their noses into other people's business.

We stood on Tash's doorstep. Claire and Polly were clutching bottles of champagne and snacks, and Polly looked much better than she had earlier in the day. She really had put on some lipstick and a smile, just as she'd said she would. When Tash opened the door, the flat immediately reminded me of when I first met Polly and Matt. It wasn't their old flat, but it was almost identical in layout. I walked in and rubbed Tash's legs.

'You OK?' Claire asked as they followed Tash into the small kitchen.

'Well, it's weird being here, but Elijah seems fine. He went to bed without any fuss, he's such a good boy.'

'Yeah, you lucked out with that one, the easiest child ever,' Claire said.

'Well, maybe compared to our girls,' Polly laughed. 'And actually he's far more laid back than Henry too.'

'He gets his laid-back nature from his father, let's hope he hasn't picked up his gutless bad points too… Sorry, I didn't mean to start with a moan.' A flash of anger crossed Tash's face. Claire hugged her.

'Hey, you moan away.'

'And in the meantime I'm opening the champers,' Polly said. 'I could do with a drink! Glasses?' As Tash opened a kitchen cupboard and located the glasses, Polly opened the champagne.

'You're pretty organised already,' Claire said.

'Well, thanks to your Jonathan. It's much smaller here so we only took what we needed. I managed to unpack most of it while Elijah was napping,' Tash explained.

'Can I ask? What about Dave?' Polly asked, cringing a bit.

'I mean, does he know about the move?'

'I haven't told him yet. Anyway, he's already moved in with his other woman. He said he's living with his mum but when she called me about seeing Elijah she let it slip.'

'So you're on good terms with his mum?' Polly asked.

'Yes, she's furious with him. We've always got on well and I've said that she can see her grandson whenever she wants. But then what about this woman?' She burst into tears. 'I'm sorry, but I still can't bear the idea of another woman around my baby.' As Claire comforted her, the doorbell went. Polly opened it and came back with Franceska.

'Oh, Tasha,' Franceska said. She was carrying bags filled with food from the restaurant. I was worried and upset for Tash but I was almost distracted by the smell of sardines. I had to shake my head to focus as I rubbed against Tash's legs.

'Men!' Polly said, handing everyone a glass of champagne. 'I'm not suggesting we toast them because, let's face it, at the moment none of us are one hundred per cent happy, so maybe we toast against them?'

'Don't get me started,' Franceska said, looking upset. Oh no, not her too!

'What's up, Frankie?' Polly asked, concerned.

'No, not tonight. We're celebrating Tasha's new flat, so back to the toast.'

'God, I'm happy to toast against men,' Tash said, trying to laugh as she took a sip. 'And hey, at least you guys can count your blessings, none of your men are in any way, shape or form as awful as Dave.'

'I guess we can drink to that?' Franceska said uncertainly, and they all laughed.

***

I tucked into my sardines with relish. It was certainly nice having a night out and not having to take care of George, although I missed him and worried about him too. I just hoped Jonathan was taking good care of him. The women all seemed to be having a good time now, after a rocky start. Men had become a banned topic and so they chatted instead about Polly's new job, Claire's adoption plans, Franceska and Tomasz's new restaurant and Tash's idea about how to make the flat her own. As Polly promised to help her with the interior, they all settled into easy chatter, and lots of laughter, which grew louder as more champagne was drunk. It seemed they were emptying the bottles at an alarming rate, which was OK because at least no one was crying.

Later that night, they all kissed Tash goodbye, Franceska got into a taxi to take her home and Claire and Polly staggered down the road with me. Neither of them seemed to be able to walk in a straight line, so I had to keep dodging them to make sure I wasn't stepped on. When we got in I ran upstairs to find George fast asleep in my bed. I felt a surge of relief, followed by a rush of love as I snuggled down next to him. I drifted off to sleep cuddling my kitten, feeling glad that, for tonight at least, the women were all happy again – or at least happier than they had been lately.

# Chapter
# Seventeen

I was incredibly excited. George was finally allowed out, further than the garden and without the lead or any humans – although of course I warned him to not go anywhere without me. He asked 'why' a million times but I was reluctantly getting used to that. It was a momentous occasion and one that felt a long time coming, mainly due to Claire's overcautious behaviour.

The cat flap had been formally unlocked. Jonathan had been pleased, saying that I had a habit of making him let me in when he was in the middle of watching something. He said it as though I did it on purpose. Anyway, freedom was once again mine. I was excited to introduce George to my friends, to my street and to the great outdoors, the world that existed beyond our small lawn. I was also going to pop in to see Matt, so George could see where they lived, and then if we had time I would show him Tasha's flat, although she didn't have a cat flap so we could only visit with her if she was in and saw us. A bit like the old days with Franceska and the boys really. Wow, freedom once more – I vowed never to take it for granted again.

I was looking forward to our first excursion very much and had taken extra time over my grooming. I wasn't sure why, but humans always dressed up for special occasions and this, George's first proper outing, was definitely a special occasion. I tried to make sure he looked his best too, but let's be honest, he was so cute that I really didn't need to worry. I jumped through the cat flap first, George following behind me. He was still a little unsure of it, although he was getting better. He had grown a lot in the time he'd been with us, and although still a kitten he was big enough now to run, jump, and climb.

George blinked as the sun hit his eyes. It was a lovely, sunny day for his first trip.

'Right, stay close to me and don't worry, I won't let anything happen to you,' I said, giving him my best pep talk.

'I know, Dad,' he said. We slid under the gate and made our way to the front of the house.

'Before we start, I need to give you a lesson about roads.' As we stood on the pavement, a number of cars whizzed past us. 'You see, those cars are dangerous.' I had nearly been hit a number of times when I first encountered roads. 'Don't cross the road unless it's clear both ways,' I continued sternly.

As we walked I gave George a full tour of Edgar Road. I pointed out Salmon's house and said it was to be avoided at all costs, although there was no sign of him anywhere, thank goodness. Our first stop was Tiger's house where we waited in her front garden, by her favourite bush. George wriggled under it and started playing with leaves. Tiger emerged a few moments later.

'Oh, hi, I was hoping you'd be here already,' she said, ignoring me and giving George a nuzzle. I looked at her indignantly. Having a kitten meant I was getting used to being ignored but it didn't mean Tiger could get away with it.

'Hello, Tiger-Mum,' George said, so sweetly that Tiger looked as if she might cry.

'Right, come on, we have to give George a proper tour of the neighbourhood,' I said, no longer feeling slighted.

'OK, but George, you're still only little so you must tell us if you get tired,' Tiger said, sounding sweet and concerned. I raised my whiskers; what had happened to my Tiger?

'I will, let's go, let's go.' George was full of excitement as he bounded off in the wrong direction.

'George, this way,' I said, and he turned round and joined us. We made our way slowly to our cat meeting point. I pointed out Polly and Matt's house on the way and explained that Tash's flat was in the other direction, although I'm not sure how much George was taking in. He was so busy looking around that I doubted he was listening.

'I bet you're glad Tasha's moved into Edgar Road,' Tiger said as we stopped and watched George staring at an overgrown plant for a minute.

'Yes. Not only is she one of my favourite people but it's good to be able to keep an eye on her,' I said.

'I like Elijah,' George said. 'He's funny.'

'I love how all the kids get on so well,' I mused as we moved on, gratified that George was listening after all.

'And any more news about the cat pictures?' Tiger said.

'Not in front of the kitten,' I said, as quietly as I could.

'What was that?' George asked.

'Nothing,' Tiger and I replied at the same time. I looked at her with concern.

I was delighted to see that our cat friends were already congregated. Nellie was sunbathing, Elvis was sitting in a shady spot and Rocky was cleaning his paws. I excitedly ran up to join them.

'Look, I've brought George to see you,' I said breathlessly.

'Where?' Rocky asked, looking up.

'Right there.' I turned around but George and Tiger were nowhere to be seen. 'They were there a minute ago.' Panicking,

I turned and retraced my steps. I found Tiger looking at George, who was sitting on a gatepost in front of someone's house.

'What happened?' I asked, concerned.

'When you ran off George decided to jump on the gate-post. He says he likes it up there.'

'George, come down now,' I said.

'No. Look, there's a funny animal in the garden.' I jumped up onto the other post and looked in. The funny animal was a small dog, who was yapping at George and now me. 'I'm going to go in there to see it.'

'No!' I shouted, a bit more forcefully than I intended. George jumped but thankfully stayed on the gatepost. 'George, dogs are to be avoided at all costs. Now come down.' I leapt down, having used my sternest voice, and George reluctantly followed me.

'Right, this is George,' I said for the second time when we re-joined the others.

'Aww, you're so incredibly sweet. I'm Nellie,' Nellie cooed. She went up to George and made a fuss of him.

'Nice to meet you, George, I'm Elvis.' Elvis looked over-joyed to see my kitten.

'I'm Rocky, nice to meet you.' Rocky stopped looking at his paw and came over to greet us.

'Wow, you're all cats,' George said. 'And there are so many of you!'

'We certainly are,' Rocky said. 'And Alfie was right, this is one cute kitten.' All three cats were immediately taken with George, I could tell.

'Come with me, George, I'll show you the bush that attracts butterflies,' Nellie said.

'What are butterflies?' he asked.

'Follow me and you'll find out.' I sat and watched proudly as Nellie took George to see the butterflies. He really is my boy, I thought, as I watched him jumping around. Of course he never actually caught a butterfly, but then neither had I, and I'd been playing for a lot longer. We just liked chasing things, usually without much success – though I did swat a fly once at home. Jonathan had been so pleased with me, until he realised it was a fluke.

'Nice youngster,' Elvis said to me. 'Look, here comes the other cat I mentioned to you, Tinkerbell.' I hoped that this wasn't another of his attempts to set me up. I know I was busy but I still thought of Snowball in any spare moment I had – usually before I went to sleep at night. But when I came face to face with the new cat I realised something strange.

'But you're a boy,' I said, confused.

'Have we been introduced?' Tinkerbell growled. Not only was he male, but he was big, about twice the size of me. I felt a little threatened.

'Sorry, I'm Alfie and I've heard about you but, well, you're called Tinkerbell so I assumed you were a girl.'

'No, I'm a tom.' He raised his whiskers. 'Look, my owner wanted a girl cat so when they got me they gave me a girl's name. To be honest I'd rather not talk about it. If you're a friend, you can call me Tinks.'

'Nice to meet you, Tinks.' I gave him my most charming look. 'And sorry for the misunderstanding. I didn't mean to be rude, it's just that my friend Elvis here seems to want to set me up with female cats so…'

'Oh yes, I heard you're the heartbroken one. But no need

169

to make a fuss, I'm happy with my name and my sexuality, thank you very much. And now that we've cleared that up, we can be mates.'

'What does it mean? Setting my dad up with a female?' I hadn't heard George approach but he was standing behind me with Nellie and Tiger.

'Well, young George, it's just that we thought Alfie might like a new girlfriend, and then you could have a new mum,' Rocky explained.

'Oh, no, thank you,' George replied. 'Tiger's my mum.'

'Aww,' Tiger and Nellie both said, and I swear I have never seen Tiger look so moved. Even Tinkerbell softened. This kitten could win any charm competition, of that I was certain.

'Goodness, Alfie and Tiger, you guys are like a married couple already, so I guess it makes sense,' Rocky laughed. I shot him one of my looks.

'Well, George, we're all your friends here, so if you need anything, then you just ask,' Elvis said.

'But don't come here on your own,' I warned. 'Not yet anyway. Either me or Tiger need to escort you.'

'As if I would,' George replied innocently.

Apart from George nearly jumping into that dog's garden – and I dreaded to think how that might have ended up – our first proper trip was a great success. My kitten was greatly admired by all and I felt so proud. Unfortunately, however, it was getting late and there was no time to drop into Matt and Polly's house. That would have to wait for another day.

'Honestly, Alfie, you're like the cat who got the cream,' Tiger said as she dropped us home.

'I have George, and he's better than any cream,' I replied.

# Chapter
# Eighteen

Back in the relative safety of home I had a quick catnap on the sofa while George was carted off to play with Summer. She was cross that we'd had been out when she got back from nursery. She kept stamping her feet and crossing her arms, saying 'bad Alfie,' which I thought was a little unfair. But Claire found it funny so I only gave a small yowl of objection. Then I went to have a well-deserved rest. As I drifted off I thought of how well George had coped with the trip, and I was pleased that the other cats welcomed him so readily. Deep down I had known they would, but it was still gratifying to see them admiring my kitten. I thought I would bask in his reflected glory as I fell asleep.

A commotion woke me. Although I had only intended a quick nap, even that had been cut short. I jumped up in fright as I heard Summer scream. Both Claire and I ran to her room.

'What's the matter, poppet?' Claire asked.

'Deorge, up there,' Summer said, pointed upwards. We all looked and saw George tucked on top of Summer's wardrobe.

'He must have climbed,' Claire said, hugging her daughter. 'It's OK, he's just playing.' She smoothed Summer's blonde hair and the tears started to subside.

'No, Deorge stuck,' Summer shouted, putting her thumb in her mouth.

'He's stuck?' Claire looked up at him uncertainly. She was fairly tall but she couldn't reach the top of the wardrobe. George looked at me and then put a paw over his eyes. Ah, I thought, he had got up there easily – at a guess he had jumped on the chest of drawers and then onto the wardrobe – but he didn't feel quite so confident in getting down. After all, it was quite high for such a little one. I looked at Claire, and then at Summer, and finally at George. Despite the fact that I didn't like heights and my legs were aching a bit from all the exercise earlier, I would have to save the day. I jumped onto the chest of drawers and then leapt up and onto the wardrobe, thankfully landing beside George.

'Look, Sum, it's OK, Alfie will help him down,' Claire said. Summer seemed happier.

'Oh, hello, Dad,' George said quietly.

'George, you must be careful. You're stuck. Why did you jump up here if you're too scared to jump back down?' I asked, trying not to sound cross. After all, we all did stupid things. I'd done too many to count.

'Oh, I'm not stuck,' George replied. 'Why did you think that?'

'Well, Summer said you were and when I looked at you you put your paw over your eyes.'

'Oh, Dad, that was to tell you I came up here to hide from Summer. She wanted me to be her baby and she tried to put me in her pushchair like a doll and I didn't really like it. I can get down, I just don't want to.'

'Well, what do we do now? Claire thinks you're stuck, and now I'm up here when I don't really like being this high. You'll have to come down with me.'

'Only if you promise you won't let her put me in the pushchair.'

'OK, get down and we'll go straight downstairs, it's your

teatime anyway.' He looked at me uncertainly.

'Promise?' he said.

'Yes, now come on.' George jumped down with ease; I envied him his youth and fearlessness as I tentatively followed. Then we both made for the stairs before Summer could object.

That night, George was fast asleep in my bed, exhausted from his busy day. Summer was tucked up in bed too, so I sat with Claire and Jonathan in the living room.

'How's Tash?' Jonathan asked.

'Actually not too bad, it's like she's a different person since she moved into the flat. I really think she's beginning to feel a bit like her old self. The solicitor's proving a godsend and has put a rocket up Dave. He's been threatened with court unless they sort out maintenance for Elijah. She's got the mortgage approved for the house, so that's all being finalised, but it's sad too. They were together for so long and it's all fallen apart so quickly. She still misses him, I think, but she's pretty brave. What with her job and her boy she's being kept busy.'

'Well, we have family day on Sunday, so she'll spend the day with us, won't she?' I pricked up my whiskers. I loved family day; every month all my families would get together and I'd have all the people I loved in one place. Sometimes it happened more often, but if not, then I always had that to look forward to.

'Yes, she'll be with us, and so will everyone else, which we all need. I mean, it seems that Polly and Matt are barely talking and Frankie says she and the boys will only get to see Tomasz because of family day. It'll be good for the kids, and everyone's coming to ours because they all want to see George.'

'That kitten is a star attraction,' Jonathan laughed.

'You'll never guess what he did this afternoon…' Claire told Jonathan about the wardrobe incident, which Jonathan seemed to find funny. Claire snuggled into him and kissed his cheek. I lay on the armchair, one eye on the two of them.

'Right, well I guess we ought to think about going to bed,' Jonathan said.

'It is going to be all right, isn't it?' Claire asked suddenly. I didn't know exactly what she meant, but I was sure by the look on his face that Jonathan did.

'Of course it is, darling,' he replied, but he sounded uncertain.

On Sunday, as everyone descended on us for family day, I think I almost understood what Claire had meant the other night. As soon as everyone arrived, George was indeed the star attraction. He purred and preened as everyone made a huge fuss of him, then of me as a bit of an afterthought, but I was mature enough to accept that. But it went downhill from there. After a bit of a strained lunch, the adults all seemed a little bit lost in their own thoughts instead of their usual chatty selves. There were three camps. The children were one, which was usual and now included George. Luckily Aleksy, being the oldest, was in charge, so I knew George was in good hands, and he'd come and get me if needed. The men had taken over the living room, and in the kitchen the women had commandeered the kitchen table. I found myself having to move between the two adult camps.

The men were more subdued than usual.

'Is something wrong with us?' Jonathan asked finally, after

even he got fed up of the silence – he usually enjoyed some peace and quiet.

'I'm just not in a great place,' Matt admitted. 'I miss working. This Mr Mum stuff isn't me. And yes, I know I sound like a sexist pig because my wife tells me often enough. And it's not even the kids, I love being with them but I would rather be at work. I miss it. Remember, I actually loved what I did.'

'So no luck on the job hunt?' Tomasz asked, eyes full of sympathy.

'Yes and no. I've got a couple of meetings lined up but nothing concrete, there's not much about at the moment. All my contacts are looking out for me but they all say I have to be patient.' Matt shook his head.

'Are you guys OK financially?' Jonathan asked. He sounded concerned.

'Yes, Polly's new job has been a lifesaver. She loves the job but I know that coming home to me, as grumpy as I am, isn't much fun for her. As it is, she's tired all the time, working long hours and then rushing home to see the kids. She gets back and then once we've put them to bed she has to work most nights. We don't spend enough time together – I'm miserable because I miss work, she's miserable because I am, and also I'm not good at laundry or something.' He laughed, sadly.

'Well, on the flip side, I'm working too much and Franceska is very not happy,' said Tomasz. 'In fact, she tells me today she and the boys are going back to Poland for the school holiday, because they never see me anyway. I know I work too much but the restaurants are doing so well now, and yes, I have a manager, but I can't hand over control yet.' Tomasz looked guilty.

'Mate, you have to trust other people. You can't do it all

yourself, what'll happen when you have ten restaurants all over the country?' said Jonathan.

'I know, it's not easy, but if I get these two right then I feel I can step back and let others do more work, no?'

All the men shrugged.

'Anyway, Jon, you're OK, aren't you?' Matt asked.

'Who thought this would turn into a sharing afternoon? Quick, better put the football on,' Jonathan replied, changing the subject.

After that depressing interlude I went into the kitchen.

'So I said to him, he can formalise the child support or we'll have to go to the CSA and I'll take him to court to sort out the house as well. I've been more than reasonable but he's just being so awful. Anyway, we have a mediation booked in. Sounds like fun, right? Means I have to see him again, which I'm dreading, but I have to do what's best for Elijah.'

I took a drink of water before going to sit with Franceska. If she was going away, I wanted to spend a bit of time with her.

'I hope it does good,' Franceska said. 'I have to tell you, we're going to Poland for the summer, me and the boys, not Tomasz.'

'Oh goodness, that sounds great,' Claire said. Really? It didn't sound good to me, a whole summer apart from her husband, not to mention me. I would miss them terribly.

'Yes, well, Tomasz is so busy, so I thought we could see family and have a holiday, and the boys don't remember much about home, so it's good for them. Tomasz is not happy but he is all work, work, work.'

'Maybe that's what Matt and I need, a holiday,' Polly mused.

'Can't you take one?' Claire asked.

'No, I wouldn't get time off work, being so new. And anyway, I'm not sure Matt would want to take a holiday, not when he hasn't got a job sorted and he's feeling so down. No, actually, I know he won't. Maybe next year.' She smiled. 'Anyway, Claire, at least you're OK.' I marvelled at the difference between the way the men and women talked. They were kind of saying the same things, but just in a very different way.

'Oh yes, we're fine,' Claire said with a loud sigh.

'Changing the subject,' Tash said. 'You know that neighbourhood watch couple?'

'Oh God, Vic and Heather,' Polly groaned.

'Yes, the ones in the matching jumpers,' Tash laughed. 'They cornered me the other day talking about the increase in missing cats. Apparently six have been reported missing from the area now.'

I pricked up my ears.

'I know, we've seen the pictures on the lampposts. Makes me really sad. Imagine if Alfie or George went missing.' I shuddered as Claire said this.

'Well, they seem to think something sinister is going on,' Tash continued. 'Apparently they're going to hold a meeting soon.'

'Oh no, not a meeting.' Polly put her head in her hands.

'Their meetings go on for days,' Claire explained.

'But these cats, no one knows what's happened?' Franceska asked.

'No. Jon thinks they just didn't like their owners or fancied a change of scene.'

'Matt said maybe there's a cat snatcher, like the child snatcher in *Chitty Chitty Bang Bang*,' Polly said.

I put my paws over my ears.

'Shush, Polly, not in front of Alfie,' Claire chastised. 'And that's ridiculous. Besides, if anyone tried to take our cats we would sort them out.' Claire looked at me as she said this and I felt marginally reassured.

It wasn't good, these missing cats – I could feel it in my fur. But for now there was little I could do, so I went upstairs to see the children, following the trail of their laughter. At least they were having fun, and I needed to join in with that while I came up with a plan for what to do with my troublesome grown-ups, and tried not to worry about this cat problem at the same time.

# Chapter
# Nineteen

It never rains but it pours. My very first owner, Margaret, used to say that a lot. I didn't always understand what it meant but I think I do now. After family day I spent quite a lot of time fretting. I worried about all my families, including Tasha, who had been in floods of tears after mediation had gone horribly wrong. She was now talking about taking Dave to the cleaners – wherever that was – and saying that her parents were going to pay her legal bills so she could do so. She was refusing to hand over the money for the house sale, which the solicitor held in an account, until it was all settled, and things had turned a bit nasty. Jonathan said that if Dave came near her he would get involved, but thankfully Tasha hadn't told her ex where she was living and anyway, she said, he was too lazy to do anything. It was all in the hands of the law now and Tasha was refusing to speak to him, or have anything to do with him apart from through solicitors. It was a bit complicated for me to follow, being a cat, but I was trying. Oh, and he'd still only made half-hearted attempts to see Elijah which upset everyone. We all loved Elijah and I couldn't understand any father who didn't want to see his child as much as possible. Look at me and George.

It was also literally pouring. As George and I sat on the windowsill watching the rain drip down the pane, I was worrying about everyone and everything.

I was feeling helpless and hopeless. I couldn't help Tasha, but actually knowing that she had this solicitor person as well as Claire and Jonathan made me feel better. I couldn't seem to help Matt and Polly, who seemed to be barely speaking whenever I saw them. I couldn't help Franceska and Tomasz, who were going to be apart. Aleksy and little Tomasz were so excited for their holiday but I worried that it meant Franceska might never come back! I couldn't imagine losing them from my life. And it seemed I couldn't help Claire and Jonathan, who only the previous night had had a massive row.

'Did you have to say that to the social worker?' Claire had shouted the previous evening as we sat in the living room.

'I only said there was no history of criminal activity or insanity in my family…' Jonathan tried not to smile. 'It was a joke!'

'Then you said you weren't sure about my mother! Did you really think that was funny?'

'Well, your mother can come across as a bit bonkers.' He laughed.

'This is just a big joke to you, isn't it, us getting a child, a sibling for Summer, another child for us to parent? I can't believe you sometimes.'

'Of course not, it was just a stupid joke, Claire. The social worker needs to know we have a sense of humour, surely?'

'Well, you're not funny.'

Claire had slept in the spare room, the room that Tash had only recently vacated. I know she cried herself to sleep too, because I slept with her, leaving George for the first time since he'd moved in, although I did check him regularly, which of course meant I was feeling a little sleep deprived myself.

The atmosphere had been strained here all day, a bit like at Polly and Matt's. So far, Claire was refusing all of Jonathan's efforts to make up and when they left for work and to take

Summer to nursery it was a relief to have that atmosphere out of the house along with them.

'What is wrong with people?' George asked me, chasing a raindrop with his paw and bringing me back to the present.

'Oh dear, where do I start?' I began to tell him all I knew. As I started feeling more and more fearful, I tried to downplay the situation for George's sake. Yes, he needed to know how humans worked, especially if he was going to take after me, but he was still so young – I had to protect him. As I was thinking of how I was going to fix each of my humans, from Tash, who had suddenly gone from the top of my worry list almost to the bottom, to Matt and Polly, Franceska and Tomasz and now Claire and Jonathan, George jumped down from the windowsill and ran off. I pulled myself from my reverie and went to find him.

When George had first come to live here, Claire was pretty careful about where he was allowed to go. All the bedroom doors were kept closed, as was the bathroom and the downstairs loo, so he was basically confined to the kitchen/dining room and living room. Despite the stair gate, he could get up the stairs, but once he was there he was confined to the landing. Now that he was bigger, however, they didn't bother to close the doors, the argument being he knew what he was doing (he didn't) and he was still never left alone (he was). But he had more freedom and now I had to locate him, with so many more places he could be.

He wasn't in the kitchen. I knew he hadn't gone outside or I would have heard the cat flap, so I did a quick look around the utility room, especially the washing machine, before heading upstairs.

'George,' I called out loudly, but there was no answer. I tried to stem my growing panic as I checked the bedrooms, telling myself that he couldn't be far, he was just a kitten after all… The bathroom door was closed, as was the door to Jonathan and Claire's en suite, so at least I didn't have to worry about him having fallen into the loo again. But still, I couldn't help but panic. I knew he was here but because I couldn't see him there was this irrational worry that I couldn't quite keep away. I went back into the spare room.

'George,' I shouted again. I heard a little muffled sound. I traced it to the wardrobe where Claire kept some of her clothes, and saw that the door was a tiny bit ajar. I hit at it with my paw until it opened a bit more and I saw George lying on one of Claire's jumpers which were piled up on the bottom of the wardrobe.

'George, I was worried! I've been calling you. Why didn't you answer me?'

'But, Dad, if I answered you it wouldn't be hide and seek would it?'

'Hide and seek?'

'Yes, the children taught me the other day, it's so much fun. One person seeks and the others hide.'

'Yes, thank you, I do know how to play, but the point is that we weren't playing hide and seek, I was sitting on the windowsill with you one minute and the next you were gone.'

'Oh, maybe I should have told you.' George had confusion in his beautiful eyes. 'Right, now why don't you hide?' He didn't seem contrite or even aware of the worry he caused me.

'I don't really feel like it.' I was still busy fretting over my families, and now that I'd found George, I had to calm myself down again.

'Please, Dad, it's the best game ever!' His eyes were wide with hope and I couldn't help but smile. I remembered when Aleksy had first played the game with me – it had been such fun. How could I disappoint? Besides, it was raining outside, so there was nothing else we could do.

'OK, you count to ten and I'll hide.'

'But I don't know how to count!'

'OK, well just give me a bit of time then.' I wasn't sure if I could count either. It wasn't the most useful skill for a cat, after all.

I went to Summer's room and decided to climb into her toy box, which was overflowing with her collection of soft toys. By my reckoning, if it took George ages to find me, I would at least be comfortable.

I woke some time later to George licking my head. I opened my eyes and stretched. 'Sorry, I fell asleep.'

'Wow, you are really good at hiding!' he exclaimed. 'My turn, my turn.' He ran off. I felt a bit better for my catnap, but I didn't rush as I climbed out of the toy box. I could hear George running down the stairs, so I waited a bit on the landing. I noticed that the rain had slowed and I jumped up onto the landing windowsill to see a glimmer of blue sky peeking through the clouds. I wondered if we could go out in a bit – it would be good to get some exercise and perhaps we could pop in to see Matt… Suddenly, there was a loud bang, which made me jump.

'Yowl,' I heard George cry. Honestly, I really must stop getting so distracted, what kind of parent was I? I ran down the stairs and into the kitchen. I stopped when I saw that one of the cupboards was open, its contents over the floor, and George was poking out of a plastic bag, tangled up in the handle.

'George, what have you done?' I asked, using my paw to get the bag off him. 'Bags are dangerous, you must be careful,' I chastised. Although of course there was a big hole, which was how he'd got in, so I didn't really need to be too worried. And us cats did like bags, I used to climb into Margaret's shopping bags all the time when I was little.

'I was just trying to move it and I fell into it,' he replied. Honestly this kitten was getting a bit too defiant. 'But I like it!'

'Not the point. What is this mess?' I asked, surveying the packets and boxes scattered across the floor.

'I managed to open that cupboard, which I thought was quite clever, and I wanted to hide but to make it really good hiding I decided to take everything out and hide right at the back, but then I didn't know how to get it back in...'

'Oh, George.' I started trying to figure out how to get things back in the cupboard before realising that I had no chance, so I left it like it was, knowing I would probably be the one who got told off. I wasn't best pleased with George but I was also cross with Claire and Jonathan. They had put those funny childproof things on most of the cupboards to stop Summer, so why hadn't they done this one? Honestly, parenting was going downhill these days.

I was exhausted after my attempts to tidy up, but George was hopping around wanting to play. He had far too much energy, so I decided that we would brave the outside. I led him out through the cat flap.

'It's wet!' he screeched as he stood in a puddle and a big fat raindrop plopped onto his head.

'OK, look, we'll go and see Matt, come on, I'll take you the back way.' I led him over and under fences in the direction of Polly and Matt's house. Luckily it was a dog-free route. Although George still didn't like the rain I was hoping that the exercise would wear him out a bit. He was one exhausting kitten at times.

We let ourselves in through the cat flap, and as we both dripped a bit onto the kitchen floor, Matt appeared, talking on the phone. He smiled at us.

'Polly, calm down. I've said it's OK. I'll pick the kids up, get them ready for bed and if they're not too tired they can stay up and see you when you get home.' He listened for a bit. 'OK, love you.' He put the phone down and then looked at us.

'You guys are pretty damp. Stay in here until you dry off.' He put the kettle on and I shook my fur. George went and lay in the warmest spot he could find. 'Right, well, nice to see you boys. This being at home on my own is a bit dull, to be honest. Don't know how Polly did it, but she never seemed to complain… I miss going to work though, I miss the pressure as well as the actual job.' I went to him and rubbed his leg, but carefully, so he didn't get too wet. 'Thanks, Alfie. Anyway, I'm trying to make the best of it. I love spending more time with the kids, I really do enjoy that, and it's nice because I'm seeing them do things I've never been around for before. But the school gate is a bit scary, all those women. And in this day and age it still is mainly women, I'm not even being sexist. I got asked to go for coffee today but I was too afraid so I made an excuse. If I'm not careful they'll draft me onto the PTA!'

'Miaow?' I had no idea what he was talking about, none whatsoever.

'I really do need to get a job. I mean, I might have got the hang of being a househusband, nearly, but it's just not me, and I miss Polly. I miss us being together and not arguing. I honestly think if I had a job then we wouldn't argue as much.'

He sat down with his tea and George started chasing his shadow across the kitchen floor.

'If only life were that simple, eh, Alfie?' Matt said, looking at George. I purred my agreement. If only I had just my shadow to worry about, but no, I had the weight of the world on my shoulders. Or the weight of Edgar Road at least.

We stayed with Matt until he had to leave to go to the supermarket before picking the kids up. George was very entertaining, being a bit of an exhibitionist, showing Matt how he could jump onto counters and climb up the kitchen blinds – which very nearly didn't end well. But at least he made us both laugh. It was nice to see Matt smile; now I understood why people watched funny cat videos on the internet for hours, it was better than catnip for lifting a mood. I was so pleased when we left; Matt was smiling, he looked smart and the house was spotless. Maybe he was turning a corner, and it seemed we had definitely cheered him up.

As we left, we bumped into Tiger at the front of the house. The rain had stopped and the sun was almost shining.

'Hey, guys, how are you?' she asked, giving George a big nuzzle.

'Exhausted and in need of a nap,' I said. I really was. I also wanted time to think about my humans, but with George it was impossible.

'But I want to play!' George said. He was still far too full of energy.

'Hey, Alfie, I can watch him. I'll take him to the park or something and bring him home after?' Tiger looked hopeful.

An offer of babysitting? How could I refuse, especially as I knew Tiger would never let anything happen to George.

'You're on. Now, George, be good for Tiger and I'll see you later.' I nuzzled him goodbye and headed home for a well-earned rest.

I enjoyed my nap but I didn't relax fully while George was out. I knew he was safe with Tiger but still… He hadn't been out without me before. When I heard the cat flap bang, I rushed to the back door. I put my head through, and saw Tiger sitting with George in front of the cat flap. I grinned; he looked so cute. They looked cute together, in fact: my best friend and my kitten.

'Hi, Alfie,' Tiger said.

'Has he been good?' I asked.

'Good as gold. We've had so much fun,' Tiger replied.

'Oh, Dad, I love the park! We climbed a tree and teased a chubby dog. It was great!' George was full of enthusiasm and I was both relieved that he was all right and thrilled to see how happy he was.

'Right, come on in, it's teatime. Thanks, Tiger, thank you so much.'

'Can Tiger-Mum come home with us?' George asked. My heart melted and I looked at Tiger and could see she felt emotional too.

'I'm afraid not, she has to get home now, but you'll see her soon. Thanks again, Tiger.'

'My pleasure. Any time you need some time to yourself, I'm there,' Tiger replied, then bade us goodbye. I stood back so George could hop through the cat flap.

'I missed you,' I said, and I really had. It was strange – I did need time to myself every now and then, but when I had it, I missed him. Was that parenthood? I guessed it must be because I was pretty sure I had heard my humans saying something similar.

'Me too, Dad. What's for tea?'

Later that evening I lay snuggled up in the armchair, with George curled up next to me. It was dark outside; Jonathan was watching the news on TV and Claire came in to join him. I felt nervous; they had been perfectly civil to each other while Summer was around, but now she was in bed, I was unsure how the land lay.

'Hi,' Jonathan said. 'Are you OK?'

'Yes, I just spoke to Tash.' Claire sat down. 'It looks as if it's all being sorted. I think Dave has had some kind of wake-up call. She's not sure, but he has apologised and said he does want to be a good dad to Elijah. They're going to meet up this weekend, with his mum, and she seems hopeful.'

'She won't take him back will she?' Jonathan looked concerned and I sincerely hoped not.

'No, I think the way he acted, cheating, moving out, not to mention the lying and the way he behaved since, means she'll never fully trust him again, but Tash is a good mum and she wants what's best for her child. At the moment that means having his dad around, no matter how useless he is.'

'I agree, although I'm not Dave's biggest fan. But I am Elijah's, of course.' Jonathan touched Claire's arm.

'Jonathan, we have our own issues to deal with, I know that, and we need to figure them out, so this weekend I want to go and see Mum and Dad with Summer, and I want you to come.'

'OK, what's brought this on?'

'I'm not going to pretend. I could do with a change of scene, but also… Dad is a social worker, you know that, and he's going to help us with the adoption – just explain how it works and what we need to do, if we decide to push forward with it. I thought it might help you to speak more to him about it.'

'You mean your dad is going to talk me into it?' Jonathan bristled.

'No, I told him that I found it all a bit confusing and I explained how you felt, and he said perhaps if he talked us through the process, and all the options available to us, then maybe we'd stop arguing and come to a decision we were both happy with.' I was proud of how reasonable Claire sounded.

'Right…' Jonathan still sounded doubtful.

'Look, I know how single-minded I get, so does Dad. I wanted us to get married when we did, I wanted Summer when we did, I know how I am and, well, I think Dad is probably more likely to be on your side than mine.'

'It's not about sides, you know that. I just don't know if I can do this.' Jonathan sounded sad rather than angry. 'I wish I had your belief, I really do.'

'And that's what this weekend is about. Having a chat, a change of scene and then hopefully we can make a decision together. Besides, Mum and Dad are dying to see Sum.'

'Blimey, you sound more reasonable than I've ever heard you,' Jonathan said.

'That's my dad. He kind of gave me a bit of a talking-to. Anyway, can we go?'

'What about Alfie and George?'

'Frankie said they could both go and stay with them. We can drop them off on the way and either pick them up on our way home or Tomasz will drop them back here. The boys want to spend time with Alfie, and George, of course, before they go on their holiday.'

Wow, I was going to spend the weekend with my Polish family, which was great, and George was going to have his very first weekend away. And we'd see Dustbin! I was already excited.

'You've got it all sorted then.' I saw Jonathan raise his eyebrows.

'Sorry, I know, I'm so bossy. But you kind of knew that when you married me.'

'True, I did. Look, Claire, about the adoption—'

'I know you're worried you won't be able to love a child that you didn't make.'

'Yes, that's it.'

'But I think you can.'

I felt a tingling in my fur. I looked at George, curled up next to me. I couldn't love him any more than I did, yet I didn't make him. I looked at Jonathan and Claire, who appeared to be deep in thought. I had adopted George, hadn't I? Yes, it had been an enforced adoption at first, but still... And now I would be distraught without him; I loved him so much. I needed Jonathan to understand this. Surely that was the answer. He had to see that, if I could love George, he could love an adopted child. I just wasn't sure how I could make him see that – at least, not yet.

# Chapter
# Twenty

'Oh, Mama, look, George is playing with the sardine!' little Tomasz exclaimed with joy. I had told George that food was not to be played with, but he loved how slippery it felt between his paws and he was chasing it around the kitchen – although of course it wasn't alive – and pouncing on it. The boys thought it was hilarious. Aleksy was laughing so hard he couldn't speak.

'George, eat the fish, is not a toy,' Franceska chastised, winking at me. She then grabbed it, chopped it up and put it back in his bowl. He obediently ate. We had arrived a little while ago, just after the boys had got back from school. They were excited, not only because we were staying with them but also because it was the start of the summer holidays. They were leaving next week for their holiday in Poland, which I felt sad about, but I didn't want that to tarnish this weekend. I wanted us to have as much fun as possible.

We ate tea and then the boys put on a film, *Star Wars*, which I couldn't quite figure out, but it was quite exuberant. There were lots of flashes of colour across the screen. George jumped up onto the TV stand and tried to chase the flashes before Aleksy moved him away.

'You'll be in trouble if you break it,' he said, echoing my thoughts. George looked at me, and I tried to give him a stern look but he just smiled that adorable smile of his. I think he was enjoying his first holiday.

Just as the film finished, big Tomasz arrived home.

'Ah, the cats, my boys, how lovely to come home to you all.' He smiled broadly and kissed everyone, and then he kissed his wife.

'*Kochanie*, I have bought some champagne home from the restaurant for us tonight.'

'What are we celebrating?' Franceska asked. Big Tomasz looked a bit sad, but didn't say anything. It was yet another 'not in front of the children' moment.

'Right, boys, bedtime,' Franceska said.

'Oh, Mum,' Aleksy said. He sounded like an English boy now, although I knew big Tomasz and Franceska were teaching their sons Polish. 'Can we stay up a bit, with Alfie and George?' he begged.

'Half an hour,' she conceded. 'Tomasz, I'll put supper on, you spend time with the boys.' I noticed that Franceska didn't exactly sound happy, but I was distracted as Aleksy picked me up while both big and little Tomasz started playing ball with George. Aleksy carried me into his bedroom. As my first child friend, Aleksy and I had been through a lot together. I had been his first friend in England and I'd also helped him when he was being bullied at school a couple of years ago. He confided in me, and as he placed me on his bed I knew we were going to have a chat.

'I'm worried, Alfie. Mum and Dad aren't really speaking and now we're going to Poland for the whole holiday without him. I'm going to miss you, and home, but I'm going to miss Dad the most.' He looked sad as he stroked me. I snuggled into him and purred my understanding.

'I'm worried we won't come home. I mean, Mum said we will when I asked her, but what if we don't? Or what if our parents split up like Elijah's and my school friend Justin's did?

I love Mum and Dad, and I get we don't see enough of Dad at the moment because he's too busy but they have to fix it.' He thumped his hand down on his bed and looked so sad. I really felt for him. Aleksy was ten but very sensitive and mature, I thought, a little like me. I tickled him with my tail, which normally made him laugh and then I put my paw up in a high five. 'You'll make sure that they're OK, won't you, Alfie?'

'Miaow.' Of course I would. I had no idea how, but I would. I was giving Aleksy my cat promise.

'I'm excited to go to Poland. I don't really remember much about it and Tommy has no memory at all. We'll get to see family and Mum says it'll be really cool but I want to come home to both my parents, Alfie. I'm relying on you.'

'Miaow.' Oh goodness, I had just been given even more responsibility.

After the boys had gone to bed, Tomasz let us out the back. He and Franceska were speaking to each other using only one word at a time, which I knew wasn't good, and he was going back to the restaurant downstairs to quickly check everything was fine. He promised Franceska he wouldn't be long, but she just grunted in response.

'It's dark,' George said as he tentatively stepped into the yard. 'Yowl!' he shrieked. 'What was that?'

'Your shadow, George. Don't worry, I'm here.' I felt brave. After all, I'd been in this yard loads of times, and yes, it was a bit scary, and there were some nasty creatures around, but Dustbin would be here somewhere and he'd take care of us.

'Yowl!' he shrieked again. 'What's that?' A figure loomed towards us.

'George, that's my friend, Dustbin.' Dustbin emerged from behind a bin, licking his whiskers.

'Nice surprise, Alfie.' He looked at George. 'And who's this?'

'This is George, he's my kitten.'

'I heard the boys talking about someone called George when they were down here the other day. I didn't know you were a kitten. Nice to meet you, George.' Dustbin's voice softened as he spoke; even he wasn't immune to George's charm.

'We aren't allowed out for very long,' I explained. 'But it's safe, isn't it?'

'Don't worry, Alfie, I won't let anything happen to your lad. Will you come to see me tomorrow?'

'Yes, I'll miaow to be let out after breakfast and we can have a proper catch up.'

'Looking forward to it, and getting to know the little lad a bit better too!'

Big Tomasz came out again, leaving a big plate of food for Dustbin, before taking us back upstairs. I noticed George was still shaking.

'It's OK, Dustbin is really nice,' I said.

'I know but it was so dark and it smelled funny in the yard. Dustbin smelled funny too.' I couldn't argue with that. He was a little fragrant, but he had a heart of gold.

George and I settled down in my bed in the living room as Tomasz and Franceska drank the champagne that Tomasz had brought from the restaurant, but neither of them looked as if they were enjoying it. They barely said a word, until finally they both started speaking really quickly in Polish, which meant that I couldn't understand what they were saying. They didn't sound very happy, I had to admit. I went to sleep worrying about them and feeling bad for Aleksy. And for myself – after all, I had promised to fix it.

The following morning, the sun was shining brightly as George and I waited to go out into the yard. In the daylight, George felt more confident, and ran straight up to Dustbin.

'MIAOW!' he screamed, as Dustbin, taken by surprise, dropped what he had in his mouth. It was a very fat mouse, or perhaps even a rat. George jumped back, the rodent jumped towards him, and before I knew what to do, Dustbin had grabbed it and flung it out of the way.

'Oh dear, that was a bit close,' Dustbin said as I went to comfort George.

'What was that?' George asked, wide-eyed.

'It was a small rat, not very nice, but my job is to keep them away from the restaurant.'

'But what do they do?' George said.

'Good question. All they seem to do is eat rubbish and spread disease.'

'Are they worse than dogs then?' George asked.

'Not exactly, but as bad as.' Dustbin was very patient with him; it was gratifying to see.

'But you know what, Dustbin, Dad, I wanted to leap on it, I had this feeling inside me.'

'That's your cat instinct,' Dustbin explained. 'Cats are natural hunters, it's in your nature and that's why you felt that urge to do that.'

'Dad, do you hunt too?' asked George.

Dustbin exchanged a look with me.

'Well, George, I'm not so keen on hunting. There was a point in my life when I had to, and I'll tell you all about that later, but now, well, I try not to get involved.' I saw Dustbin smirk but he didn't contradict me.

'But I can do it?' he asked.

'Look, George, come with me and I'll give you a lesson. But honestly, I do this as a job, it's not something you domestic cats need to worry about too much.'

'Thank you! Can I, Dad?' he asked, looking at me hopefully.

'Of course, George.' I sat back on the doorstep as I watched my boy go hunting with Dustbin. And I have to admit he was already much better at it than me. My boy, a total natural.

'So, Alfie,' Dustbin said, when we were all sitting in the sun by the restaurant back step. 'How's your broken heart?'

'Oh, well, now you come to mention it, it's still a bit sore.' I gestured to George. 'He keeps me busy, which may have been Claire's idea, but there are moments when I feel pangs of loss. I still wonder what Snowball's doing…' I looked wistfully at the sky, although I wasn't sure why.

'You know, I thought about it after you left last time,' Dustbin said. 'It's as if you give a bit of your heart to everyone you love, and sometimes they stay around and sometimes they don't. The point is, Alfie, that you have a very big heart, with enough pieces for everyone.' I felt emotional as he said this, thinking of those I'd loved who had taken pieces of my heart with them: Margaret, Agnes and Snowball. I knew Dustbin was right.

'For such a feral cat you're very wise,' I said, touched and full of love for him.

'That's what friends are for.'

'But I don't understand,' George said, looking bewildered at both of us.

'You're far too young,' we both said at the same time.

We had a lovely time with Dustbin and I filled him in on the lamppost cats. I did it while George was distracted, as I didn't like talking about them in front of him. I didn't want to scare him.

'Interesting,' Dustbin said after a while. 'I wonder what's going on? They can't all have decided to leave home.'

'That's what I think. My humans have been all preoccupying me as usual with their own problems, but this is beginning to make me worry. What if the worst is right and there's some kind of threat to all the cats in the neighbourhood? No one from Edgar Road has gone missing, but still, it seems a bit close to home to be comfortable.'

'Look, Alfie, I can ask around.' Dustbin had this amazing network of cats who generally knew or could find out anything; they had helped me in the past.

'I'd be really grateful if you could.' I still wasn't sure what the lamppost cat issue really was, or if I should be worried about it, but having Dustbin dig around for me wouldn't hurt at all.

When we went back inside, big Tomasz took the boys out for lunch so Franceska could pack. George and I followed her into her room where there were two suitcases on the bed, one big and one small.

'So much easier to pack for the boys than for me,' she sighed as she started putting clothes into the bigger case.

'Miaow,' I said, staying close to her. I followed her to her wardrobe and then, when she had an armful of clothes, back to the bed.

'Where's George?' she asked. I looked around; he was nowhere to be seen. Oh no, not hide and seek again. I started looking round the room as Franceska put the clothes in the suitcase. Suddenly they all flew up in the air.

'Ahhh!' Franceska screamed as George jumped out from the suitcase. 'You gave me such a fright!' Then she started laughing. George purred with joy, and I felt relieved he was all right, although he'd made a mess. After that, he kept climbing into the suitcase as if it was a new game. In the end, Franceska shut us both in the living room, saying if she let us stay she'd never get packed before the boys got back. I told George off; although of course he had just been playing, I had hoped to spend some time with Franceska.

'Right, I'm done,' she said a while later, coming into the living room, closing the door behind her, and flopping down on the sofa. 'Having a kitten is like having a baby, you can't take any chances,' she said. I purred in agreement as I jumped onto her lap. 'I'll miss you, Alfie. I know it's only for a few weeks but it will be the longest I haven't seen you since we met,' she said, stroking my fur and scratching my head – which I loved. I snuggled further into her lap, hoping she would miss her husband too. 'I'll miss Tomasz of course,' she said, as though reading my mind. 'But he works so much, I hardly ever see him anyway. I tell him he needs to spend more time with his family. The boys, they grow up so fast.' I miaowed: yes, they did, all the children did, even George seemed to be growing at an alarming rate. I often found myself asking where my tiny kitten had gone. 'I guess we'll be back before you know it but, just in case we don't get time alone again this weekend, take care and be good.' Franceska kissed my head. She often talked to me a lot when it was just the two of us. I liked to think I was one of her best friends – I almost had too many to count.

'Mama, Mama, look what we got, a Happy Meal!' little Tomasz ran into the living room carrying a box. 'It has a toy in it!'

'You took them to McDonald's?' Franceska asked, sounding surprised.

'Mum, we begged Dad to take us, we never get to go and all our friends do,' Aleksy said. He looked worried – being such a sensitive child, he didn't like arguments.

'It's fine, your dad is soft. It's not good for you, but it won't hurt. Tomasz, I guess it was a special treat.'

'It was, *kochanie*, and I would have taken them wherever they wanted to go. I'm going to miss you all, you know.' He sounded a bit down.

'I know, and we'll miss you too.' Franceska sounded warmer towards her husband than she had done in a while. I wondered if she meant it or if it was for the boys' sake. 'But later we eat healthy food, no more junk,' she smiled.

'Pizza?' little Tomasz asked.

'I said healthy,' Franceska laughed.

'Pizza with vegetables on it?' Aleksy suggested, and everyone laughed.


The rest of our weekend whizzed by. Aleksy and little Tomasz made an assault course for George, which he loved. It had tunnels, jumps, balls and toy cars, and George enjoyed being the centre of attention – which he usually was anyway – as they timed him going round it. It wasn't without incident: at one point he got stuck in one of the tunnels, which was made out of cardboard and a bit small. But after much pushing, prodding and coaxing, he was freed at last, no worse off for his experience. Franceska was in a better mood too, and Tomasz stayed with us, which seemed to prove to me that he didn't need to be in the restaurant all the time.

As we said goodbye later that evening, I was sad. I would miss them all, including Dustbin, who had really helped me yet again. It was good to know he was going to try to get to the bottom of the lamppost cat mystery. Aleksy, of course, I would miss so much, but little Tomasz and Franceska too. When they all went to Poland they would each take a piece of my heart with them. I just hoped – really, truly hoped – that they would return with their pieces before too long.

# Chapter
# Twenty-one

Polly was at our house when big Tomasz drove George and me home. Matt and Jonathan had gone to the pub. Matt was no further forward in his job search and Polly was worried that he might still be feeling depressed. Claire thought a trip to the pub might do both him and Jonathan some good.

We settled the children in front of the TV. Claire said it was frowned upon to use it as an unpaid babysitter but she defied any normal mum to actually be the one who frowned on it. They were arguing about who got to cuddle George and so they all had to take turns. George didn't mind being passed between them – as always, he quite liked the attention. Polly, Claire and I sat in the kitchen; all doors were open so we could hear the kids, but at least we could also have some grown-up time.

'How are things with work and Matt? I feel I haven't seen you in ages,' Claire said.

'That's the job. Honestly, I do like it but I want to cut down a bit on my hours. I can't though, we need the money and at the moment I have two big projects on, and of course everything has to be finished yesterday so I'm working most evenings. I feel I hardly see the kids and when I do, I'm so knackered I just let them watch TV.'

'Like now, like me, you mean? Don't beat yourself up, Polly – you need a break. It's not like we're terrible mothers, you need to cut yourself some slack.'

'You're right. Been there, done that. I know I can be tough

209

on myself sometimes, but it's hard not to feel guilty, you know?'
When Polly had post-natal depression with Henry, she felt she
wasn't a good mother to him and I know she still beats herself
up about it, but she's a great mum – I see it every day.

'You're enjoying your job though?'

'I love it. And I love that they appreciate what I do. I know
it sounds silly but I feel really proud of myself. I don't think I
could go back to not working again. But I don't know what
the future holds. I just wish Matt would get a job, not because
I want to give mine up – to be honest, I really don't – but
because he hates being at home so much. I can't bear how
miserable he is.'

'There's nothing you can do though, is there? I mean, apart
from being supportive. And he'll find a job soon, Pol. He's
applying for them, isn't he?'

'Yes, and I'm trying to be optimistic but, well, his glass is
definitely half empty at the moment. You know how happy go
lucky he normally is but now he's all doom and gloom.' She
sighed. 'Anyway, how was the weekend?'

'Good and bad. Dad put it all into perspective for me. If we
want a child sooner rather than later, then we need to be open
to adopting an older child. The process still takes a long time,
although, thanks to Dad, and the contacts he has, we are quite
a way along. But as soon as we're approved, if we're approved,
if we want a baby or a young child, then the wait begins. I
think an older child would be great, they'd be at school and it
would be an older sibling for Summer, like Henry, maybe, but
Jonathan thinks it'd be even harder for him to love an older
child than a baby.'

'His argument?'

'It does make sense. Well, to him it does, only because it's the way he feels. He thinks that he loves Summer so much because we made her. He's scared that if we adopt a child he won't feel the same and he doesn't want a child to live with us and feel second best.'

'It's kind of sweet, in a way,' Polly pointed out. And I agreed. Jonathan did have a sensitive side, it was just kind of buried beneath designer suits and bluster.

'Oh yes, he wouldn't want to treat the child differently, but more importantly he wouldn't want to feel about them differently, even if they didn't realise it. He said it was important for him to love any child equally and if he didn't he wouldn't be able to live with himself.'

'So what are you going to do?' Polly asked.

'We agreed to see if we got approved before we made any decisions, but to be honest, he's freaked out a bit and let's just say we aren't on the best of terms right now.'

'Oh God, we're all arguing.' Polly looked at the table.

'Yes, we all are. And Tash, who is the only one of us whose relationship is actually broken, is probably doing better than we are now!'

'I'm glad for her. She's really been so strong through all this, it's amazing.'

'Yes, well, that's the thing. I have someone I want her to meet, one of Jonathan's colleagues, so I thought I'd arrange a dinner. Here, next Saturday night. Can you get a babysitter?' Claire asked.

'I can, but are you sure it's wise to fix her up? It hasn't been very long since she split up with Dave.'

'No, and it might be terrible, but she's been stuck in that flat since she moved in, she only sees us and she needs a confidence

211

boost. It might end in tears but, on the bright side, they'll probably be mine.' Claire laughed and Polly smiled at her.

'OK, I think you're mad but I'll come. I mean we'll come. What does Jonathan think?'

'That I'm too bossy for my own good! But I think he loves me for that in a weird kind of way.'

'And Tash?' Polly drummed a manicured finger on the table. 'Surely she has a say?'

'Well, she's not exactly jumping at the idea but she eventually agreed with me that a night out with some company and food would do her good.'

'So you wore her down too?'

'I absolutely did.' Claire grinned and gave Polly's arm a squeeze. 'We'll work things out, our little gang, we always do.'

'Miaow!' I jumped onto the table. Thank goodness, some positivity at last, although I knew that I would be the one to sort it out in reality.

'Mummy, Mummy! Summer won't let me have my turn with George.' Martha appeared at the door looking cross.

'Come on,' said Claire. 'Let's go and sort this out.' The two women smiled as they went into the living room. It seemed there was only so much the TV could do.


Jonathan came back from the pub quite late. Claire had waited up and so had I. George was sleeping next to me, snoring softly. I loved hearing the sounds he made while sleeping – I could watch him for hours. Well, until I fell asleep anyway.

'Hi, Jon, how was your night?' Claire asked as he kissed her.

'Good. I did try to come home ages ago but Matt wouldn't let me,' Jonathan said.

'That's OK. Was he all right though?'

'Not really, but I think he'll be fine, he just needs time. Right, I've got a really busy day ahead of me tomorrow so I'd better get some sleep.' Without waiting for Claire to respond he left to go upstairs. Claire looked a bit sad as she cleaned up the kitchen before following him.

'George,' I said, nudging him gently. I did think about leaving him to sleep here but I wanted my bed. He opened one eye and looked at me. 'Bedtime.'

'Dad?' he said, stretching his little legs out.

'Yes?'

'Why is everyone so unhappy?'

'What do you mean?' I asked, but I felt a quiver in my fur; had my boy picked up on the tension?

'I had a lovely weekend, but it was clear that Franceska and Tomasz were sad, then Polly looked a bit miserable and Claire talked about them all falling apart. Tash as well. I only just met these people but what happens if they don't get better?' He sounded so sad, and although my heart was breaking for him, I was also incredibly proud. He was learning to be a very perceptive little cat: a chip off the old block, as Jonathan would say.

'George, please don't worry, we are going to fix this, both of us. My job is often to help my families, and you're right, now they need us more than ever, but we'll figure it out. Trust me.'

'I do trust you, Dad,' George said as he got up and made his way to bed.

Snuggled up next to little George, I began fretting. I had now promised both Aleksy and George that everything would be all right, but I had no idea where to start. There were often hurdles to get over but this time there seemed to be so many.

One thing my families had in common was that they did love each other, and I knew they wouldn't ever fall properly apart, but I could also see they needed help. Urgently. Yet again my to-do list had grown.

I also had to deal with my own heartbreak – although that had been pushed far down the list – George, who needed guidance and a lot of taking care of, as well as all my humans, or the adults anyway. At least the children seemed to be all right. Although Aleksy knew something was amiss with his parents, so how long would it be until all of the children were affected by the less-than-congenial atmospheres in their respective homes? Children, just like kittens, did pick up on things, even the little ones. So, I had the children to protect, the adults to sort out and I had promised George and Aleksy we were going to find a way to do it soon.

I tried to sleep but my brain was whirring.

Franceska was going to be so far away, so how on earth could I get big Tomasz to see that working these long hours for his family was making him risk them all? How could I get Polly and Matt to see that although they had a role reversal, and it wasn't perfect for either of them, they could make it work? And Claire and Jonathan, well, they worried me most of all in a way. They were so far apart, despite Claire's dad trying to talk some sense into both of them. Jonathan still thought he couldn't love someone he didn't make but that was crazy – look at the way I felt about George. Even if he were biologically mine, I couldn't love him any more than I already did. So why couldn't Jonathan see that? Why couldn't Claire point it out to him? Yet again, it all came down to me. I had a heavy burden on my little cat shoulders and a long, hard road ahead to ensure everyone was happy. And on top of that, there was the mystery of the lamppost cats to solve. If there was something sinister going on, we needed to get to the bottom of it. And quickly.

My whiskers ached at the thought of how I was going to do it, but somehow, do it I would.

# Chapter
# Twenty-two

Franceska had gone and Tomasz had been round to have a beer with Jonathan and see us. He seemed very lost without her. Matt was no closer to getting a job and he was feeling useless. Polly was settling into a routine now; she was juggling the job and the children quite well, I thought, but she still didn't talk to Matt properly about work because she was afraid how he would react. Claire and Jonathan had had lots of meetings with a social worker and were told that they would hear if they were approved for adoption soon. This seemed to create an even bigger gulf between them and they were still very distant with each other. I heard all of this, and yet I still had no idea what to do.

Tonight, Tash was coming over for dinner with all of them and one of Jonathan's friends or colleagues I hadn't met, and I was hoping the dinner might give me some inspiration. When little George kept asking if things were going to get better, I kept fobbing him off, saying that soon they would and that I was working on it. But really I had no idea.

'Tiger, this is different,' I said.

'It's always different, Alfie. Remember what you've done so far – you've been in more scrapes than I can count, from getting yourself stuck up trees to almost being killed. Don't you think that now, with George to think about, you'd be better off keeping out of it and letting the humans sort themselves out?' Tiger made a good point but she wasn't going to deter me. That wasn't the sort of cat I was.

'The reason I'm doing this is *for* George. Well, for him and all the children. The adults need to see what they're in danger of losing. It seems to be only when I put myself in danger that I manage to bring people together, you know that.'

'Yes, but what are you going to do this time? Set fire to yourself? There's only so much danger you can get away with and I think you've probably reached your limit.' Tiger looked stern.

She had a point. I had been through a lot in my life and perhaps there wasn't much more I could do. How many more of my nine lives could I afford to lose? I might have to come up with a less dangerous way of fixing things.

'OK, look, I know you're right, so I'll give it some time, and maybe, just maybe, they'll all sort themselves out. But if they don't… then we'll have to come up with a plan.'

'Deal,' Tiger said. 'But what about the missing cats?' She knew me too well.

'I've asked Dustbin to ask around about them. I'm still hoping it's just something weird rather than something serious. But all we can do on that one is wait and see.'

'Mew, mew, mew.' I looked up to see George clinging to a branch by his front paws.

'I tried to catch a bird,' he said, 'but now I'm going to fall.'

Oh my goodness, my poor little boy. 'Just stay where you are, George, I'm coming,' I shouted, starting to panic. Tiger shot me a look.

'It's OK,' she said calmly, 'George, you can jump from there. Look it's grass here, and if you let go, you'll land on your legs.' George looked at us uncertainly and I realised that, actually,

Tiger was right – he wasn't far from the ground. I must learn not to panic so much.

'Tiger's right, George, you'll be fine and we're right here.' Eventually George let go and landed on all fours.

'Wow, that was fun, can I do it again?' he asked, giggling.

'Another day,' Tiger and I said in unison. I smiled at her and she grinned back; we were getting good at this parenting lark, I thought, as a flash of affection for Tiger flooded me. But I couldn't think about that, I had bigger fish to fry.

Talking of fish, a little while later, George and I made our way home to eat our supper of sardines. I told him to make sure he bathed thoroughly: we had company coming so we both needed to look our best. Claire looked very pretty as she started to cook the food that she'd prepared earlier in the day. She was wearing a dress and high heels and her hair was swept back off her face. She had put on some make-up but still looked natural. She hummed to herself while she worked. I heard Jonathan upstairs. He was bathing Summer and getting her ready for bed, and seemed in a slightly better mood as he laughed with his daughter. We heard splashes and shrieks of joy coming from her. I was always excited when we had friends coming round. Being a sociable cat, I enjoyed people, and I also guessed that no one would argue tonight, because they tended not to in public. So we were in for a nice, harmonious evening with friends and I for one felt it was just what the vet ordered.

Tash arrived first. She was wearing jeans, a sparkly top and heels. George jumped up at her, and she scooped him into her arms after handing a bottle of wine to Claire.

'Easy, George,' she said, smiling. He was mesmerised by her

top. It was like lots of tiny mirrors and I knew he was trying hard to look at his reflection in it! She petted him before carefully putting him down and accepting a glass of wine from Claire.

'Are you OK?'

'I'm nervous. Not only because of tonight and you trying to set me up with some bloke I've never met, but because Elijah's with *him.*'

'I know, honey, but he's also with Dave's mum.' The stipulation to an overnight visit had been that it had to be at his mum's house, because Tash seemed to think that Dave would expose Elijah to danger if his mum wasn't there. I didn't know much about it but the situation seemed to be good for Dave's mum, who adored her only grandchild.

'I know, thank God for Pat. Poor woman feels so guilty on her son's behalf but I keep telling her that it's important she feels she can see Elijah whenever she wants. Anyway, I need to stop being so silly about it.'

'And as for tonight, it's just dinner with friends. Yes, there happens to be a single man you've never met coming but what's the worst that can happen?'

'I get drunk and make a fool of myself?'

'Tash, you don't do that, it's more likely to be me, now sit down and relax.'

I went to sit on Tash's lap, and as she stroked me I could feel her calming down. I purred 'you're welcome' to her as she smiled at me. Jonathan entered the kitchen. He looked very handsome in his jeans and a clean, pressed shirt.

'Hi, Tasha,' he said, kissing her cheek. He then kissed Claire before grabbing a beer from the fridge and hovering. 'Can I do anything, darling?' he asked.

'No, it's all under control.' And it was, but then Claire was pretty organised when it came to things like this. The table was set with candles and cutlery, but it wasn't too cluttered; wine glasses gleamed and the food smelled delicious, although I could tell there was no fish.

'So, tell me about this guy,' Tash said. 'I know I'm supposedly not being set up, but I certainly feel like I am!'

'Tash, you are being set up, my beautiful wife knows what she's doing!' Jonathan laughed. I saw Claire smile, which was rare lately, but tonight was a great example of how united they could actually be. 'Anyway, Max is forty-four, divorced, one child who's at university – so he started young by the way – and he was married for twenty years. No big drama, he and his wife just drifted apart apparently.'

'And he works with you?'

'Yes, he trades the same stocks as me. Good job, nice guy and actually quite fun, although he does like to play golf but I try not to hold that against him.' I didn't know what golf was but Jonathan was a strictly football guy, and whether he watched it at home or in the pub it always involved beer. Maybe golf was like that?

'He sounds great, but I'm just not sure how I feel about dating again, it might be too soon,' Tash said.

'Oh, nonsense,' Claire cut in. 'I'm not saying marry the guy, but it doesn't hurt to meet new people and maybe even have the odd date. After all, a girl's got to eat.'

'Anyway, aren't you ladies forgetting something? Tash might not fancy him,' Jonathan teased.

'Oh, she will, he's really good-looking,' Claire said. Jonathan shot her a look of mock hurt.

George was grinning as I joined him on a soft chair in the corner of the dining area. I knew what he was thinking, that it was lovely to see everyone laughing and relaxed for once. We were interrupted by the doorbell, and as George and I settled down to watch the evening's events unfold, I began to feel positive. Maybe Tiger was right and everything would sort itself out after all?

Well, Claire turned out to be right. Max was very good-looking: he was tall, with greying hair, and he had a lovely smile. I immediately liked him as he made a huge fuss of both me and George. I could see that Tash was quite taken with him too, she kept blushing and twiddling with her hair. Polly and Matt were on good form, and were even being affectionate to each other. They were usually the most touchy-feely of my couples, always holding hands or hugging or doing that kissing that you see in films, but lately they hadn't been doing that so much. So to see them back to their old selves was heart-warming. They weren't doing film kissing but Polly kept putting her hand on Matt's arm and he had his hand on her leg when he wasn't holding a fork. There was more laughter and fun than we'd had in a long time and I think, for George, ever in the time he'd lived with us.

I couldn't help marvelling that even though he'd only been with us for such a short time, I almost couldn't remember life without him. I hadn't forgotten my time with Snowball, but it was as if George belonged in my life more than anyone or anything else ever had. The time before him felt like it had happened to a different cat. Did that sound crazy?

'So, Claire, we have to go to this dinner with my bosses next week, can you babysit?' Polly asked.

'Sure, what night? I'd be happy to if Jon can stay home.'

'Thursday.'

'No problem,' Jonathan said.

'It'll be funny, Polly often had to endure dinners when I was working, but now I'm the spouse who has to charm her bosses. Not sure I'll be as good at it as she was,' Matt said, but he didn't sound bitter.

'They'll love you, but I agree it will be odd. Gosh, over the years I've been to so many of these corporate dinners with you.'

'I know, and you've always dazzled. Never mind, I'll just have to do my best,' said Matt, kissing her cheek.

'Well, you are charming all the school mums I used to hang out with,' Polly teased.

'Charming?' Matt replied, 'I spend most of my time running the gauntlet so I don't get cornered by them. Not only are they scary but they keep wanting me to join them for skinny lattes and Pilates.' Matt laughed and everyone else joined in.

'What do you do, Matt?' Max asked. I held my breath.

'At the moment, nothing. Well not nothing, I'm a house-husband. I worked for a digital design agency, which went belly-up. And despite numerous applications there aren't any posts senior enough for me at the moment.'

'Oh God, you'll have to take up Pilates, mate,' Jonathan teased.

George had fallen asleep beside me, but I was concentrating on the conversation. It seemed that Max's brother co-owned a company like the one Matt used to work for, and Matt had heard of it. And although Max didn't know if he had any vacancies, he said he'd be happy to ask. Matt seemed very pleased and I thought about what a small world it could be. As Tash flirted, Claire and Jonathan looked happy and Matt and Polly were affectionate; I wondered if they would sort everything out without my help. For once. With that lovely thought swimming around my head, I fell asleep.

I woke as Tash and Polly came to say goodbye to us. George didn't stir, but I decided to follow them out, just to make sure that everything was all right. I don't think anyone noticed as I went out the front door, they were all so effervescent and excited. As I stood by our gate, I saw Matt and Polly head off in one direction holding hands, which made me feel warm in my fur. Then Max offered to walk Tash home before getting into the taxi that was waiting for him. I hung back slightly as Max spoke to the driver and then he and Tash set off the short walk to her flat, the opposite way to Matt and Polly.

'I know things are raw but I had fun tonight. So if you fancy going to dinner sometime…' I heard Max say. I decided I really liked him: not only was he handsome, he was kind.

'I would like that,' Tash said. She could barely keep the smile from her face and she looked so pretty in the moonlight. Max stopped and pulled out his phone as Tash gave him her number. Satisfied, I made my way home.

I went to jump through the cat flap.

'Yowl!' I flew backwards. Yet again, I had forgotten that the cat flap was still locked at night. When would I learn? I panicked slightly; what if I was locked out for the night? What if George woke and I wasn't there? I jumped on to the kitchen windowsill and was relieved to find myself looking at Jonathan. He was holding a glass and seemed to be staring at the sink.

'Miaow!' I shouted as loudly as I could, tapping the glass with my sore head.

'What the?' Jonathan jumped and dropped the glass. I ran to the back door. 'You gave me the fright of my life, Alfie!' Jonathan shouted. I walked past, giving him my sternest look. Take away your freedom and then see how you feel, I wanted to say, but of course I couldn't, being a cat.

# Chapter Twenty-three

Vic and Heather had called a neighbourhood watch meeting. I watched through our living room window as people crammed into their house. Polly and Claire went; Polly said that Matt was so down she didn't think he'd survive it, so Claire offered to go with her in solidarity. Tash couldn't go as she had to look after Elijah and to everyone's amusement she was actually a little disappointed. But as they told her, there would be plenty more meetings to attend in the future. But despite the joking, I knew the nature of the meeting might help me so I was disappointed that I couldn't go either.

I felt a little sad as I watched Polly, still in her work suit, and Claire, wearing jeans and a jumper, walk through the Goodwins' door. All I could do was settle down with Jonathan and wait for Claire to come home. Summer was in bed, George was asleep on the armchair and Jonathan and I sat side by side on the sofa watching the news. There was no mention of any cats on it as far as I could see, so I didn't think that this lamppost cat thing had reached epic proportions yet, but still I found it troubling. Despite the increase in posters, none of our cat friends had gone missing, so it didn't make sense. I still hadn't heard from Dustbin, and I wondered if Edgar Road was somehow protected from whatever was going on. But then just what *was* going on? Anyway, I was sure they would be discussing it at the meeting, so I would hear about it later.

Jonathan fell asleep on the sofa at some point, as he often did, snoring a bit and dribbling sometimes, but then when he woke up denied he had been asleep at all. Glancing at George, who was also fast asleep, I went to stretch my legs in the garden. As I slid through the cat flap I was surprised to see Tiger by my back step. Her fur glinted in the moonlight, and she looked very serious.

'What are you doing here?' I asked.

'Thank goodness you're here, I thought I'd have to risk coming in.'

'Tiger, I've told you before, I'm sure Claire and Jonathan wouldn't mind!' Jonathan would probably huff and puff a bit but actually he'd be all right. Besides, he was snoring away just now anyway.

'I've been waiting for ages and getting cold, but I had to come and see you.' Tiger's eyes shone with fear.

'What is it, Tiger?'

'The lamppost cats, it is serious after all.'

'Ah, I worried it was. That's why the Goodwins called their meeting.'

'Yes, it is. My owners were fussing, telling me to be careful, saying they might have to stop me from going out! Anyway that's not the worst bit. There was a new poster tonight and it's…'

'Come on, Tiger, spit it out.' Tiger often got a bit flustered when she was upset. I tried to be patient but it wasn't one of my strong points.

'Pinkie! It's Pinkie on the poster.'

'Are we sure she isn't just in a fridge somewhere?' I asked, but I had a bad feeling.

'She's missing, Alfie. Her poster is on a lamppost. So finally, after all our musing about whether this was a proper problem, someone we know has gone missing, an Edgar Road cat. It's time we stopped burying our heads in the sand. I think that something bad is going on and you know I'm not a dramatic cat. But I can't just sit by and watch our friends go missing.' I had never seen Tiger this agitated before.

'Calm down, Tiger. Right, let's think this through. Pinkie wouldn't just leave home – she liked her owner.'

'Exactly. She really was happy there.'

'OK, so you're right, something is going on. I need to think about this, and I need to go and see Dustbin again. I mentioned it to him before but with Franceska and the kids in Poland I haven't seen him since. I need to go there but what will I do with George? It's too far for him to walk.'

'How about I look after George and you go. I'd go with you but one of us needs to take care of the kitten.'

'OK. And don't worry, Tiger. Alfie is on the case.'

'Oh, Alfie, I just don't want anything bad to happen to any of us.'

'Hey,' I said, with all the confidence I could muster, 'I won't let it.'

I went back inside, legs shaking. I was more troubled by this latest development than I cared to admit. It had hit home now and no longer could we ignore the problem. Jonathan decided he was too tired to wait up, so I took George to bed, and although I tried to stay awake, sleep claimed me. I was asleep before Claire came back.

At breakfast, I was delighted that Claire discussed the meeting with Jonathan.

'I know they are quite mad but it does seem there are a spate of cats going missing. The Goodwins have done a spreadsheet and everything. And you know, Jon, it's more than is comfortable, even for London.'

'You're kidding?' Jonathan said through a mouthful of toast. 'What's a spreadsheet going to do?' Trust Jonathan to focus on that.

'Well they have charted where the cats went missing and it does seem to be a triangle of streets around us. They've also got all the owners together and everyone is searching. Jon, you have to admit that it's too many now for it to be cats running away or getting run over.' As Claire looked worried, I thought of poor Pinkie. 'And for once the Goodwins are actually being helpful, not just interfering.'

'Yeah, they have got a point. But what are they going to do?'

'They've asked us all to search around the area, look out for anything suspicious and most of all keep our cats safe.'

Jonathan looked at her. 'You don't think anyone would take Alfie or George do you?' Finally he sounded as if he was taking it seriously. 'Has anyone spoken to the police?'

'Yes, but I don't think missing cats are their top priority, and the point is that if we can get to the bottom of it soon then they won't get the chance to take our cats. We were all wondering if we should keep them inside.'

'But Claire, Alfie would hate that. Look, maybe we use that as a last resort.'

'Well, this better get sorted, Jon, or we'll have no alternative.'

'Right, I'll call Matt and after work we can go and do a bit of a search.'

It didn't sound like much of a plan but at least it was something. I really didn't want to be locked in the house – how would I help the lamppost cats or my families then?

\*\*\*

'George, stop that and come here,' Claire shouted. She had been cleaning up after Jonathan left for work and George had taken the opportunity to play. Having recently discovered the cupboard where the plastic supermarket bags were kept, he had decided they were his favourite things. He had climbed into one now and was sliding all over the kitchen floor. Summer was chasing him and giggling, but Claire was cross.

'It's dangerous,' she shouted. I knew it wasn't, there were holes in the bag and he could definitely breathe, I wasn't that neglectful a parent. Finally Claire caught him and removed him from the bag. 'When Jonathan gets home I am getting him to childproof that cupboard, George. No more bags for you.' George looked distraught. I made a mental note to tell him how much fun boxes could be later on. Claire looked flustered as she put George down on the floor and went to get Summer dressed. She was going out with Tash for the day with the kids, as they both had a day off work. Tash had had a date with the lovely Max last night so Claire wanted to hear all about it. I did too, but disappointingly I couldn't go with them, although it did mean I could go and see Dustbin, with Tiger kitten-sitting for me.

'I wish we could go out with them,' George said.

'Well, they won't let us. It would mean stowing away in Summer's pushchair or something,' I mused as I strolled towards the living room, where I could watch the world go by through the window.

'Bye, Alfie, bye George,' Claire shouted later. I lay down on the sofa and thought about having a nap, before I suddenly sat up with a start. Something was wrong. I wasn't sure what, or if I was imagining it, but something didn't feel right. I went to find George. I searched the house, but couldn't see him. I sighed, it was tiring but he kept playing hide and seek without telling me, which was beyond annoying. So I looked for him in all the places that he normally hid, but there was no sign of the mischievous little kitten. Once I was certain he wasn't in the house, I went out. He might have snuck out while I was in the living room. Honestly, what kind of parent was I? I searched the garden, but he wasn't there so, trying not to panic, I went to find Tiger. Thankfully she was in her front garden.

'What do you mean "gone"?' Tiger asked.

'Claire went out and I can't find him anywhere.' Oh, this was so worrying. I felt a bolt of real fear as I thought of the lamppost cats. My George!

'Are you sure you looked everywhere?' asked Tiger. She looked panicked too.

'Yes, of course, I checked and double-checked. You haven't seen him?' I was frantic.

'No, Alfie, if he went out he didn't come this way. Let's check the park, he loves the park.' Tiger was staying calm, something I was finding difficult. I felt an emotion I had never felt before: total fear. I was always a bit panicked when he was hiding, but in the house I was a little more confident. However, outside… anything could happen to him.

'I told him never to go out without me!' I knew I shouldn't have taken my eyes off him, but then I didn't expect him to be so irresponsible. Hadn't I warned him about going out on his own? Of course I had – time and time again.

Tiger and I were silent as we made our way to the park as quickly as possible. I had never felt fear like this before. He was still so young, and didn't even really know how to cross roads on his own. There were dangers everywhere and I had taught him so much, but still, it wasn't enough.

He wasn't there.

I collapsed back at my house. I wanted to cry, my back legs ached from all the running and I still hadn't found my boy. I couldn't help but yowl.

'Look, you wait here, Alfie, and I'll go and see if the others have seen him.' Tiger was distraught but was trying her best to hide it.

'Tiger, I don't know what I'd do without you.'

'I'll be quick,' she said, and bounded off. I lay in the front garden and said a prayer to the god of cats to bring my boy home safely. We had checked the park, every tree, bush and flowerbed, anywhere he could possibly hide, but there was no sign. Where on earth could he be? I promised if he was brought back safely to me I would never take my eyes off him again, not for a minute. How could I have been so irresponsible?

It felt like ages before Tiger came back. She looked downcast.

'No sign. Oh goodness, now I'm beginning to really worry. Although if he had come outside, someone would have seen him. It doesn't make sense,' she said, and I had to agree with her. 'Not even Salmon, and he's been watching for ages. He said he saw Claire leave with the pushchair but nothing else. The other cats are all looking for him right now.'

'What could have happened? It's as if he's just disappeared into thin air. What if the lamppost cats are something really bad and someone's taken him?' I was feeling so hysterical that I didn't think I could breathe anymore. 'I can't bear the idea that someone could have taken my boy.'

'Oh, Alfie, I don't know what to say—' She stopped suddenly. 'Look.' I turned and saw Claire and Tash approaching. Claire was pushing Summer in her pushchair, and Elijah was walking next to them, holding his mum's hand. I was flooded with relief as I saw, sitting bold as brass on Summer's lap, George. I tried to slow my breathing down to a normal level as they approached us but my heart was still beating out of my chest.

'Oh, Alfie, were you looking for George?' Claire said as they reached us. 'The naughty little kitten stowed away in the pushchair, in my bag.' She lifted George out. 'We were on our way to soft play but of course we couldn't take him in. Now, George, stay here. We have to go back before the kids get mutinous.' She shook her head, gave me a pat and left.

When they'd gone, Tiger and I exchanged a glance.

'Don't ever do that to me again,' I said crossly. I had never felt so cross and yet so relieved in my life.

'Why?'

'We were worried sick,' Tiger added. 'George, you can't just go with humans, and if you do then you need to tell Alfie.'

'Why?'

'Because we were worried and we love you, but at the moment I am very cross with you. What were you thinking?' I didn't want to scare him by telling him about the lamppost cats – he was too little for that – but he needed to be aware of the dangers. Parenting wasn't as easy as it looked.

'You said you'd like to go to hear about Tash and that man. And by the way, she had a lovely time, he took her to something called French restaurant, they drank something called champagne and they had a great evening, and they are going to see each other again but they've both agreed to take it slowly. Tash doesn't know if she's ready but actually she admitted she really did enjoy herself,' said George.

As much as I liked hearing this, I was still angry and scared. Although I was delighted for Tash, and it was brilliant that George had listened so well, I wasn't going to tell him that.

'I know I said I wanted to go but I also said that we couldn't go. We just can't go anywhere we fancy it, no matter how much we want to.' I once stowed away in a bag and went all the way to the seaside with my families but I wasn't going to tell George about that. 'It's dangerous, it's reckless and your mum and I were worried sick. Now you will go inside and stay there, and think about your behaviour,' I said crossly.

'But I'm sorry,' George said, trying to look cute.

'No, George, you need to be punished. Come on, inside now and never, ever go anywhere without telling me again.'

I hustled him round the back, with Tiger following us. As I told George to get through the cat flap, Tiger hung back.

'I'm so relieved,' Tiger said. 'The feelings I had when he was missing were awful.'

'I know, it was horrific, I really can't begin to tell you.'

'I think I understand. I love him too, you know.'

'I know we're his parents, and just like with my families, I've seen how parents worry and I totally understand it now. I worry enough about all my humans, but even that isn't the same as the way I feel about George,' I tried to explain.

'Because he's your kitten,' Tiger said. 'Anyway, I'd better go and let the others know he's safe, they're probably still looking for him.'

'Great. And Tiger…'

'Yes?'

'He's not my kitten, he's *our* kitten.'

Tiger nuzzled me and left. I went inside to deal with our kitten feeling an odd cocktail of emotions.

George behaved impeccably for the rest of the day. He didn't go near anything he shouldn't and he asked me before he did anything. I wished he could always be this good, although of course I'd probably miss his mischievous side just a tiny bit. When Summer came home, she grabbed George and took him upstairs to play dress up. After having to wear bonnets, scarfs and dolly dresses, I think he'd been punished enough. However, the idea that he could really go missing haunted me. I needed to get to the bottom of the cat mystery sooner rather than later.

# Chapter Twenty-four

I knew I couldn't wait any longer. That morning, after delivering George into Tiger's care, I set off to see Dustbin. She was such a good mum, and I felt lucky to have her. Glancing back, I saw the two of them looking after me and I felt a pang in my heart. I needed to do this for all my friends, but especially Tiger and George. I went as fast as my legs would carry me, knowing the way and knowing what dangers to look out for – usually just cars and maybe the odd dog. I took the back route into Dustbin's yard without too much trouble, feeling pleased with myself for making such quick time.

'Hi, Alfie,' Dustbin said. 'This is a pleasant surprise.'

'Well, Dustbin, you might not feel that way when I tell you why I'm here.' I filled him in on the latest developments. 'So it seems the lamppost cats might actually be more of a problem than we first thought. God forbid any more cats are in danger.'

'Right, Alfie, sounds like we need to sort this out before it gets out of hand. I'll go this afternoon and talk to my colleagues again and we'll ramp up the urgency. I'm sure that between us we can get some information. In the meantime, you stay vigilant and let me know of any developments as soon as you can.'

'I think I'll set up a network here, so that when I can't get to you I can send Tiger or something. I really do need to keep a close eye on George, I shudder to think anything might happen to him.'

'Right, well, it might take a bit of time, but I'm on the case and I'll come and find you if I have any news.'

'But do you know where I live?'

'Yes, I was interested once so I followed Tomasz.' I raised my whiskers.

'OK, so maybe I was being a bit nosey. I fancied seeing where you lived. I miss the boys by the way.'

'Me too. I wish they'd come home. And I wish all the missing cats would get to go back to their homes too. Oh, Dustbin, I wish the lampposts were just lampposts again.' My eyes were full of worry, but Dustbin, more than anyone, reassured me.

Life has a funny way of turning round in circles; time passes, things change. One minute everyone's sad, then they're happy, and then, well, where do I start?

Tash was over at ours when I got back from seeing Dustbin, gushing about Max, who she'd been on another date with. I couldn't believe how happy she seemed. She'd come to realise that perhaps she had fallen out of love with Dave before he left her, without realising it, and although she was cautious, she was beginning to see that she deserved happiness. And as Claire said to her, you didn't know when it would come along so you had to snatch it when you could. Also, because Max was a father himself, he understood her need to put Elijah first. I felt very hopeful although I did worry she would get hurt again. But I was a cat who worried about things, that was just what I did.

'Anyway,' Tash said, 'he's great, puts no pressure on me at all. But you know, whatever happens, he's made me see that I tried so hard to make the relationship with Dave work, whilst he did nothing. If I'm honest, I think having Elijah was my last-ditch attempt to save us. I don't think I realised it at the time, but it does make sense.'

'I had no idea,' Claire said.

'He was just so lazy. Anyway, I put up with him for so long and I really believed I loved him. Well, I did love him, but actually, he's not worth it,' said Tash as she watched Elijah eat his sandwich at the kitchen table. Summer was sitting opposite him, pulling her sandwich apart and dropping bits on the floor, where George was waiting, hoping it might be something he liked. Luckily for him, it was grated cheese. George loved cheese.

'Summer, eat that – don't drop it,' Claire said, sounding exasperated. 'Well, sometimes you lose something and you realise how much you miss it, and other times you lose something and realise that actually it wasn't right in the first place.'

'Was that what it was like with your first husband?' Tash asked. I had never met Claire's first husband. She moved here after they divorced and she was sad then.

'He was a control freak and then, remember, I moved on to Joe who was the same only worse. I think with Dave, you were together so long you were used to him, you know, he was part of your life, you might not have seen that you weren't actually happy.'

'I think you're right. But did you see it?'

'Honestly? No. I mean I never really got to know him that well, and Jonathan was never overly keen, but then Jon's ambitious and he doesn't understand men who don't have ambition.'

'Dave didn't, did he? I thought he was laid back but I didn't realise how lazy he was. I worked twice as hard as him, I found the house, I did pretty much everything. Anyway, enough about me, what's going on with you? Elijah, do you want some fruit?' I marvelled at the way parents managed to have conversations but always seemed to remember what they needed to do for their children. I needed to learn that skill with George. Elijah nodded, and Claire handed Tash a banana.

'Look,' Claire said. She took an envelope out from behind the toaster and handed it to Tash.

'What's this?' Tash took the letter out and read it.

'But, Claire, that's fantastic, you've been approved!' Tash jumped up and hugged Claire.

'Yes, we've been given the green light for adopting and the social worker said that if we're willing to take an older child it won't take as long. But, well, I haven't told Jonathan yet.'

'When did you get this letter?' Tash asked.

'Last week. I know it's silly, but I want this more than anything, I don't know how I'd feel if Jonathan said no.'

'And you're sure about taking care of an older child?' Tash looked concerned, as did I.

'Yes. Tash, I'm doing this for the right reasons and I've thought long and hard about that. I want Summer to have a sibling, and I want to add to our family. A baby isn't realistic. We're a bit older now and the waiting list is so long, Summer would probably be at university before we even got a baby.' Claire looked thoughtful. I thought she was being optimistic: Summer at university? She was so bossy she'd probably be kicked out of school long before then. 'Anyway, we have a lovely home and a lot of love here, so any child would be welcome. And I hate to think of any kid not having a loving family, I really believe that this child needs us and we need them.'

'That's lovely, Claire.'

'But the thing is that Jon is scared and I can't seem to get through to him, so I just don't know what to do.'

I jumped onto the kitchen table. I wanted to tell Claire that if she was a bit more supportive as to how Jonathan felt, and told she him understood, yet explained why they would be such great parents to any child, then he would come round. But how could I convey that? It seemed that she was on her road and he was on his and they didn't seem to be going to the same place. I nudged Tash.

'Claire, tell him you understand,' she said, as if reading my mind. 'Do it gently.'

'I railroad people, don't I?' Claire asked.

'You do make up your mind and then go for it, which is great, and a real asset in so many ways and why we all love you, but in this case, maybe try a more gentle approach?'

'I'll try but I can't promise. In my head I'm already decorating the spare room for him.'

'It's a boy?'

'It would be a boy, yes, I just feel it.' Claire laughed. 'I see what you mean.'

I tried not to despair. She knew what to do but, being Claire, she wasn't sure she could do it. I wanted another child here. I could see the value for all of us, and with the way I felt about George, I knew that adoption was a great, positive thing, but Claire needed to convince Jonathan, not tell him, and that was where I worried. If they couldn't agree on this, then what would happen to them?

Tash took Elijah home for a nap, and as Claire took Summer upstairs for hers, George and I went out. None of the cats seemed to be around so after playing with some leaves and chasing a fly we decided to go and see if Matt was in. I missed Polly on days like this, she and I hung out together quite a lot before she got her job, but I loved Matt too – it was just that these days he wasn't quite as much fun.

George and I headed through the cat flap and into Polly and Matt's house. Imagine my surprise when we went to the living room and saw big Tomasz sitting in the armchair with Matt on the sofa. It had been ages since I'd seen Tomasz – since the rest of the family had gone on holiday – so I jumped up onto his lap and snuggled in. George sat at Matt's feet.

'Ah, our friends the cats,' Tomasz said, making a fuss of me. I purred happily, it was so lovely to see him. 'I know, I miss you too, Alfie,' he said. 'And of course my wife and children.'

'Jeez, Tom, it feels like they've been gone for ages, although I know it hasn't been that long,' Matt said, which I agreed with. 'When are they back?'

'Another two weeks, before school starts. I asked her to come home sooner but Franceska says they're having a lovely time and anyway I'd only be working.'

'Tom, you know, me being at home this way, not the way I'd choose, by the way, has taught me something. I see more of my children than ever and they do something different, something new, every day. I love that. I spent so long worrying about losing my job and the fact I was no longer the "man" of the house, but actually, when I think about it, I really enjoy spending more time with the kids. I've made myself a promise that if, or when, I get another job, I'll always make sure I spend enough time with them.' George hopped onto Matt's lap and licked his face. Which was very clever of him because I would have done the same had I not been busy being stroked by Tomasz.

'I know you're right, but the business… We have two restaurants now. And I do this for my family, you know.'

'Yes, and you're brilliant – look how successful you've become. But mate, you have managers, you need to delegate, take more time off. There's no point in doing this for your family if you don't see them.' I couldn't have put it better myself. Matt had come a long way since learning how to load the dishwasher.

'I know, you're right. And since they've been gone I've missed them like crazy, I just need them to come home so I can let them know.'

No, I felt a tingling in my fur. Tomasz was wrong, he didn't need them to come home, he needed to go and get them. He needed to go to Poland. But how did I tell him that? I looked at Matt, willing him to have the same idea.

'Changing the subject, I've got a meeting. Long story but the brother of one of Jon's colleagues has a design agency. He's got some work, it's freelance, not a permanent role, but it's a good company and if I get it I might be able to be more flexible, so Polly can keep working if she wants to, and I can still do more with the children.'

'Have you spoken to Polly about it?'

Matt shook his head. 'We're not communicating very well right now either.'

'When did our lives get so complicated?' Tomasz asked. I didn't know the answer to that. It was complicated, and I couldn't help but feel a little exasperated that neither man seemed to know what to do about the situation.

# Chapter
# Twenty-five

'So what you're saying is you need yet another plan?' Tiger said, sighing. We were all crouched under a bush in the park: me, Tiger and George. George was making a pile of leaves to nestle into and his nose was covered in mud. He looked very sweet.

'Basically, yes. I tried to leave them to sort it out but to no avail. The thing is, it has to be a big plan,' I pointed out. 'The biggest plan of my life.'

'What are you hoping to achieve?' she asked.

'Well, I want Tomasz to go to Poland to get his family back. I want Claire and Jonathan to work together on this adoption, not both on different paths. I want Matt and Polly to talk again, to be as close as they normally are and to agree on how they can both work with jobs and the children. Oh, and I want Tash to feel more confident about having a new relationship because my cat instinct tells me Max could be wonderful both for her and Elijah. Although out of everyone, Tash actually seems the happiest right now. And of course I want to get all the lamppost cats back with their owners, including Pinkie.'

'Is that all?' I could detect sarcasm in Tiger's voice. She could be one sarcastic cat.

'I know it's a lot but hey, there's a lot to do at the moment.'

'But how are you going to do it? Where do we even start? I mean, nearly getting yourself killed or being stuck up a tree won't achieve all that,' she said, referring to my previous plans.

'I know, and I'm also aware I only have so many lives left,

253

so let's not risk them.'

'But Dad,' George piped up. 'How can you make Tomasz go to Poland?'

'I don't know. What I need to do is find a common thread.' I started thinking. Thinking made me hungry. It wasn't lunch-time but I could hear the gentle rumble of my stomach, and then I saw a butterfly, which I decided to jump for. I missed, of course, and landed in a flowerbed. I rolled off and Tiger laughed.

'Right, well Dustbin is on board with the cat problems but for all the others I want us to have a good think. We'll meet tomorrow to see if we're any closer to a grand plan.' George looked confused, Tiger amused. As I brushed a petal off my head, I tried to muster all the dignity I had left.

As George and I walked home, we saw Tash approaching.

'Hello, boys,' she said. George rubbed up against her legs. She scooped him up, holding him so tightly he began to wriggle.

'Sorry, my little angel, hope I didn't squeeze too tight.' George purred in response; he was such a flirt. Then I saw her eyes were red. Although we were still in the street, I rubbed against her legs. 'Oh, Alfie, I'm so confused,' she said. She slumped down on someone's front wall, still holding George. I jumped up next to her.

'Miaow?'

'It's Max. I really like him, but I'm so afraid, and I've been arguing with Dave about Elijah and money.'

'Yowl,' I said, to show my disapproval of Dave.

'I know, I know, he's such an idiot. But Max… Well, he's lovely, but I told him I needed to take some time out from us. I just don't know if I can do it, a relationship, it's too confusing.'

I was cross. Not because of Tash – I understood how she was feeling. After all, I still couldn't even contemplate replacing Snowball, but then she wasn't an idiot like Dave. I needed Tash to remember that thing about snatching happiness whenever you could. As I tried to comfort her, along with George, who was being so affectionate, I remembered that when I got Claire and Jonathan together, after Claire had had a disastrous relationship with a man – I couldn't bring myself to say his name – Claire had said it was too soon for her to think about dating Jonathan, and Tash had pointed out that if she lost a good man like Jonathan because of a bad man like *him*, then she'd regret it. Where were her wise words when it came to herself?

'Miaow!' Give yourself the chance to be happy, I tried to say, but she didn't seem to be listening.

That night, yet again, I couldn't sleep. I was wide awake, wracking my brain for a plan. George was fast asleep, thankfully, but I could hear voices coming from Claire and Jonathan's room. I moved closer to the door to listen.

'Just shut up, Jon, you're being really mean,' I heard Claire shout. Her voice wobbled and she sounded close to tears.

'No, I'm not. But, Claire, this is the truth, you wanted the truth, I don't think I can love a child who isn't mine, especially an older one. They will already have a personality, probably come from a terrible background and will need extra-special care. It's not about whether I want to do it or not, it's that I simply don't feel I can. How many times can I tell you that I don't think I can do this!' He sounded particularly angry.

'I think you can. I think we can. This isn't about just you, Jonathan, this is about us as a family.'

'A family which at the moment seems close to falling apart,' Jonathan hissed.

'So now you're threatening me?'

'No, Claire, I'm trying to tell you how I feel but you can't seem accept it, or even have a rational discussion about it.'

'No, I can't, because the man I love wouldn't threaten me.' Jonathan made a frustrated noise and then went quiet. I watched from the shadows as the door opened and Claire went into the spare room, where once again she cried herself to sleep.

# Chapter
# Twenty-six

'We are now in a state of emergency,' I announced the next day, having gathered all my cat friends at our usual spot. I needed the whole gang. I felt a little bit like I was commanding an army as I strode backwards and forwards, although they weren't exactly standing to attention. Elvis was lying on his back, enjoying the sun; Tiger sat with George lying between her paws, looking very sweet; Rocky and Nellie were sitting together; and Tinkerbell was cleaning the back of his legs in a move that would make most yoga enthusiasts jealous. Only Pinkie was absent, which was a stark reminder of one of the reasons we were here.

'Oh, that sounds very incredibly serious,' Nellie said excitedly. She loved drama.

'Not only do we need to find those missing cats, but I also need help with all my humans.'

'Right, Alfie, so what do you want us to do?' Elvis asked.

'Firstly, the cats. We are all feeling under stress now that Pinkie is gone. I mean, we don't know who or what this threat is and when it might come for any one of us.' I glanced at George, who thankfully was being nuzzled by Tiger and didn't seem to be listening.

'I heard that in some places they eat cats,' Nellie said. We all shuddered.

'Don't be ridiculous,' Rocky said, but he looked terrified. 'No one would eat a cat.'

'What could be happening to all these cats though?' Elvis said.

'I have no idea, but listen, my pal Dustbin is on the case for us so I think our best course of action is to wait until we hear back from him. If anyone can find out anything it's him. But then I also have the other issues and I need you to help me come up with a big idea. A grand plan.' I explained the problems with all my families to them, leaving no stone unturned.

'When my family wanted to go overseas they went to a travel agent,' Rocky said, not very helpfully.

'I don't think that's the issue,' I pointed out. 'I know I can't literally make Tomasz go to Poland to get his family but I need to make him realise that that's what he needs to do.'

'Oh, I think I understand,' Tinkerbell said. 'You need to do something to make all your families understand how much they love and need each other.'

Thank goodness. 'Yes! Exactly!' Tinkerbell was suddenly my new favourite cat. I was glad that he had become a regular part of our gang. I shot a look at Tiger but she was gazing lovingly at George. Oh blimey, everyone was so obsessed with that kitten, me included. 'Tiger, can you drag yourself away from George for long enough to pay attention?' I snapped.

'That's it!' Rocky said.

'What?' I asked. Tiger looked up.

'The boy. Everyone is besotted with the boy, so use him in your plan.' Rocky looked pleased with himself.

'Everyone loves me,' George said.

'Um, George, it's important you don't become too big-headed,' I said.

'Well, we all know who he takes after,' said Tiger. The others laughed; I did not.

'But anyway, he's got something there,' said Elvis. 'For

example, you could put the kitten in danger and then the humans will all come together to save him, or something.'

'You can't put him in danger!' Nellie snapped. George looked scared and hid behind Tiger.

'No, of course you can't. I didn't mean literally, but if they think he is,' said Elvis. 'Look, we need to try to find the lamppost cats, but what I was thinking was that if your families thought George was one of them, then they would put their problems aside and all get on with it.'

'Make them think that George has been taken like one of the lamppost cats?' I felt my brain whirring. 'You might be right, Elvis. Remember when I was very ill at the vet, it brought all my families together – Claire and Jonathan even fell in love and the others all became friends because of me.'

'Yes, but you absolutely can't put him in danger,' Tiger said. 'Not like you do with yourself.'

I felt an idea hatching, and my whiskers and fur tingled with excitement. 'What if we just pretend he's missing?' I asked.

'How do we do that?' Tiger asked.

'Well, Tiger, I'm not completely sure yet but let's say we find somewhere to hide him, and you go with him. He'll be safe because you're taking care of him, but everyone else will think he's lost.'

'How long? You couldn't do it for too long, it wouldn't be fair,' Tiger pointed out.

'Yes, that's true,' I agreed. 'Not too long, I mean, he was only missing for a short time the other day and I was terrified, but he has to be lost for just enough time to trouble them all and get them talking.'

'Ohhh,' said Nellie. 'Then we can all look for him.' We all turned our eyes on Nellie.

'He's not actually going to be lost, so we won't have to look for him,' Tiger said scathingly.

'Oh, I see,' Nellie said, but she didn't look as if she did.

'Isn't it mean? To make people worry?' Tinkerbell asked, looking uncertain.

'Not in the long run. We need something drastic to make them realise that they love each other. If we hide George, they'll all look for him and talk properly, and then when we find George alive and well they'll be so relieved and happy that they'll sort out their problems. It's foolproof.' Well, I hoped it was.

'Are you sure about this?' Tiger sounded dubious.

'No, but have you got any better ideas?'

'Other than me kidnapping George, making everyone sick with worry before he's found, and then bringing them all back together again? No, not really.'

'You aren't really kidnapping him,' I pointed out.

'You know what I mean. Look, Alfie, think about this for a while. They'll be really worried, and Tinkerbell's right, it does seem mean. If they're already upset they don't need any more stress.'

'I know, but these humans need a wake-up call, they're all forgetting about what's important. Yes, it's awful that they'll worry, but it won't be for too long. We've been here before: if they have something else to focus on they begin to see how much they really love each other. It's the way humans work. I don't think we have a choice, Tiger, we have to do this. And in the meantime, Dustbin is going to get to the bottom of the real lamppost cats, I just know he is.' I felt excited; I knew this was going to work out. I just knew it.

'On your paws be it,' Tiger snorted. 'But yes, before you ask, of course I'll help you, it goes without saying. And I'd be happy to keep George safe for a while, although we need to work out the logistics. Where will we go? What will he eat? How do I keep him warm?'

'We'll all help you, Alfie,' Nellie said. 'It brings us together too, doesn't it, these plans of yours?' I was relieved, Nellie had finally got it.

'See, Tiger,' I said. 'I know what I'm doing.' I couldn't help but feel a little bit smug. It made sense. Everyone chasing after a lost George would make them all see how much they needed each other, and then they'd talk, really talk, to each other. Matt and Polly, Claire and Jonathan, and then Tomasz would realise he had to go to Poland to get his family, and Tash would see how important love was and would give Max a chance. I know it seemed I was always chasing a happy ending for everyone I loved, and I was, but there was nothing wrong with that. It's just what any loving cat would do.

# Chapter Twenty-seven

I was busy working out the finer points of my plan; I was still not one hundred per cent sure of all the details. Though my idea for getting my humans together was not dangerous, it was logistically complicated, and that was keeping me occupied. I also had a visit from Dustbin, who, true to his word, had his cat network – some feral like him, others domestic – all working on the mystery of the lamppost cats.

He caught my attention while I was looking out of the front window. I ran round the back and we met in the garden.

'Any news?' I asked.

'It is a problem. Some cats' owners are so worried they won't let them go out. It's causing havoc among local cats. I think your street is the last street to be hit by whatever's going on.'

'So no one knows?'

'Not yet, but a very good friend of mine – Mr B, the cleverest cat I know – is on the case and he's going to come and see me tonight. Just try to relax, keep an eye on your kitten and hopefully I'll have news. I'll try to come at the same time tomorrow, look out for me. I'd better go, it's time for my lunch and I have to see off those pesky rodents too.'

I said goodbye and went back to the house to worry. While the plan for my families wasn't dangerous, we didn't know what we were dealing with with the lamppost cats. There was so much piled up on my plate at the moment and it seemed to be mounting up.

And George was getting into more and more trouble, which

was threatening to distract me from the task at hand. He was becoming quite a paw-full. The other day, he had played with Jonathan's favourite work tie and it looked a bit worse for wear when he'd finished with it. Jonathan was really angry, and of course somehow he blamed Claire and me. Claire told him he should focus on what was important, which just made him madder. They weren't really talking to each other by the end of the day and George was still unsure what he'd done wrong. I tried to explain but actually I was trying to focus my energy on the bigger picture. I remember one of my families saying that with children you had to pick your battles. Stealing Jonathan's tie didn't really warrant too much of my attention – after all, he had loads more. Claire was right: Jonathan needed to worry about what was important and it wasn't a silly tie. Although George hid from Jonathan for a while afterwards, I did tell him, yet again, that Jonathan was prone to flying off the handle but he usually calmed down quite quickly. I was used to him getting cross with me but quickly thawing anyway.

And then one morning George had noticed that Claire was eating smoked salmon for breakfast, so while her back was turned he jumped onto the table and actually ate from her plate. Jonathan found this funny but Claire, who was a bit keen on everything being clean and not having cats on the table while they were eating, didn't. This time she was cross; she put George on the floor and gave him a long lecture on hygiene, which I know he didn't listen to, because I got bored halfway through and he had an even shorter attention span than me. After that I had taken him to Matt and Polly's so we could lie low for a bit.

Matt had been getting ready to go to a meeting with his

potential new employer. They would be discussing something called 'terms' and he was stressed because he still hadn't really discussed it with Polly yet. He kept putting it off because he wasn't sure how they would cope with both of them working or something. As he blustered on, in quite an unlike Matt kind of way, George, who was growing and as a result was going through a clumsy phase, got under Matt's feet, causing him to trip up and bash his elbow. As a result he became even more flustered. I had decided to take George to the park in the end, hopeful that no trouble would follow us. Thankfully it didn't.

Later that day I had found George scaling the curtains in the spare room, gleeful about discovering that he could climb them. However, he got almost to the top and then realised he didn't know how to let go. He had started to panic and I had to coax him down. It took a lot of time and effort, his claws were stuck firmly into the material, and when he was finally persuaded to let go – one paw at a time – I noticed he had made quite a few little rips. I hoped no one would notice and I told George that we should give the spare room a wide berth for a bit, just in case.

And this morning, George had knocked a cereal box off the kitchen counter, pouring the contents all over the floor. He had then climbed into the empty box and started running around the kitchen. Summer was laughing and Claire was shouting while Jonathan shrieked, 'We should be filming this for YouTube, we'd at least make enough money to buy more cereal out of the blooming kitten.' Of course it was left to me to get him out of the cereal box. Although he'd been covered in cornflake dust, he was so adorable when he was happy, it was almost impossible for me to be cross with him.

Thankfully, or not, everyone else was too cross with each other to really tell us off. I mean, I know I hadn't done anything wrong, but I was responsible for George, so I could have been given a bit of a ticking off too – like I had with the tie incident.

With Dustbin working on the lamppost cats, I was focusing on my plan for my families. I decided to go and round up our cat friends to finalise the details for my grand plan. Poor George didn't really understand, it was a lot for a kitten to take in, even though he was getting bigger, but I remained patient as I explained that he was going to be the most important cat in solving everyone's problems, which he quite liked the sound of. And every way I had looked at it there was absolutely no danger involved at all. If Tiger wouldn't let anything happen to me, she absolutely would never let anything happen to our George.

I was just about to start the meeting when a large shadow loomed.

'What are you up to?' Salmon asked, approaching us. Oh no, this was the last thing I needed. He couldn't get wind of any plan; if he did, he might sabotage us.

'Well,' George said, before anyone could stop him, 'I am going to save the whole wide world.' Bless him, he had interpreted the plan in a slightly different way.

'What are you talking about?' Salmon asked, in a kindly way, but I knew he was looking for gossip in that salacious way of his. Tiger gently put her paw over George's mouth and motioned for him to be quiet.

'It's just a game we're playing, Salmon,' I said, trying to sound friendly. 'Nothing for you to be concerned about.'

'You guys are always here, plotting things,' he spat back. So much for friendliness.

'Well, that's not true, most of the time we're napping, sun-bathing and playing with leaves,' said Rocky.

'And just hanging out. With friends. You should try it sometime,' Elvis said. 'If you have any friends, that is.'

'As if I have time for such frivolities. Honestly, if I was like you then this street would go to wrack and ruin. Well, carry on with your silly game, I have more important matters to attend to.' He turned and stalked off.

'What was he talking about and why did you put your paw over my mouth?' George asked.

'I'll teach you about him later,' I said. 'But right now we have to finalise our plan. Right, Rocky, you go first.'

As each of my friends gave their ideas, I listened to them all. It seemed they had all thought carefully about it and had done a pretty good job. I beamed with happiness; it was all going to be so straightforward, the easiest of my plans but also the most important.

D–Day was set for tomorrow, Saturday. It had to happen then, because everyone would be home from work. So today was the only day we had to get it right. But I was confi-dent; we were all working together and we had left no stone unturned. I was one hundred per cent sure that nothing could go wrong.

'My idea,' Nellie said. I almost didn't want to hear, she could be a bit silly sometimes. 'My idea is that you use the shed at the bottom of Tiger's garden.'

We all looked at her. Our sticking point had been where we could hide George. After all, Tiger couldn't take him to her house, her humans doted on her but they weren't keen on other cats. I had been chased out of there a few times and I'm not only charming, but Tiger's best friend too. But Nellie had come up with a genius idea. Tiger's shed was quite tatty, and had a gap in the door they could easily slip through. And her humans didn't use it, ever.

'That isn't a bad idea,' Tiger admitted grudgingly. 'So what do we need? Food, something to keep us warm and comfortable, water, something to play with?'

'You're only going to be there for a few hours, not the whole summer,' Rocky pointed out.

'But we can get enough food for George, a blanket and yes, he will need a source of water,' I said.

'I can sneak him into my house for food and water,' Tiger said. 'Because how on earth are we supposed to get food and bowls and stuff into the shed?'

'Good point. So you sneak him in when it's safe. They always give you too much food anyway, so you'll have plenty for George.' It was true, Tiger was totally overfed – she had to exercise a lot to keep the weight off.

'I'll drag a blanket down there for you,' Elvis offered. 'We have loads at home and I am the strongest cat here.'

'That's debatable,' said Tinkerbell. I wasn't sure which of them was right but I knew I wouldn't like to fight with either of them.

'Why don't you both get the blanket, it'll be easier with two of you,' Tiger sensibly suggested. They looked at each other and nodded. I liked how everyone was working together.

'What about toys? I don't want George to get bored,' Tiger said.

'We can bring some from home,' I said, although I wasn't sure how we would carry them. 'Right, we need to get this settled because we're going to do this tomorrow.' My voice shook with nerves.

'Alfie, it's fine, we have planned this brilliantly, what on earth could go wrong?' Nellie asked.

I didn't answer. In my experience those sounded like famous last words.

Later I quietly ran through the plan with my little boy again. He still didn't understand fully but he was super excited about being a hero, which of course is what I had convinced him he would be if everything went the way I hoped. But I had to say, I was more nervous about this plan than I had been about my others. Not because of any danger – this was the least dangerous plan I had ever come up with – but because so much was at stake.

Walking back from our planning meeting, we'd popped in to Matt and Polly's. Polly had taken an afternoon off because Martha had to go to the doctor, and Polly wanted to be with her. I thought that was a good sign, but I quickly realised things weren't good. George had run off to play with Henry and Martha in the living room, while I listened to Polly and Matt arguing in the kitchen.

'Well, yes, I agree we should be celebrating you having got a new job, but you seem to have forgotten that I'm working now and we have two children.'

'I haven't forgotten, but I don't know what you want. Do you want to keep working?'

'Yes, I do. I was dubious at first but I did the interior design course so that I could go back to work at some point and now I love my job. I've cut my hours lately, now I know what I'm doing a bit better, and I feel I've got the balance right. And now that it's all sorted, you want me to give it up!' Polly wasn't shouting but I could tell she was angry.

'I didn't say that, but what are we going to do about the kids? I mean, yes, Henry's at school, but the days aren't long enough and Martha is only at pre-school three days a week.' Matt sounded frazzled.

'It's not like either of our jobs are permanent. I know I'm on a rolling contract but yours is six months and then we might be back to square one,' Polly ranted.

'Thanks for the optimism.'

'Oh God, I can't talk to you when you're like this, I'm going to see my children,' said Polly, storming out of the room.

I went to get George and told him it was time to go home. Before we left, I made a fuss of Henry and Martha. I worried for those two lovely children.

Claire was sitting at the kitchen table, crying, when we got home. I looked at George, who seemed very sad. This day was not going well. I was wondering where Summer was just as Jonathan walked into the kitchen.

'Claire, please don't cry,' Jonathan said, sitting down next to her.

'I asked Tash to give Sum tea so we could talk, yet we're not talking.'

'I don't know what to say, Claire.'

'I want this child,' she said.

'There is no child, not yet.'

'You know what I mean.' Claire had tears streaming down her face and I felt so sad for her.

'I do, but I don't know what you want from me.'

'Yes, Jonathan, you know exactly what I want from you.' So much was unsaid between them, but they both knew what they meant.

'Look, I'm going to the gym and then I said I'd pop in to see Tomasz at the restaurant.'

'Right, that's more important than this?' Claire snapped.

'No, but I made plans and I'm sticking to them. Tomasz is really struggling without his family. Besides, we're not getting anywhere right now.'

'Oh, just go then,' Claire screamed at him. I had never heard her so angry.

By the time Tash brought Summer home, Claire had stopped crying, and she also had a glass of wine in her hand.

'Can I tempt you?' she asked Tash. Her eyes were red and Tash hurriedly took Summer and Elijah into the living room with some of Summer's toys.

'OK, just a quick one. My boy's tired tonight.'

'Nursery wears them out. Oh, Tash, sorry. I've had another row with Jonathan.'

'I thought so. Come on, sit down.' They both sat down and as George again went to play with the children, I stayed with the adults.

'I'm not going to bore you with the details, it's nothing new anyway. Distract me, tell me about your budding romance.'

'Ah, well you might regret asking that. I've asked Max for some space. He wasn't being anything but charming and wonderful, but I freaked out when we were last out.'

'Why, Tash?'

'I'm falling for him, Claire, and I got scared. I'm not sure I can cope with being hurt again.'

'Oh, Tash, look at us both. Two great men and we're pushing them away.' Claire's eyes filled with tears again.

'I know, that's exactly what we seem to be doing,' Tasha said sadly.

It seemed that tomorrow couldn't come quickly enough, and we only had one chance to get it right. There was so very much resting on our plan. I hoped and prayed with all my heart that we got it right.

# Chapter Twenty-eight

I was yet again facing a sleepless night. I was so worried about tomorrow. George slept soundly at least, which was good. Despite the lack of danger involved in this plan, I was still worried that George would be spending his first night away from me, and although he'd be with Tiger – she had promised to sleep in the shed overnight with him – I wouldn't feel comfortable without him. I knew that I would feel as if something was missing, being apart from him. But at least I would be busy. I would have to rally all my families to look for George and make sure they bonded over it. I did have quite a big part to play in the plan – the biggest, in fact. All George and Tiger had to do was lay low, I actually had to mobilise the humans and somehow ensure that they actually came together over this, rather than falling apart. I had to admit that I was a ball of nerves: from the tips of my claws to the ends of my whiskers, I felt like jelly.

Oh, life was so hard and so complicated. It was a lot to cope with. Not just for me either. As I watched my kitten sleeping, I hoped that I could protect him from the worst that life had to offer, but failing that, I hoped that I could at least equip him to deal with it. Being a parent was just so fretful, and I didn't think that I would ever stop fretting about George.

I must have drifted off, because I woke with George tickling my nose with his whiskers.

'Dad, it's the day!' he squealed.

'Shush,' I said. 'Let's not draw too much attention to

ourselves. We need to go before the others wake up.'

George was an early riser, waking at dawn most days, so our plan was that we would leave the house, I'd deliver him to Tiger and then come back to bed. I'd pretend to be asleep and when everyone else woke up they would find me alone in the bed. I could make lots of noise to show them I was worried and then our search would begin. Part one of the plan was simple.

I made George drink some water before we left. There was no food as Claire still didn't leave food down for us overnight, but hopefully Tiger would get him into her house for breakfast. We then left, as quietly as we could. I walked George to Tiger's house and we stood by her back door. I pushed the cat flap to let Tiger know we were there.

'Good luck, my little boy,' I said, feeling affectionate, emotional and a little bit terrified all at once.

'Thanks, Dad, and don't leave me too long.'

I nuzzled up to him. 'I won't, but you know Tiger will be there for you. There's nothing to worry about. But, George, listen, it's important that you do what you're told. Do you understand?'

'Yes.' He looked serious. I hoped Tiger had woken up. She had said she would get up when the birds started singing. After a short while, she appeared.

'Here we are,' I said, shaking.

'It's OK, Alfie, it'll be fine, and I'll take it from here. Right, George, wait there, I have to go and make sure the coast is clear – my family are early risers – and then I'll come back and sneak you in for breakfast. I'll be really quick,' Tiger said.

'Do you understand, George?' I asked. He looked a bit like he hadn't been listening as he stared at the emerging sun and then a bird flying overhead. Tiger disappeared round the back of her house.

'Yes, of course. Wait. Breakfast.'

'Right, I have to go. Remember, do whatever Tiger says.' I touched my nose to his and then, before I got more emotional, I left to go home. George would wait, Tiger would be right out and then the plan would begin to unfurl.

'I'll listen to Tiger-Mum,' were his parting words for me. I felt so proud.

I rushed home and luckily made it back to my bed before anyone in the house woke up. Because I was so tired, before I knew it I'd actually fallen asleep.

'Where's George?' I woke up to see Claire and Summer standing over my basket. I looked around and then yawned.

'Miaow?' I said.

'Jon, Jon,' I heard Claire shout. She then went into the bedroom. A sleeping Jonathan emerged.

'Alfie, is George downstairs?' he asked me, rubbing his eyes.

'MIAOW!' I don't know, I tried to tell them.

'Oh God.' Claire practically flew downstairs and Jonathan picked Summer up and followed her. I went after them. Of course, after looking everywhere we didn't find him.

'I told you it was too soon to leave the cat flap open at night,' Claire snapped.

'Um, Claire, everyone said it was OK and anyway, Alfie nearly got locked out the other night. I mean, you can't keep them in forever.'

'Oh, Alfie, why did you let him out of your sight!' Claire stormed back upstairs to check again.

So at the moment she was blaming Jonathan and me – a bit unfair, but it was early days and it was early in the morning. Neither of them had had coffee and that said a lot. I normally avoided them in this state.

I stood by the back door and made a lot of noise. While Jonathan strapped Summer into her highchair, made coffee and gave Summer a drink of milk, Claire could be heard slamming doors upstairs.

'He's definitely not up there,' Claire said, coming back into the kitchen. 'Jonathan, where on earth is he? He's never out without Alfie and he's always here first thing in the morning.' She had searched the whole house by now and of course found nothing.

'Look, darling.' Jonathan gave her a hug. 'You sort Summer out and I'll throw on my tracksuit and go out and look.'

'Can you get Matt to help you?' Claire asked.

'Of course, don't worry.' He kissed her and I felt a little tiny moment of triumph. See, it was working already.

I went out with Jonathan, and followed him to Matt's house. Luckily they were already up and dressed and Matt came straight out when he heard what had happened.

'Oh God,' Polly said as she came to the front door. 'Let me know what I can do. I'd go to yours, Jon, but then George might come here, so maybe I should stay?'

'Babe, I think you should stay put. I've got my mobile so we'll keep in touch.' Matt kissed Polly and she hugged him tightly. 'I'm sure he's fine, you know what kittens are like, they get into all sorts of trouble.'

As the guys decided to go and check the street, I followed them. But I heard a hiss by Tiger's front gate and I turned to see her, trying to get my attention. I waited until the men were at a safe distance.

'Tiger, it's working already!' I exclaimed.

'But where's George?' Tiger asked.

'What do you mean?'

'Well, I told you I'd check the coast was clear at home, but when I came back out, George was gone. I looked everywhere and couldn't find him, so I assumed there'd been a change of plan and he was with you.' Tiger sounded slightly panicked.

'You mean he's not with you?' I felt fear bubble up in the pit of my stomach.

'No, he wasn't there when I came out of the house, nowhere to be seen. So I assumed he was still with you and the plan had somehow changed! I was literally gone for a flap of a butterfly wing!'

'Oh God, Tiger, no. I left him on the doorstep so I could get home before everyone woke up, and that was the last I saw of him. I thought he was with you! I told him to wait and he said he understood.' Now I sounded hysterical.

'Right, OK, let's stay calm. He's definitely not in my house, so shall we check yours?'

'We can pop back there but Claire's there and she checked everywhere.' I was finding it hard to catch my breath. 'When I got home, I went straight to bed. I dropped off, but it wasn't for long, and that's all I can tell you.'

'So George really is missing?'

'Oh no, my boy is missing!' It dawned on me. 'Jonathan and Matt are looking for him and now we're going to have to *really* look for him.' I felt terrified; I couldn't quite comprehend what had happened.

'Oh no, Alfie, this plan has gone wrong before it's even started.'

'And I never even saw it coming.'

As we quickly ran to my house to see if he'd gone home, I felt increasingly worried – but also a bit angry with George. I had explicitly told him to wait for Tiger, he had only been left alone for a matter of minutes, and he knew not to go off. But I was angrier with myself. I should have waited with him, or told Tiger to risk taking him into her house. We had specifically chosen the back of the house in case there was a lamppost cat snatcher – after all, they wouldn't have known George was there would they? Unless they'd been watching us. No, it couldn't be that, that made no sense.

Oh goodness, all he'd had to do was stand there, why couldn't he have done that? Where could he be? I felt as if my mind was running round in those circles George was so fond of. Oh, little George. I tried to breathe calmly, despite feeling as though my life was spiralling out of control. I wanted my boy back!

He wasn't back at ours and I heard Claire on the phone to Tash. She sounded as upset as me. The plan was so simple, but it had fallen apart from the moment it started and I only had myself to blame.

'Alfie,' Tiger said, as we checked every inch of our back garden. 'Beating yourself up really isn't helpful. We need to think about this. Let's round up all the cats and get them to spread out. We need to check his favourite places.'

'He's not at our house, if he was at Polly's we'd know and Tash is looking out for him. So the park, or the end of the street? But then if he goes there the other cats will see him…'

I couldn't think of anywhere else.

'Right, I think you need to stay central and also keep an eye on the humans, and I'll keep checking my house, because he might remember he's supposed to be there. How does that sound?'

'I have no better ideas. I wish I did.' I felt like lying down and yowling but then that wouldn't find my boy, would it?

'Look, come with me to find the others and you can help me organise them. Oh, Alfie, we have to find him, where on earth could he have gone? Why did I take my eyes off him?' Tiger seemed to feel the same as me.

'I just don't know where he'd have gone. And, Tiger, it's not your fault – you had to check the coast was clear. I mean, I know I keep saying it, but he was supposed to sit on the step and wait for you! Why didn't he do that? I was sure he understood.'

'I didn't take long, Alfie, I promise I just ran in, checked downstairs and was out again.'

'I know. I mean it, Tiger, it's not your fault. I should have waited with him.'

'But then you might not have been home before your family woke up and that was a crucial part of the plan.'

'OK, let's stop going round in circles and just find him then.' I turned to run off and saw Dustbin appear. I'd never been so pleased to see him.

'Oh, thank goodness you're here. George is missing,' I said.

'What? Not the lad?'

'Yes.' I explained the plan to Dustbin. 'It was still dark when I left him in Tiger's back garden. Oh, what have we done? What if I've lost him for good?' I yowled.

'Right, Mr B is on the case, honestly he's the best cat in the business. I'll go to him right now and tell him of this latest development. Don't worry, Alfie, if I've got anything to do with it, he'll be found safe and well.' I tried but failed to feel reassured.

Rocky was the first cat we saw. He went to get Elvis, who went to find Nellie, who rounded up Tinkerbell, and we all met at the end of the street. I outlined the situation.

'So you want us to pretend to find him?' Nellie said. Honestly!

'No, contrary to our plan he is actually missing.'

'Oh my word, the gorgeous little baby is actually missing?' Nellie started yowling and Elvis had to calm her down. Although I could see all my friends had panic in their eyes.

Once roles had been allocated, Tiger headed back to hers. I went with her to check but there was still no sign of George. I felt as if I had a paw missing, I missed him so much. I hoped he wasn't scared or in danger.

I went back home and slipped through the cat flap.

'Have you found him?' Claire, who was still not dressed, rushed up to me. I just looked at her, my eyes full of sorrow. She picked me up. 'Don't worry, Jon and Matt will find him. Oh, Alfie, I'm sorry I shouted at you.' She hugged me close before putting me down. I purred sadly. The doorbell went and Claire opened it to Tash.

'Where's Elijah?' Claire asked.

'With Granny today. She picked him up really early, so it means I can help. What should I do?'

'No sign of him on the way here?' Claire asked without hope.

'No, I looked the whole way, on both sides of the road. I read somewhere kittens like to hide though, so he could just be hiding.'

We had checked all the usual places more than once, so I knew that he wasn't hiding.

'Has Summer had her breakfast?' Tash asked.

'NO!' Summer shouted. Tash grinned.

'Claire, go and get dressed and I'll make Summer some toast.'

'Oh, thank you, Tash.' Claire had tears glistening in her eyes as she made her way upstairs.

By lunchtime everyone was in our kitchen. Claire, Jonathan, Polly and Matt sat at the table. Tash had set up a sort of playgroup in the living room for the children. The doorbell went again and I hoped it was someone with George, but we opened it to find Tomasz standing there.

'Right, I am here now, so let's make a plan,' Tomasz said, sitting down.

'Aren't you supposed to be at work?' Claire said.

'Some things are more important. Don't worry, my Alfie, we will find him.' As he stroked me, I felt reassured, Tomasz was so big and comforting. I felt a slight sliver of hope.

'I don't know what we'll do if we don't find him.' Claire started crying and Jonathan wrapped his arms around her.

'We will find him,' he said, but I heard his voice crack. He was such a softy underneath the bluster, but he sounded determined.

'We have to,' Polly said, her beautiful face ashen. Matt hugged her. Somehow the fact that everyone was being brought together didn't make me feel any better.

'I think I'll call Max,' Tash said, her cheeks reddening. The others looked at her. 'He might be able to help, he's quite practical.'

'Good idea, Tash,' Jonathan said, and I saw Tash brighten. I followed her into the other room, and when I heard her speak to him, I knew that she was letting him in. By asking for his help she was trusting him, and although I felt as bad as I ever had in my life, I felt a little better for that.

It was decided that Tash would stay with the children and Claire and Jonathan would go on foot to the park at the end of the street, stopping at the Goodwins first – if anyone could find George it would be those nosey parkers, Jonathan said. Matt and Polly would go to the other end of the street and Tomasz and Max would drive around looking at the surrounding area. The plan was that if we hadn't found him by nightfall they would put alerts on the local Facebook and then maybe even make posters… My baby might become a lamppost cat! But we all hoped it wouldn't come to that. I prayed and prayed it wouldn't come to that.

I did actually see the flaw in my plan then. Even if it had worked, I had planned on George staying away overnight, but the amount of worry that that would have caused was unfair. No matter how much my humans needed to have their eyes opened, it wasn't worth this distress. But now he really was missing, and it was all my fault.

If anything happened to my kitten, I would never, ever forgive myself.

# Chapter Twenty-nine

It was nearly teatime and I had had enough. I still cared about my humans, but not as much as I cared about getting George back. The adults were still looking for him, to no avail, so I went to round up my cat friends in the hope that they might have some leads. As I set off though, Salmon loomed over me.

'Right, Alfie, what is going on?' he demanded, narrowing his eyes. 'I've seen the neighbourhood cats running around like headless chickens, your family have been to see my family and I heard them say they had to go and look for George before dashing out.'

'So you know exactly what's going on then. George is missing. It's a long story but the fact is we need to find him.'

'I was afraid that was the case. I was actually hoping this was just one of your hair-brained schemes.'

I wanted to be affronted, but for once Salmon was right. 'Well, he's missing, and I'm frantic, we're all frantic. What if he's become one of the lamppost cats?'

'My family said they were afraid that that might have happened to George. Look, they're looking for all the cats, George now included, and with so many of us we're bound to find him. And I'm off now, so if there's any news I'll report back.' Salmon sounded kind, which was a first for me.

'You will?' I was wide-eyed.

'Yes, the boy is very cute and, well, I've got a soft spot for him. Don't worry Alfie, we'll find him.'

'But what if he's with the other lamppost cats?' I asked.

291

'Then at least he'll be among friends. Alfie, try not to worry.'

I watched in amazement as Salmon bounded off. My kitten had bewitched even him.

I was sure now that George was lost, not hiding, and the idea of him being afraid was almost too much for me to bear, especially now that night was falling. My cat friends had paired up to search the area: Nellie had gone with Tinkerbell, Rocky with Elvis. Tiger and I were sticking together – I needed her more now than I ever had. It was as if her physical presence was keeping me in one piece. Or almost. I wanted to curl up and yowl but I had to try to keep going until he was found. Not finding him was not an option.

When we met up, all the cats reported where they had looked so far, and we all shared our frustrations that no one had come close to finding George. Despondency filled the air around us; I didn't know how much more of this I could take.

'I'll go home and see if the humans have any news,' I decided. 'You wait here for Dustbin, and I'll be back as quickly as I can. They all nodded solemnly. Nellie had said that my plans brought them together, but this was a step too far. We were all distraught: for Pinkie, because of the fear that someone might be out there to hurt cats, and especially for George, who we all loved.

My legs felt heavy as I made my way inside. I saw, to my dismay, all my humans at the kitchen table. Why weren't they out looking?

'Miaow,' I said angrily. They all turned to look at me: Jonathan, Claire, Matt, Polly, Tomasz, Tash and, surprisingly, Max. I saw that Max and Tash were holding hands – what was that about? I then saw that on the table were posters, just like the lamppost ones, only these had a picture of my George on them. I felt my heart tear in two.

'Hi, Alfie. No luck?' Claire said. She looked terrible, as if she had been crying. In fact, none of my humans looked good. I just looked at her. I didn't have the energy to even wonder where the children were.

'Thanks for doing these posters so quickly, Max,' Jonathan said. 'We can't risk wasting any more time.' He issued instructions to everyone on where they should put them up. I climbed onto Claire's lap, and looked at George's beautiful face.

'You are such a star, Max,' Tash said, and I saw her cheeks were again pink. It seemed they had resolved their issues, but I didn't have any energy to be happy for them, not now at least. I jumped down and headed back out. We weren't any closer to finding out where George was.

'Dustbin?' I asked hopefully as I approached Tiger, who was waiting by my gate.

'Sorry, Alfie, he's not here yet. The others have gone to do another search, no one has any idea what else to do.'

'And for once I'm all out of plans. Tonight will be the first night I've spent away from George since he came to live with me. I'm not sure I can bear it.'

'Alfie, look, why don't we wait here until Dustbin comes? We'll stay all night if we have to. And if either of us need to go inside then the other will be here.'

'That would be great,' I said. 'I just feel so useless.'

'Alfie, we'll get him back, I just know it.' Tiger and I snuggled together by a bush, although I didn't think sleep would visit that night.

\*\*\*

We saw Matt, Jonathan and Tomasz emerge from the front door, armed with posters.

'Right, guys, meet you back here when they've all been put up,' Jonathan said. They headed off, Matt and Tomasz in one direction, Jonathan in the other.

'They're putting up pictures, on the lampposts,' I explained to Tiger. She looked distraught as the reality of what was happening hit us once again.

'If only I hadn't insisted on that stupid plan,' I lamented.

'Oh, Alfie, it's not your fault. You only left him for a few minutes.'

'I know, but I shouldn't have left him at all. I should have waited with him until you came back. No matter what the plan was, he should not have been left alone.'

'Well, we can't turn back the clock, and blaming yourself isn't going to help anyone. Come on, Alfie, let's try to be positive. You're the most positive cat I know.'

'I just don't feel it right now.'

'I know, it's horrible. I didn't think I could miss anyone the way I miss George.' Tiger looked sad. 'But we will find him. We have to.'

'I just wish Dustbin would turn up.'

The front door opened again and Tash walked out carrying Elijah. Max was next to her.

'Are you sure I can't carry him for you?' Max asked.

'I'm used to it,' Tash replied.

'But, Tash, you don't have to. Look, I promised you we'd take things slowly, and I mean it, but let me help you.' He sounded so genuine; I really liked this guy.

'You're right. I guess I'm so used to doing things myself.

Max, you have to be patient with me.'

'Hey, Patience is my middle name.'

I really hoped it wasn't.

Tiger and I watched them walk off towards Tash's flat, with Elijah now in Max's arms. It was very sweet and had I not been so worried about my kitten my heart would be full of joy.

'George needs you, Alfie,' Tiger said, suddenly. 'He needs us both. We sort of promised him we were his parents now and we have to protect him. No matter what.'

'Tiger, you're right. We need to be strong; no time for moping.' We were going to find him. I closed my eyes and wished it with all my heart.

# Chapter
# Thirty

I woke with a start. I was still lying under a bush; obviously I'd fallen asleep at some point, but it was still dark. Tiger slept beside me, looking so peaceful I almost forgot the turmoil we were in. I stretched out and took a look around. Still no sign of Dustbin, or any other cats for that matter. I paced around a bit, to loosen my legs up and also for want of something to do. I was just about to lie down next to Tiger again, when to my surprise I saw big Tomasz walking down our street. What was he doing? Had he found George? I barely dared to hope. I ran out onto the street to intercept him, and as soon as he saw me he scooped me up in his arms.

'Alfie, is the middle of the night,' he said as he sat on the garden wall, still cradling me. I miaowed – I knew that. But what was he doing here? 'I have been thinking a lot. Seeing how lost you are without George makes me see how lost I am without my family – my wife and kittens. Alfie, I am coming to look for George tonight, while everyone else sleeps, but I feel so useless.' I nestled into his neck; I felt the same. 'Alfie, I'm sorry, but as worried about George as we all are, I know what I need to do. Tomorrow I am going to fly to Poland to get my family back. I hope we find George by then but if not I have to go. I hope you understand.'

Tomasz was such a big, solid man but he sounded so sad. I did understand. After all, part of my grand plan had been to get him to go to Poland. I thought of the miserable irony of my life: Tash had opened herself up to Max and Tomasz was going to get his family, yet here I was having lost my kitten. There was no triumph, only pain, and I tried to ignore the horrible feeling that I would rather have George back than any of this. It was selfish of me, wasn't it? I was suddenly realising that my kitten was more important to me than anyone, and his happiness and safety came above all else. I loved my humans, and I wanted their happiness, but not at the expense of George. I nestled into Tomasz again; I wanted to feel a bit of warmth because suddenly my fur was freezing, and so was my heart.

After a while, Tomasz left to go and look for George. Poor Tomasz, he felt guilty at leaving us before George was found, so he was sacrificing his sleep to have one last look, but I had a terrible, sinking feeling it was fruitless. I was beginning to give up all hope. How could I continue to put one paw in front of the other? How could I eat, sleep, ever be happy again? I was pretty sure that unless George came back, I couldn't.

The next morning Tiger woke up and stretched; we had spent the entire night outside and I had been unable to get back to sleep. The sun was beginning to come up and as I saw Tomasz coming back again. I looked, hopefully, to see if he had George, but his arms were empty. As he came up to our front door, I looked at Tiger, who nodded. I was going to go inside to see if there was any news. He rang the doorbell and I stood at his feet as Jonathan, wearing his dressing gown and with hair messier than I'd ever seen it before, opened the door. His skin was pale and I guessed he hadn't slept much either. Wordlessly, he stepped aside and let Tomasz and me in.

'No luck?' he said, as they made their way into the kitchen.

He began to fiddle with the coffee machine.

'I walked around for hours. No sign. But, Jon, I need to say something. I have decided that I am going to Poland today. I book a flight, I leave the restaurants with the managers.'

'Mate, you're going to get your family back!' I saw a faint glimmer of a smile on Jonathan's lips.

'I feel so bad leaving when George is missing but I need to tell Franceska and the boys how important they are to me.'

'Yes, Tom, you do and you know we'll find George. I just feel it. So you go and I'll text with any news, but first you need coffee, you look like death warmed up.'

'Then looking at you is like looking in a mirror,' Tomasz joked.

'Who knew how painful this could be. And for poor Alfie too. You know, we will find him,' Jonathan said again, but I wasn't sure who he was trying to convince – me, Tomasz or himself.

I watched the house come alive but there was a flatness to everyone. Even little Summer wasn't her usual self, she must sense that something was wrong. Children can be quite perceptive, I had learnt, though not quite as perceptive as cats. Claire wore her emotions on her face and I knew she had been crying. She kept hugging me and saying how sorry she was. Jonathan kept giving us both worried glances as he filled Claire in on Tomasz's revelation.

'I'm so glad he's come to his senses,' Claire said. 'But honestly I wish it hadn't taken losing George to do it.'

'No, darling, nothing is worth losing George for,' Jonathan agreed.

I had some water and tried to eat, although it felt as if the food would choke me. Spotting George's bowl sitting empty in the cupboard was almost more than my heart could bear. I cleaned myself up a bit and listened to Claire and Jonathan trying to come up with a plan.

'We've looked around, we've put posters up and we have Vic and Heather on the case. I think our best bet might be to sit tight here and hope the phone rings,' Jonathan suggested.

'I agree. Tomasz has been looking all night, we searched everywhere all day yesterday, and Vic and Heather even spoke to the police. If we stay close to home we might hear news or maybe, just maybe, George will come home.'

Oh, how I envied their optimism. Though I felt a little angry with them – they seemed to think they could sit around and do nothing. There was no way I could that. I had to be out there, doing something. Even if it was fruitless.

I left the house and made my way round to the front of the house to see Tiger looking uncertainly at something.

'What is it?' I said, rushing up to her.

'Your friend is coming,' she said, sounding nervous, 'and he has someone with him.' I squinted as I saw Dustbin approaching from a distance. My heart swelled with hope but the cat with him wasn't George, it was a big black cat. Tiger and I both sat upright, waiting for them to approach.

'Alfie, can we talk somewhere a bit more private?' Dustbin asked, gesturing to his companion. I wordlessly led them under our bush, where we'd be hidden. 'Right, first things first. This is Mr B. And Mr B, this is Alfie and Tiger.' We all nodded our hellos. 'Mr B is the best in the business, an expert at finding stuff. In fact, he helped me when your Snowball was lost.'

'I remember it well,' said Mr B. 'Pretty white cat, got herself into a bit of a scrape. Anyway, the thing is, Dustbin told me about the lamppost cats, and I've spent a bit of time looking into it, and I think we've got the answer.'

'Really?' I couldn't breathe. They had found George?

'Look, it's been a bit of a job, but we got lucky, or we think we have. It seems that someone's going round picking up cats off the street when they aren't expecting it.'

'You mean there really is a cat snatcher?' Tiger looked terrified.

'Yes. We don't know who it is or why they're doing it, but after extensive work we have found the house we think the cats have been taken to. *Think* is the operative word here – we can't be one hundred per cent sure. But after doing some surveillance around this area we heard reports of unsocial levels of cat noise.' Mr B sounded very professional, I thought. Once again I was indebted to Dustbin.

'George is there?' I asked.

'We don't know, Alfie. We know where the house is, it's not far from here, but getting in isn't going to be easy. The front has a high gate, which we can't see over – it's too tall to get up there. Attached to it is a wire fence which leads around a garden. We could see in but the curtains were all drawn and the house was in darkness. However, we were able to verify that indeed there were a large number of cats there.'

'How?' Tiger asked.

'Good question,' Mr B replied. 'There's a lot of noise, although be reassured we didn't necessarily hear cats in distress, just cat chatter, and more than would be normal for a domestic house. Then there's a shelter at the back which is packed full of tins of cat food and big bags of biscuits.' I shuddered, I didn't like cat food from tins myself. 'The house is also being guarded by some kind of creature right next to the wire fence. With the high gate, the drawn curtains on every window, the cat food and these guards, the evidence points to the fact that the person living there is hiding something – or rather, is hiding lots of cats.'

'I guess it makes sense.' I felt doubtful but we had nothing else.

'Alfie, we can't be certain, but if George is there then we need to find out soon. We need a plan,' Dustbin said. I felt a tiny bit of hope swell inside me. This was the first bit of news since George had gone missing and I needed to be strong now, for my boy.

They needed a plan. Well, they had come to the right place.

# Chapter
# Thirty-one

I felt nervous. Of all the plans I had ever put into play, this one had the most riding on it. Not only George but potentially all the lamppost cats would be saved by this. I had rounded up as many of my friends as I could to explain what we needed to do.

After long discussions with Mr B and Dustbin I had all the information I needed, and they had even taken Tiger and I to the house. As they had said, it was in total darkness, but we could hear faint cat noises coming from inside. The front gate wasn't going to help us but the back fence, which stretched around the house, was wire, and although it wouldn't be easy, it provided a possibility.

The best thing though was that the creatures guarding the house turned out to be hens. Their run followed the fence all the way along its length, so the only way to get into the garden was via them. I managed to poke my nose through the fence, and although they were angry, squawking and wobbling their heads at me, when I explained that I had many hen friends in the country – only a slight exaggeration – they were more welcoming. At least they didn't try to peck me through the fence with their beaks, anyway. We didn't exactly communicate easily but we managed to establish that I would need their help, and as they calmed down I think they agreed to it. I was thankful for my time in the country: my understanding of hens looked as if it was finally coming in handy.

'Impressive,' Dustbin said as I came back. 'But that fence will be tricky to climb.' He was right: it was tall and there was spiked wire along the top. It didn't look very safe.

'I know, I think I can do it though, if I put my mind to it,' I said, trying to sound brave, although I was quaking all the way down to my paws.

'Oh, Alfie, are you sure, it looks as if it could really hurt you and your leg…' Tiger sounded worried.

'Tiger, if my boy is in there I have to do it. I'll get over there somehow.' The others looked worried but it was agreed that Dustbin would accompany me. Tiger and I then left Dustbin and Mr B to keep watch on the house. They were going to wait there, because we still had a lot to do before we were ready for the actual cat rescue.

'So, Alfie, what can we do?' Rocky asked as I told them about the house.

I outlined our plan from start to finish, leaving no stone unturned, and by the time I had finished speaking everyone understood how serious it was. 'So, guys, I'm going to go. Dustbin and Mr B are waiting.' I looked at Tiger, the only other cat who knew where the house was. She was needed in case anything went wrong. 'I have to sort out the humans too, but if you guys could find Salmon for me then that would be great. Tiger, can you direct Salmon to the house?' I explained exactly what I needed Salmon to do. I wanted to give all my friends a part in the plan, although many of them were just going to be supportive roles. I knew how important it was for them to feel useful. Tinkerbell was going to assist Tiger, whilst Rocky, Nellie and Elvis were going to ensure they knew what was going on and would warn either Tiger or Tinkerbell of any problems. I could see how fired up they all were. Frightened, yes, but adrenaline was pumping through all of us. We were going to rescue George.

This plan was risky because I couldn't do it with my cats alone. I had to get the humans involved and that wasn't going to be easy. However, everyone agreed they knew their parts and what they had to do, so I felt as confident as I could.

'Good luck, Alfie, we're all supporting you, and we'll be waiting to see you come home safely with the boy,' Elvis said.

'You're such a brave cat,' Nellie added.

I took a deep breath, and went to put the plan into action.

My first stop was home. I needed some humans with me and my preferred ones were Jonathan and Matt. They were phys-ically fit and if I could get them to come with me then that would be half the battle won. Or quite a bit of it anyway. I still had quite a bit of work to do, as did Dustbin, who being such a tough cat was my chosen sidekick.

Once we got to the house I knew everything would happen very quickly, but first I had to get there and hope that I could get at least some of my humans there too.

I walked into the kitchen. It was funny how wrong it felt without George. He had only lived with us for a short time but the house needed him. I padded my way over to where Claire and Tash were feeding the children. Polly was pacing, as was Matt. Jonathan was on his phone.

'Oh, Alfie, there you are,' Claire said. 'I guess there's still no news?'

'Miaow.' I took a breath. 'Miaow, miaow, miaow, miaow,' I screeched as loudly as I could. Everyone stared at me. Right, so I'd got their attention. I ran around in circles, still yowling, then I ran towards the front door, the idea being that someone would follow me.

As I sat by the front door, listening to them all talking about me in the kitchen, I began to realise that might not happen.

'Has he gone mad?' Tash asked.

'Blimey, who knew he could even make that noise,' Jonathan said. OK, I told myself, trying to keep calm, this wasn't going to be as easy as I thought.

I went back and repeated the routine, yowling, miaowing and making as much noise as I could, but they all just stared at me dumbfounded, and then Summer burst into tears. I was feeling frustrated as Claire comforted her, telling her not to worry, though she looked worried herself. I went to Jonathan. He was my only hope it seemed, and that was slim. Honestly, they say humans are clever, but really? These guys were not showing it very well. I tried to sit up and swipe at his leg, but he just looked at me.

'What, Alfie?' he asked.

'YOWL!!' I replied, but still he looked confused. I hated to do it, and hoped he would forgive me later, but I had no choice. I scratched him as forcefully as I could.

'Ow! What on earth did you do that for?'

I took my chance as he looked at me angrily. 'MEOW,' I said, running towards the front door.

'I think he wants you to follow him,' Claire said at last. 'Do you think he knows something?'

As I sat by the front door, bashing it with my head to further illustrate my point, Matt, Jonathan and Polly finally appeared. At this rate I would have to knock myself out before they did what I needed them to do. As Jonathan opened the door I ran out, glad to see he followed me.

'What is he doing?' Polly asked as she stood at the door.

'No idea, but Jon and I will follow him, you guys stay with the kids. I'll call you if anything happens,' Matt shouted as they started following me down the road. I took the route that I had memorised so carefully. I was tired but we had to hurry. If George was in that strange house then I wanted him out of there as quickly as possible.

I remembered the route perfectly, which was a huge relief, and as I reached the house, Mr B and Dustbin were waiting for me. I wasn't sure what Matt and Jonathan would think but Mr B slipped into the shadows, leaving only Dustbin and me.

'I think I saw your boy,' Dustbin whispered. 'There was a moment when the curtain went back and I can't be sure but I think it might have been George.'

'I hope it was.' My heart sang at the idea. 'Are you ready?' I asked, and Dustbin indicated he was.

Matt and Jonathan were standing by the high gate, trying and failing to open it. They banged on it loudly but to no avail.

'What is this?' Matt asked.

'No idea, maybe Alfie really has gone mad? Mad cat's disease or something,' Jonathan said. I yowled at him – this was no time for jokes. 'OK, sorry. Right, Alfie. What is this place and who is that enormous cat?'

'I can't be sure but I think it might be Tomasz's restaurant cat,' Matt said, looking puzzled.

'Nothing would surprise me with these guys,' Jonathan said, as we led them to the fence. I miaowed a lot to get the chickens' attention. They stared at me with their small beady eyes but stayed quiet, which I took to mean they were ready for us. I took a breath and then started scaling the fence. It wasn't easy: the wire was slippery and it was high.

'Blimey, what's he doing?' Matt asked. I noticed neither of them tried to help me.

'Do you think, I mean, is it possible, that maybe George is in that house?'

'I can't see why else Alfie would do that. He doesn't like heights remember.'

As I climbed with Dustbin by my side, encouraging me, I ignored the humans. At least they had figured out why we were here, so hopefully they would actually do something useful now. After what seemed like forever, I made it over the spikes and prepared to begin my descent. Going down looked so much scarier than coming up. I froze.

'I think we should call the police,' Jonathan said finally.

'And say what?' Matt replied.

'That there might be a cat snatcher in that house,' Jonathan said. I glanced back at him from the top of the fence and he pulled out his phone.

'What evidence do we have though?' Matt asked.

'Well, they have our cat, or they will in a minute anyway. Look, Alfie's about get in there.'

Out of the corner of my eye I could see Jonathan pull out his phone and start to dial, looking anxious.

'They might not believe us,' Matt said. 'Although yes, if you say our cat is in there it might work.'

'Exactly. Unless you've got any better ideas? If there is a cat snatcher in there they might be nasty, so we can't take them on.'

'True, right, get the police,' Matt said, still sounding uncertain.

'It's OK, Alfie,' Dustbin said quietly. 'Watch me, just go

quickly, gripping where you can, and you'll be on the ground in no time.

I was still terrified. Matt was right, I didn't like heights – and what if Dustbin and I were heading into terrible danger? I was glad Jonathan was calling the police.

I gave myself a little pep talk and, as I saw Dustbin reach the bottom, I knew I could do it. I could do it for my boy. I landed a little roughly but I made it. Dustbin still looked scared of the chickens but he managed to jump out of the coop easily. I looked at the chickens.

'I hope you understand this. I'm going to chase you, but I promise I won't hurt you, I just need you to make a lot of noise,' I told them.

'Cluck, cluck, cluck,' they replied, which I was pretty sure was hen-speak for 'yes'.

I took a breath and started running after the chickens. They flew everywhere, and thankfully they must have understood me as they made a huge racket. Even though I was tired, I kept going, and the chickens made more and more noise. Probably a bit more than necessary, but then chickens could be quite dramatic. Feathers started flying. I hadn't even done anything.

'Blimey, why is he chasing chickens? He was scared of them when we were on holiday – didn't want to go anywhere near them,' Jonathan said. 'Alfie, stop that, stop that now!' he shouted, but of course I wasn't going to stop for him.

Finally a door sprang open and a scruffy lady emerged. As she ran at me screaming, Dustbin managed to sneak into house. Great, the first part of our plan had worked!

'Get off my chickens,' the woman shouted; she sounded a bit like the queen. 'Get off them!' Yeah, as if, I thought. I chased the chickens even harder, until I was sure Dustbin was safely inside. Thankfully the woman had forgotten to shut the door too. The idea was that he would tell all the cats to come out, so there could be no doubt that this person had the missing lamppost cats. I just hoped she did have them, after all of this. It would be a bit embarrassing otherwise.

'We're sorry,' Jonathan said, his voice shaky as if he was nervous, when the woman noticed them. 'Alfie, get out of there!' I did as he asked, hopping into the woman's garden to stand by her feet. I noticed she was wearing one boot, but the other foot only had a holey sock on it. She didn't exactly look dangerous, although her grey hair was wild and she wore a huge jumper over what looked like pyjamas.

'Right, well, I'm sorry about this but if you could open the front gate, then Alfie can come with us,' Matt said, glancing at Jonathan. He and Jonathan turned around; they were looking for the police, I guessed.

'I will do no such thing. This cat is mine now,' she said, looking at me. 'Ahh, I don't have a British Blue and you are very handsome.' I raised my whiskers – how kind of her to notice – but then I remembered where I was and why I was there.

'He's our cat,' Matt said angrily. 'Give him back!' He stood as close as he could to the fence and Jonathan joined him.

'Yowl,' I said angrily.

The woman stared at me, then at Jonathan and Matt before turning around and looking at her back door.

'Arrrghhh!' she screamed as Dustbin emerged, followed by a horde of cats. My heart quickened as I saw George next to Dustbin.

'Miaow,' I said, running up to him. 'Thank goodness you're all right.' I nuzzled him with all my might.

'Dad, I knew you'd come,' George replied.

'Right, no time for that just now, we need to stick together.' I saw Pinkie emerge with the others; there must have been about twenty cats there! She ran over to me.

'Thank goodness,' she said. 'Alfie, thank goodness you're here.' She looked upset. 'I'm so relieved to be out. I really didn't like being there, not even her fridge was a comfort to me.'

'It's OK, you are all free now,' I said.

Although I realised with a sinking feeling that actually none of us were; we were still stuck in the woman's garden.

'You really are the cat snatcher!' Jonathan shouted above the noise, as cats of all shapes and sizes ran around the garden, miaowing loudly.

'I most certainly am not,' the woman replied.

'But you've got our kitten, and you're trying to take Alfie!' Matt said.

'They are all mine. Mine I tell you,' she screeched. I looked at her, worried she was deranged. As she tried to round up the cats, including me, two things happened. We heard a police siren coming closer, just as Vic and Heather Goodwin ran up to Matt and Jonathan, with Salmon at their heels. I had never been so pleased to see them. Actually before now I had *never* been pleased to see them, so this situation really was very odd.

'What is going on?' Vic shouted.

'She's the cat snatcher,' Matt said.

I snuggled close to George; we didn't know how to get out but at least I had my boy. The other cats all seemed happy to be outside as they ran around in circles, enjoying their freedom.

'What, this old lady?' Heather asked, incredulous. 'Citizen's arrest!' she shouted, although how she was going to do that from the other side of the fence I wasn't sure.

'I am not the cat snatcher. These are all my cats,' the woman maintained.

'The police are on the way,' Matt told them.

'Good. And that's not true, lady.' Vic waved a bunch of papers at the woman. 'All these cats have been reported missing.'

'And George is one of them,' Jonathan said.

'You are a cat-napper of the worst kind,' Heather shouted.

'But…' The woman looked defeated. 'I just wanted them to be mine.'

The police car pulled up and two policemen got out.

'What on earth is going on?' one of them asked, as Vic took it upon himself to explain.

In the ensuing madness, I was able to check that George was all right. He said that Pinkie had looked after him and the other cats were all very friendly. They were all very upset to have been kitty-napped, as they thought of it. But the cat snatcher, who it turned out was called Henrietta, was kind to them, although she wouldn't let them go out, so the house was a mess and the cats were all stir-crazy. She hadn't been mean though, which to me was the main thing.

It transpired that she had grabbed George from Tiger's back step in the few seconds he had been there alone. She must have been watching us. I shuddered to think that I had been so careless.

'Let us in,' one policeman said.

'I'd rather not,' the lady replied uncertainly.

'Either let us in or we will have to force our way in, and you're in enough trouble as it is.'

As the police eventually gained entry, with Matt and Jonathan alongside them, Vic and Heather also barged in. They were doing their best to tell the bemused policemen what to do.

'You should arrest her,' Vic said.

'Lock her up and throw away the key,' Heather concurred.

'Well, perhaps first we should sort out what to do with all these cats. It's not like we can take them to the station,' one of the policemen said, looking slightly afraid.

'No need,' said Heather. 'We can call all the owners and they'll come and collect them. Look, I've got the posters. We took a copy of each so we knew what cats to look out for. We don't run the neighbourhood watch for nothing, you know.'

'Well that is good, Mr and Mrs Goodwin. Right, Ms…'

'Babbington-Smythe. But you can call me Henrietta,' the strange lady said. She even held out her hand to the officer, who looked confused but shook it.

'Come with me,' said one of the policemen. 'I'm afraid I'll have to ask you to wait inside while we sort this out.' The other policeman used his radio to inform someone that they had a cat situation which may take a while. As Matt scooped up George, Jonathan phoned Claire to tell her what was going on and I managed to get a quiet moment with Dustbin and Mr B.

'I don't know how to thank you, Mr B, you did a sterling job. And, Dustbin, you proved, yet again, what a great friend you are. None of these cats would be free without you.'

'I dunno about that, Alfie, but I'm just glad the boy is all right,' said Dustbin. 'The other cats too, of course, but especially him.' We nuzzled. 'And, Alfie, it took real guts to do what you did, that fence, your fear of heights, the hens. Good job.'

'I'm sorry to interrupt, but I must get back, you never know when I'll be needed next,' Mr B said. They both managed to get away without anyone noticing or trying to rehome them, thankfully.

After what seemed like ages with the policeman, we were allowed to go. Heather and Vic agreed to wait for the other cat owners, only to help the police, of course. As I gave Salmon a grin, I realised the Goodwins were in their element. They were loving every minute, although possibly disappointed they didn't get to make a citizen's arrest.

As we made our way home, Matt carrying George, Jonathan carrying me, I realised that this plan had worked pretty well. No one was hurt, I hadn't got more than a couple of scratches from the fence, no chickens had been harmed, and I had George safe and sound with me.

'Thank you all so much,' I said to the chickens. I felt as if I was friends with the creatures now.

'Cluck,' they replied, bobbing their heads in what I could only assume meant 'you're welcome'.

My relief was palpable. I had relied on a team, and that team had really come through. As we approached Edgar Road I saw Tiger at my gate. I miaowed and Jonathan set me down.

'He's safe,' I said, grinning.

'Oh, Alfie, you did it!' Tiger looked so happy and I felt closer to her than ever in that moment.

'No, Tiger, *we* did it.' I nuzzled her and felt like the luckiest cat in the world.

# Chapter
# Thirty-two

It was pandemonium when we got back with George. Claire burst into tears, as did Summer, who ran up to George, clutched him to her little chest and told him, 'Bad kitten.' George looked confused at this telling off, but I gave him a reassuring look. Polly and the kids all crowded round him and of course they wanted to hear the story.

'Alfie did it, really,' Jonathan said, looking confused. 'After that whole thing here, the kerfuffle, he made us follow him and he led us to the house. How did you find it when no one else had?' Jonathan asked me. I tilted my head to the side. 'I think he had help, cat help, that is. And then he took his life, or one of them anyway, into his own hands...' Jonathan told the story, but it sounded a bit more like one of his action films than what really happened. I mean yes, it was dramatic, but not quite as dramatic as he made out.

'So it turns out that poor Henrietta worked at a cattery, but she hated giving the cats back so they gave her the boot,' Matt said. 'Which sent her a bit mad and she basically scooped up all the cats she came across. There were about twenty there, all in this big dilapidated house.'

'Imagine the smell, Claire, you would not have coped,' Jonathan added. It was funny what humans dwelled on.

Everyone was so happy and made a huge fuss of George, but I got a hero's welcome after Matt and Jonathan finished explaining what had happened. Claire went to get us some smoked salmon, which was very welcome after our ordeal.

We ate as everyone stayed close by, all chattering with relief. 'Have you told Tash?' Jonathan asked.

'Yes, I texted her. She's at home with Elijah, he wasn't feeling too well, but Max is with her so she said she would celebrate. And Tomasz? Has anyone let him know?'

'I texted him,' Jonathan said. 'And look.' He held up his phone, which had a photo of my Polish family on it. 'Family selfie, so it's all good with them,' Jonathan grinned. I began to relax. George was back where he belonged. In fact, it seemed everyone was where they belonged right now.

As I snuggled up with George, after we'd eaten and cleaned ourselves, I wanted everyone to see how much I loved him. I hoped they would then see how much they loved each other.

'It's amazing, really,' Polly said. 'Alfie has really adopted George as if he's his own. Even if he'd fathered him he couldn't love him any more.' Claire looked at Polly and then at Jonathan. I saw Jonathan looking at me and then he reached over and grabbed Claire's hand.

'And we love those cats as if they're our children, almost,' Matt pointed out.

'We do,' Claire said, and I saw she had tears in her eyes as she held tightly onto Jonathan's hand. I made a note to make an extra fuss of Polly later. How clever she had been with what she said.

'Polly,' said Matt, 'I was thinking a lot today, when we were looking for George. I felt so scared for him, I know we all did, but it was as if we'd lost a part of the family. And so I think we need to decide, for the good of our family, how we can both work, because I don't think it's good for anyone if either of us are miserable.'

'We have been awful lately,' Polly said. 'Poor kids, we must have been a nightmare to live with.' I purred my agreement from where I was resting: they had been.

'You can get a nanny or an au pair or something,' Jonathan said. 'Plenty of parents do that.'

'And I can help you find one,' Claire said. She was so efficient that I knew she'd probably find them someone in no time. 'And you're right. We've all made a bit of a mess of things lately, perhaps this was the wake-up call we all needed to start putting things right.' She looked at her husband.

'We'll talk, properly talk, later,' Jonathan said, leaning over to kiss her.

Henry walked into the kitchen and up to his dad. He looked cross.

'What's up, mate?' Matt asked.

'Martha and Summer want me to dress up as a girl and go to a pretend tea party with them.' He didn't sound happy.

'Oh boy, those girls are so bossy. Right, Henry, come with me and I'll find you something else to do,' Jonathan said, taking his hand.

'Can I play on the iPad?' Henry looked hopeful.

'OK, but you'd better use it in the kitchen or the girls will squabble over it.' Jonathan ruffled Henry's hair as he went to get his iPad. Henry sat on a chair in the corner of the room, happy once again now he was safe from the girls.

Oh, I thought as I felt the warmth of my little boy, it could all be so easy, if only people would let it.

'I'm going to open a bottle of champagne,' Jonathan announced. 'We need to celebrate George's safe return.' He went to the fridge to get a bottle.

'You know, the last time I was as scared as I was today was when Alfie was ill and I didn't know if he'd survive,' Claire said. She was talking about my first plan, which had been incredibly dangerous. Although it had worked, it did almost kill me.

'And to think we didn't know each other then. Gosh, Claire, I can't imagine not having you guys in my life,' Polly said.

'If it wasn't for Alfie, and now for George, we wouldn't all be talking like this, like we haven't done for ages, so I reckon we should toast them,' Matt suggested.

'You'd almost think he planned the whole thing,' Jonathan laughed.

'Oh, Jon, you are so ridiculous where Alfie's concerned, of course he didn't. But Matt's right, our lives are richer for having them in it, so let's toast them,' said Claire, giving Jonathan an affectionate pat on the arm.

Jonathan stood up and cleared his throat.

'To love, family and friends – and that includes our lovely, clever cats, without whom we would be lost. As lost as little George was. To Alfie and George.' He raised his champagne and everyone echoed him as they clinked glasses.

My heart swelled, so full of joy, I wondered if it would burst.

Apart from the fact that George actually did go missing, and my plan had gone totally awry, the end result was exactly what I had hoped for. No, it wasn't worth losing George for, and I would never leave him ever again, not for a moment, but we had him back and it was time to stop dwelling on the bad times and look to our future. Which, as I listened to Claire and Jonathan talk that night, seemed to be exactly what they were doing.

'I think adoption is important for so many reasons,' Claire said. 'A child needs a loving family, and we have one, we are one. There are too many children in the world that don't have what we can offer,' she said.

'I know and I want to, but I'm scared. What if I don't love the child like I love Summer? I can't believe how much I do love her, it takes me by surprise even now.'

'But what if you do love them? Jonathan, you don't real-ise how big your heart is, you treat all the kids – Aleksy, little Tomasz, Elijah, Henry and Martha – as if they're family.'

'I know, and I love them all, but they don't live with me. I'm not their father.'

'But you are like Alfie and George's dad now, as well as Summer's.'

'I sometimes think that perhaps I could do it, but I'm scared, Claire. And by the way, I know we treat them like they're children but Alfie and George are cats.'

I did fleetingly think that Jonathan hadn't exactly wel-comed me when I first met him, physically ejecting me from this very house a number of times, but then I knew that was a very different Jonathan to the one I had now. I had won him round and Claire had fixed whatever was wrong with him. Now he was the best father anyone could have. Well, apart from me of course!

'I know that, and it is scary. I'm sorry I've been so deter-mined to do it that I haven't really thought how frightening it is. I'm not just thinking about me, you know. I think that expanding our family in this way will be good for all of us.

Summer would really love a sibling, we have a loving home to offer any child, and who cares if he's older than her.'

'He? Don't tell me you've already got a child and haven't told me.'

I thought I wouldn't put it past Claire actually. Jonathan looked even more terrified.

'Of course not.' Phew, I was relieved. 'But in my head it's a boy. A big brother for our Sum, someone to take care of her. To protect her while we protect him.' Claire had tears in her eyes, and I felt a hit of emotion. It would be so perfect, to open our home, our family to a child who didn't have one. That's what they had done with me.

'I would like that. I'd also like to have another child, but Claire, what if I don't feel the right way about them, what if I don't feel that I'm their parent?'

'Trust me, you will. When the right child comes here, you will feel it.'

'But how can you be so sure?' he asked.

'Because of Alfie and George.'

# Chapter
# Thirty-three

It was over six months since George had gone missing. He was big now, and never got into any trouble. Pah, who am I kidding? He was always up to something. Luckily he had grown out of hide and seek – I think being trapped in Henrietta's house for so long had put him off hiding. The local paper had called her a mad cat woman – I have to admit, I actually felt a bit sorry for her. She was actually a woman who loved cats, although of course that didn't mean she could just nick us off the street. Anyway, despite his ordeal, George still loved playing with bags, boxes and curtains, jumping up and climbing. I was forever telling him off but I had learnt that was an important job for any parent, cat or human.

However, I also made sure he knew he was loved. I was always on hand with a nuzzle whenever he needed one – or if I'm honest, whenever I did. Making sure George knew how loved he was was my most important job. It was so funny, how reluctant I had been when he first arrived, how I wanted to be alone with my heartbreak, but Claire had obviously known what she was doing.

I was teaching George how important us cats actually were in the lives of our humans. He did get a bit carried away, telling me that his latest goal was to make Summer less bossy. I wished him luck with that; it was too ambitious a plan, even for me. And for him, I thought, as I watched her still insisting that he pretend to be her baby. But the boy was taking after me, and although there was no blood shared, I could never love anyone more. A chip off the old block, he was eagerly lapping up information and charming all the neighbourhood cats, even Salmon; he pretty much had us all wrapped round his little paws.

Tiger had become such a great surrogate mum to George too. We spent so much more time together and although she was still sarcastic, judgmental and a little scathing of my more sentimental side, she took George under her paw as if he was her own. We were quite a team, the three of us. We had a bond I knew no one could ever take away from us, and we spent more time together than ever. Even Claire and Jonathan had noticed the time we spent together, calling Tiger and I an 'old married couple'. They thought it was funny. I did not. There was nothing old about me.

And our other cat friends were all part of our lives in a way they hadn't been before. Losing George and Pinkie had bonded us in a way that took us all by surprise. The cats of Edgar Road were a force to be reckoned with, and not to mention Dustbin, whose friendship I valued highly.

My families were all doing well again, and I had my paws crossed that it stayed that way. I didn't for one minute think that it would – after all, it never did – but I had learnt to enjoy the good times and only worry about the bad when they actually came.

Tash was now a fully-fledged resident of Edgar Road and George and I visited her flat regularly. She was seeing Max and apparently their status was 'in a relationship'. She was cautious, but happy. And though it hadn't been plain sailing, they weren't friends, Tash and Dave had reached a level of agreement over Elijah which, according to Tash, was the most she could hope for. And lovely Elijah was so laid back and happy; he was getting big but he was the loveliest boy. The adults joked that he and Summer would get married one day but to be honest I wasn't sure it was a good idea, Summer would run rings around him. He'd be totally henpecked – I had learnt what that phrase meant from my holiday in the country and my rescue mission. Of course, I loved Summer and I loved her bossiness, I just didn't wish it on anyone else.

I had been to stay with my Polish family, with George as well, because Claire and Jonathan had had something important to do. They were much happier now and Aleksy told me he was no longer worried about his parents. Big Tomasz was busy, and they were planning on opening their third restaurant, but they had put such a good formula in place that he didn't have to actually be working all the time. He was the brains behind the food, his business partner looked after the business side, and they had good chefs and managers working for them. They were even talking about moving to a bigger home, so the boys, who were growing so fast, would have more space. I could see their point but I worried that I would miss Dustbin. George and I loved hanging out with him. He'd declared that George was a very good hunter, which I didn't approve of; but I couldn't really stop him, it was natural for most cats and I knew I was an anomaly. But I enjoyed spending time with Dustbin, who was one of the wisest cats I knew; even if they moved, I would find a way to see him, I knew the way to his home by now. Franceska was saying how wonderful it would be if they could live on Edgar Road again, although they hadn't seriously looked at anything at this stage. Jonathan joked that they were turning into 'The Waltons', although I didn't know what he meant. I would love to have them back on our street – I would have another home to visit regularly and I would feel like a proper doorstep cat again. You could never have too many homes.

I'd tried explaining this to George when I'd settled him back home. He had been a little traumatised by his ordeal but mainly because of the noise of the other cats.

'This is your home,' I'd said. 'Always remember that.'

'But what about Matt and Polly's?'

'Well, yes, that's your home too.'

'And Franceska and Tomasz.'

'Yes, that's your home too, but nowhere else.' I was getting a bit frustrated.

'Tash?'

'OK, George, what I am trying to say is that these are your homes, all the ones you mentioned. But the easiest way to look at it is that your home is wherever I am.' He seemed to accept that.

It had taken a while, but Polly and Matt had ironed their issues out. They both worked now and they both loved their jobs, but they made their family life work too and had employed a nanny, who the others shared sometimes. Lucy, the nanny, was so nice and we all liked her. Polly and Matt also made sure they spent time together once a week. They were all lovey-dovey like they used to be. Polly looked so much like her old self, beautiful and happy. Matt was relaxed and he enjoyed the time he spent at home – even the tidying. They were planning a big family holiday, but I was pretty sure that George and I weren't going to be invited. Martha was getting bigger, as was Henry. He now refused to play with Martha and Summer and was relieved when Aleksy and little Tomasz returned from Poland and he had boys to play with again.

Claire, Jonathan and Summer were all great too. George and Summer were so close, and I liked that, because I wanted her to have that relationship the way I did with Aleksy. We both loved all the children but we did have an extra closeness with those two, because I felt as if I had grown up with Aleksy and Summer was growing up with George. Summer had turned three recently and we'd had a lovely family party, and it was then that Claire and Jonathan told us their big news. It hadn't happened overnight, but it didn't matter, because today was a big day. Everything was about to change yet again, only this time I hoped it was going to change for the better.

We were all very nervous and excited at the same time. My stomach fluttered. We were all looking our best: Jonathan wore a pair of smart trousers and a shirt; Claire was wearing a pretty floral dress; and Summer was wearing a princess costume that she'd got for her birthday, which she insisted was her best outfit ever. To be honest, she barely took it off, but she did look very cute. I had made sure George groomed himself thoroughly and I had done the same. We both looked incredibly handsome, even if I did say so myself.

We all waited, fidgeting and not quite knowing what to do with ourselves. Time crawled by so slowly, which it always did when you were waiting for something.

Claire and Jonathan had met him, of course – our potential adoptee. They'd had lots of visits and trips with him, but now he was coming to our house to see if we were all going to live together. He couldn't move straight in, he had to be happy here, but why wouldn't he be? Our home was so full of love it radiated out of every room. He would fit right in, once he had time to get used to it. Just like me, and like George.

I stretched as the doorbell went.

'Oh goodness, they're here. Do I look OK?' Claire patted her hair and looked flustered. Claire's mood had been so great lately, she was so happy and excited about the future. She kept saying that this was fate and she knew it was meant to be. And I think Jonathan believed her, finally.

'You look lovely,' Jonathan said, taking her hand. I could see he was sweating a bit as they made their way to the front door.

'Me too!' Summer shouted as she followed them, George and myself on her heels.

Jonathan opened the door, and in walked a lady holding the hand of a boy about Henry's age. He looked terrified, and clutched the lady's hand tightly. My heart went out to him; if anyone needed a cat it was this boy, I could immediately tell.

'Hi, Marie,' Claire said, shaking hands with the lady.

'Hi, guys, Summer,' Marie said.

Claire knelt down on the floor. 'Hello, Toby, welcome to our house,' she said gently. The boy looked at her and smiled uncertainly.

'Toby.' Summer jumped forward and smiled at him. 'I'm a princess.'

'Hi, Summer.' He seemed a bit more at ease with her, but still shuffled from foot to foot. I watched Claire kneeling before him, with Summer next to her. Jonathan hung back slightly.

I decided to introduce myself. He must have been feeling so mixed up, and he was so young to have to handle such emotions. I lost my first home when I was too young to fully understand and it had been the hardest time of my life. I wanted him to know I knew how he felt, in my own way.

'Miaow,' I said, rubbing his legs.

'A cat!' he exclaimed, and sat down on the floor to stroke me. Claire followed suit as did Summer. George joined us.

'Another cat!' Toby said, even happier to see George, who crawled into his lap. This boy was all right, he clearly loved cats. Summer giggled, and Toby looked at her and giggled too. I felt choked up as I saw Claire's eyes fill with tears. We were both thinking the same thing, I was pretty sure. This is our boy.

We all played on the floor for a while. Marie the social worker hung back but Jonathan still seemed rooted to the spot. I decided to go and give him a little nudge.

'Who's hungry?' he asked finally, looking at me and then at them.

'Me!' Summer shouted.

'Toby?' Jonathan asked. Toby nodded shyly. We all looked at Jonathan. He had tears in his eyes, which was rare, and his voice was choked. I was so proud of all of them, but especially him, at that moment.

He reached out his hand to Toby. Toby looked at it for a few seconds, but then he put his hand into Jonathan's. Jonathan pulled him gently to his feet and held onto that little hand so tightly.

'Come on, son,' he said.

# Chapter
# Thirty-four

When Toby had to leave, he said he didn't want to go, and nor did anyone want to say goodbye. Although he was still shy and uncertain, he had enjoyed being with us, I could tell. I found it hard to accept that a boy who was five years old had to come and live with a new family. It was part of life that I would always find upsetting, confusing and just wrong. But then I also knew, watching how Claire, Jonathan and Summer were with him, that if he had to go to a new home, ours was the best.

Marie took Claire and Jonathan aside and said the visit had gone very well and so they would be increasing the time Toby spent with us until it was decided he could come and live here, which she hoped would be sooner rather than later. Claire looked relieved and Jonathan beamed, proving us right, he could love a child that wasn't biologically his. His eyes were already full of love. After Toby left, with many hugs and kisses and promises that he could come back soon, we were all emotionally drained.

'So Toby's going to come and live with us?' George asked when I was trying to settle him in bed.

'Yes. Claire will be his mummy and Jonathan will be his daddy.'

'Like you and Tiger are to me?'

'Yes, just like that.'

'Because I love you, Dad, and I love Tiger-Mum too.' I kissed him goodnight: there was only so much emotion one cat could take in a day and I had reached my happiness limit.

\*\*\*

'Jonathan, I didn't want him to go,' Claire said when we were alone later, after Summer and George were fast asleep.

'Me neither, I almost couldn't bear it. You were right. The minute I saw him, I knew he was my son. I don't understand it but I looked into his eyes and I loved him. Right away, I loved him.' Jonathan was crying again – this was a regular occurrence today.

'Oh, Jon, I love you so much and Toby will be the luckiest boy having you as a father.'

'He deserves it after what he's been through.'

'Jon, don't talk about that, let's look to the future.'

'Can't wait to take him to the football.' Jonathan tried to laugh.

'Summer might want to go too,' Claire pointed out.

'Of course. I'm not being sexist, I'll take them both. But I think you're right, you know, it feels as if our family is complete now. Us, Summer, Alfie, George and now Toby. It feels right. It feels really wonderful, in fact.'

'I know exactly how you feel. I'm just so happy right now. I can't wait to have that lovely little boy living here.'

'It might be hard at first, he's going to need a lot of time and attention and we need to make sure Summer doesn't feel left out.' Jonathan was always the voice of reason.

'I know, Jon, and that's why I'm taking a year off work, remember. I'll have time to give them both the attention they need. Nothing worthwhile is easy but we are going to do this and we're going to do it really, really well.'

'Maybe I should listen to you more in future,' Jonathan laughed.

'Finally! It's about time you realised that. But seriously, Jon, we're going to be all right.'

'No, Claire, we're going to be more than all right.'

I checked on George, who was snoring gently, before I got ready to go out. I went past the living room, where Claire and Jonathan were snuggled on the sofa, and left the house. There was someone I needed to see. I had taught my humans a lot, and of course my plan had ultimately worked, despite it going terribly wrong, but they had taught me a great deal too. Seeing my families pulling together, all of the parents reaffirming their love, or looking for new love, had opened my eyes. Being a parent, whether of a child or a kitten, gave you a different perspective. Love and parenting worked in so many different ways. For example my first human, Margaret, didn't have human children, she had Agnes and then me, we were her babies and she parented us brilliantly. She showered us with love and affection, not to mention pilchards. And it was the same with Claire and Jonathan before Summer came along. You were parents to your pets, your pets were parents to you. There were no rules when you loved – you just took care of each other.

That was what I had learnt. I had also discovered that nothing is forever, so you need to snatch whatever happiness you can, when you can. You need to hold tight to what's important to you and nurture and cherish it. You need to appreciate everyone you love every single day. Everyone had learnt something when George was missing, and I wondered if perhaps I had learnt the most.

It wasn't late, but I gently bumped the cat flap and waited

in the back garden. After a few moments, Tiger emerged. The sky was dark blue, the moon bright and round; stars sparkled at us, it was a beautiful night. We sat on the back step, the place where our plan had gone wrong, looking up at the moon together, sitting side by side in silence.

'How did today go?' she finally asked, flicking her whiskers at me.

'Wonderful, brilliant, it couldn't have gone better if I'd planned it myself. Toby is a lovely little boy. I feel sad he doesn't have a forever family already, but we're also so lucky that we're going to be it for him. You'll love him too!'

'Another kitten to worry about,' Tiger grinned. 'Although perhaps it's time to hang up your hat when it comes to plans to fix things.'

'As if I will ever do that! Anyway, I don't think he's as naughty as George, or as bossy as Summer, but yes, of course I'll worry about him, and love him, and do all I can to take care of him.'

'Because that's the kind of cat you are.'

'It is. But I also need to appreciate those who help me, with George and my families, a bit more than I do at the moment,' I said. My thoughts were clear but I was finding it hard to articulate them.

'Anyone in particular?' Tiger asked.

'You know who I mean, Tiger. You. You've always been there for me, even after that business with Snowball you still were my best friend, and now you're my co-parent.'

'I've never heard of a co-parent,' she said. She looked slightly embarrassed, probably because I had alluded to the time she told me she was in love with me.

'You know I've learnt that love comes in all shapes and sizes. I think with Snowball it was young love, my first ever romance, I suppose, but we didn't have too many responsibilities back then. I'll always miss her a bit but life is different now and I wouldn't change it for all the pilchards in the world.'

'You wouldn't?'

'Tiger, what I'm trying to say, which I'm not doing very well, is that you've been by my side when it matters and I want us to be like that for a very, very long time.'

'What do you mean?'

'Our relationship – we're best friends, we're parents and we love each other. All that teasing about us being an old married couple, well, I see it now. Maybe not the passion of youth but a more mature kind where we love each other properly.' I felt so flustered by this conversation.

'So you think we're like an old married couple?' Tiger asked, her voice slightly mocking.

'Yes, well, less of the old, but a married couple who have the utmost respect for each other, who both love George in a way where he will always come first, but also a couple who have fun, who laugh with each other, and have deep, deep feelings of love for each other – that's how I feel, Tiger. And vanity aside, none of us are getting any younger, it's about time I saw what was right in front of my face.'

'Me.'

'You.'

'Oh, Alfie, I never thought you'd say this, I mean, I never dreamed after Snowball…'

'Shush. Some things take longer to figure out. Like with Toby, that's not an overnight thing and we aren't either.'

'But… we're rock solid?' Tiger asked. Her eyes were full of everything I loved about her: warmth, fun, friendship, beauty. I had taken her for granted for so long but now my eyes had definitely been opened.

'Unbreakable. Like the best things in life, we've been worth waiting for, and now, Tiger, my love, the wait is over.'

'I've loved you for so long, Alfie.'

'I know, and I'm sorry it hasn't been plain sailing, but now I can return that love. And I know one little kitten who will be incredibly happy.'

As we both looked at the moon, my heart was full – of my families, of my cat friends, of Tiger and, most of all, of our kitten, George.

I feel so lucky to be able to write a third Alfie book, so firstly I think a big thanks needs to go to my readers – thank you for buying my books and I hope you will continue to do so! Alfie has become such a part of my life, and my family, so it means a lot to me.

Thanks as always to my wonderful agents, Diane Banks Associates and everyone there, Kate, Diane, Chloe and Robyn. Also to all at Avon but especially my lovely editor Helen Huthwaite – still such a pleasure working with you!

To my family and friends who have been as supportive as always. You know who you are and how invaluable you are to my life. And my son, Xavier, who has been amazing as always.

I ran a Twitter competition to have someone's cat as a small character in this book, and so I want to thank everyone who entered, it was so difficult and I would have loved to have chosen all the cats! There could only be one winner though, so congratulations to Pinkie, who is such a gorgeous cat, and her owner, Victoria Nikiforou – thank you both for being part of my book.

A special mention for Moira and Charles Huthwaite. I hope you like our tribute to Mr B: always missed but never forgotten.

Again, it has been a joy to bring Alfie to life once again, so a massive thanks to anyone who has made this possible and I hope you enjoy *Alfie & George.*